EL TIGRE DE NUEVA ORLEÁNS

The Tiger of New Orleans

A Novel from the deMelilla Chronicles

D1412120

MR. STEPHEN V. ESTOPINAL

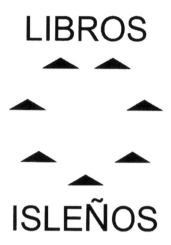

LIBROS
ISLEÑOS

Libros Isleños Publishing

Gonzales, Louisiana 70737

ISBN-10: 1492807753

ISBN 13: 9781492807759

To
Dr. Elaine Boston
8/14/2015

DEDICATION

TO THE LOVE OF MY LIFE
MARIE ELAINE RUSSEL

CHAPTER *1*

"*Era Septiembre* (It was September)," Grandfather began.

Bartolomé deMelilla knew very well the story that was to follow, *La Derrota de Baton Rouge* (The Fall of Baton Rouge), for it had been told many times. He had memorized every word of every story his grandfather had recited, in the tradition of oral family history. Still, the old man mesmerized Bartolomé with his memorable images of war and adventure.

Bartolomé's grandfather, Diego deMelilla, had been a soldier in the Spanish Louisiana Regiment. He had been recruited in the year 1778, at the age of thirty, by the army of King Charles III of Spain. Charles wanted to increase the population of Louisiana with as many Catholics as could be recruited, so that they could serve as a barrier between Mexico and the Protestant British colonies along the Atlantic coast. The king had enlisted Spaniards, French Acadians, Irish, Germans, Canary Islanders, and others to colonize Spanish Louisiana.

Diego was a native of the village of Aguimes, on the island of Gran Canaria. Gran Canaria, one of the seven islands off the African coast known as the Canary Islands, had been conquered by the Spanish at the end of the fifteenth century. He was typical of the people of Aguimes. Spanish in name, language, and to some extent custom, he yet retained many of the traits of the native side of his ancestry. He was tall compared to most, for which he received an enlistment bonus, and he had the sparkling blue eyes frequently found amongst *Isleños*, as the Canary Island colonists came to be known in Louisiana. The Spanish Army brought Diego to Louisiana to serve in the newly created Louisiana Regiment. He was transported to New Orleans along with his wife, Maria, and two children, Pedro, who was ten, and Maria, seven, to populate the colony. Pedro was Bartolomé's father.

The battles that Diego participated in under the famous Governor General Don Bernardo de Galvez were legendary. Britain and Spain were at war from 1779 to 1783. While Britain contended with the rebellion in the American colonies, Galvez succeeded in expelling the British from the southeast corner of North America. Beginning at Manchac in Louisiana and culminating at Pensacola, Florida, Diego was in every fight. The Spanish Louisiana Regiment never lost a single battle. The stories he told not only kept Bartolomé rapt with awe and wonder, they provided Bartolomé an opportunity to keep his Spanish sharp.

Today's story begins just after the fall of Fort Bute at Manchac. Don Bernardo de Galvez's force had originally consisted of a hundred and seventy veteran regulars, three hundred and thirty new recruits of the Louisiana

Regiment, and about a thousand others, mostly Acadian and German militia. Disease and the rigors of the march up from New Orleans had already cut the force in half when the trek to Baton Rouge began.

An alert observer along the trail would have first noticed the scouts in advance of the main force. Scattered in small groups to the left and right of the trail, the scouts were constantly moving. Forging ahead or circling back to report, not one scout would set a foot on the trail itself. They were followed by the Spanish veterans and the Louisiana Regiment, four hundred *soldados* marching four abreast and filling the rough trail from side to side. Two dozen oxen and horses followed, towing field guns and wagons loaded with supplies. The militia and wagons carrying the sick or injured followed over a trail flattened by the hosts before them. Finally came the trailing scouts, insurance against an attack from the rear. The army required over an hour to pass a single spot on the trail. Less than twenty miles from Fort Bute to Baton Rouge, it took the army five days to deploy for the attack on Baton Rouge.

Diego paused in his recitation. He stared at Bartolomé. "Always learn as much as can be known about where the enemy is, how strong he is. Knowledge is the key. You must know your enemy to defeat him." He wrapped a weathered hand around the back of Bartolomé's head as he repeated, *"Estar enterado* (Be informed). Satisfied that his grandson was suitably impressed, Diego continued the history lesson.

When they approached Fort Richmond at Baton Rouge, the scouts sent back word of what lay ahead. The British defenders numbered about five hundred, of which three hundred and fifty were regulars. The walled fort bristled with thirteen guns, and those within were well aware of Galvez's force. Diego knew that this was not going to be a repeat of the easy victory at Fort Bute. Security forces spread out around the fort, and the army began to establish a camp as the long caravan trickled in. It was late afternoon before the last of the force arrived. The scouts, officers, and Galvez gathered to plan the next move. Diego did not have long to wait. The orders were for the regulars to ground all accoutrements except musket, bayonet, and cartridge boxes. The oxen were unhitched from the cannon, and squads of regulars were assigned to each gun. This group was to follow a trail to the north and east, well out of sight of the fort. They marched out without drum or voice command. The guns were towed by hand and everyone was ordered to remain silent. Diego was amazed at how silently they moved.

As they departed, Diego could hear the militia that remained moving about, followed by the horses and oxen towing wagons. He later found out that Galvez had directed the militia to march across an opening in full view of the fort, just out of cannon range. The wagons followed, making a great show of their movement. This display masked the militia as they circled back to march across the gap, again and again. To those in the fort, it appeared that Galvez had arrived with a force of thousands.

Diego and the regulars arrived as night fell, at a location on the opposite side of the fort from the demonstration. Even at this distance, Diego could hear the commotion that the militia was creating. Working all night by the light of the moon, they dug emplacements and set the cannon on a small knoll. By the time it was barely dawn, all was ready. The first volley from the Spanish guns smashed into the wooden palisade and low earthworks. Splinters and great clumps of earth flew about with every volley. Galvez kept the guns working for several hours. The British could not bring their own cannon into play. Most of the British ordinance had been gathered at the far wall to oppose the Spanish militia that had formed into a line of battle far out of range. As soon as a British gun was moved into position near the battered rampart, it was smashed by a Spanish volley.

Then the order came for the regiment to form up in column, four abreast, and to shoulder their muskets. Diego was on the right end of his rank. As the guns bellowed, the regiments moved out until the lead rank was just beyond the farthest gun. The column began a left turn, followed by another left, until it resembled an enormous, long, white, snake slithering out of the tree line and turning to cross in front of the guns. As the head of the column continued along the front, the cannons fell silent, each in turn. Finally, the four hundred Spanish Infantry, in white uniforms, white trimmed tricorne hats, and glistening bayonets, halted. At a command, all moved as one, facing right to form a battle line. They brought their bayoneted muskets to the position of "charge" with a great shout. The shout echoed off the remains of the palisade.

Diego interrupted his story again. "The battle had been won before we had formed our battle line," he said. "It was won when the British blinded themselves by hiding in the fort. They did not patrol. They had no scouts in the surrounding forests. We could move our forces in secret. The enemy concentrated on what Galvez wanted them to see and ignored all else. They were not wise." The old man nodded his head. These interruptions were important to Bartolomé's education. It was not enough to tell the boy what happened. He needed to know why. Diego resumed his tale.

Diego advanced. The butt of his musket was firmly pressed against his hip. His right hand was around the throat of the stock and his left firmly grasped the fore-stock, so that the musket canted forward with the point of the bayonet about eye level. He glanced to the left and right. Every bayonet was perfectly positioned. He looked into the ruins of the fort. He could see a Redcoat run from the rubble, but nothing else. They advanced at the regular pace until the officer ordered "quick march." Now the battle line surged ahead with new vigor, but still disciplined and in formation. Diego was surprised that he felt no fear, just a strange kind of excitement. Perhaps fear would come when the fighting began.

The Redcoat returned to the wall with a British officer. The officer produced a white handkerchief and gave it to the Redcoat. The British solder waved the cloth over his head and both of them advanced into the field. They were calling for a truce.

Diego heard his officer order the ranks to halt. In a single instant, as one, the four hundred-*soldado* battle line halted. On command, they placed their muskets at "order arms" and snapped to attention. Dust drifted past the white-uniformed ranks as silence covered the battle line. The British pair seemed tiny, insignificant, defeated as they stood before the regiment.

Diego was no more than twenty paces from the two Redcoats when the order was given to halt. He watched as Captain Fernando Leyba appeared from the left and approached the Redcoats. He could hear them talking in English. Diego had never heard the language before. It all sounded like "oo ah oo ah" to him and he did not know what was said.

Captain Leyba then walked over to Diego's *pelotón* (squad). He ordered them to form a guard around himself and the Redcoats. When this was done, the tiny formation marched back into the demolished fort. Diego was on the front right corner of the guard. This was the first time he had witnessed the aftermath of a real battle. Fort Bute had not been a real fight.

The small contingent moved quickly through the narrow, debris-cluttered alleys. They were never challenged by any of the Redcoats along the way. Instead, the sullen and often wounded British stepped aside to make way. Several British dead, perhaps seven, were laid out in a row at one location on the route. When they reached the British command post, Diego and another *soldado*, Gonzales, were posted at the doorway. They held their bayonet-tipped weapons so that crossed blades blocked the doorway. Their orders were to deny entry to anyone. The rest of the group went in. More than two dozen Redcoats gathered a short distance away and glared.

The door opened and Captain Leyba stepped out. Diego and Gonzales came to attention. A British officer, not the same one Diego had escorted in, followed the captain. The officer issued orders to those gathered about and reentered the building. The Redcoats dispersed in several directions. Captain Leyba turned to Diego and instructed him to return to the regiment, find General Galvez, and report that the surrender had been accomplished according to the terms the general dictated. He had Diego repeat the message and then sent him off.

Diego jogged with his bayonet tipped musket at the "port" position across his chest, retracing the route they had taken. He was glad his position in the guard had provided him a clear view of the surroundings and that he had paid close attention to the landmarks. By this time, civilians were also about, fear in every face. Everyone he passed glanced at him then looked down or away. When he cleared the remains of the palisade, he saw that the regiment was still formed in a line of battle, but at the "rest" position. The regiment, without a command, came to attention as Diego approached. Every man in rank strained to hear what it was that Diego had to say to the officer who stepped out to meet him. They were disappointed, for all they heard was *"un mensaje para el general* (a message for the general)." The officer led Diego through the formation and to the rear to a command tent. The tent had not been there when the regiment had begun the assault.

Standing before Governor General Don Bernardo de Galvez himself, a man he had only seen at a distance and on horseback, Diego came to attention and, when ordered to speak, delivered Captain Leyba's message verbatim.

"Gracias, Sargento deMelilla," General Galvez said as he dismissed Diego. Diego was stunned. First, the general knew his name and, second, he mistook Diego's rank. Anyone could see that Diego was a private soldier. He left the tent in wonder.

The aide-de-camp stopped him and gave him the sash of a *sargento*. As Diego wrapped the sash around his waist, the aide instructed him to return to Captain Leyba with the message to proceed with the surrender.

When he returned to the British command post, Gonzales and Perez were standing guard. They were surprised to see Diego. A private had left and returned as a sergeant. They halted Diego. Gonzales, with a wry smile, asked the sergeant to state his business. *"Un mensaje para el capitan, Soldado Gonzales,"* Diego said, mocking formality. Both the men on guard laughed, congratulating Diego, then let him enter to deliver his message. Diego learned later that when Captain Leyba was dispatched to deliver the surrender demands, he said that the man he would send back would be a private soldier who had shown exceptional leadership ability and he requested that Diego deMelilla be promoted to sergeant.

The surrender terms paroled all the British militia, civilians, and others to their homes and farms where they could return to their normal, daily lives. They were even allowed to keep their personal weapons. The Redcoats were disarmed and loaded on a barge to be transported to New Orleans where they would remain prisoners of war for some four years. There were more battles to come for the regiment, but this one was done. In less than two years, Diego went from being a goat herder in the mountains of Grand Canaria to a Spanish Army sergeant in the swamps of Louisiana.

"Cómo cambia la vida," Diego said. He always ended this story with the expression, "How life changes."

* * *

Diego looked at his grandson as he concluded his tale. Bartolomé was strong and tall. He looked very much like his father, Pedro. His hair, which was white until he was about eight, had become a light, sandy color. His eyes were hazel or light brown, depending upon the light. He was broad shouldered and solidly built. These were traits often seen among the pre-Spanish natives of the Canary Islands.

The fever took Pedro shortly after Bartolomé was born. It saddened Diego a little that, of all of his grandchildren, this boy was the only one being raised in another culture and in another language. He could also see ambition, determination, and a strong desire to learn in Bartolomé. Bartolomé's mother, Aimée Bourg, had remarried. Her new husband, Jacques Troyles, was a farmer who knew nothing but farming, though he knew it well and was good at it.

Bartolomé got along well enough with his stepbrothers and half-sisters. The stepbrothers, born of Jacques and his first wife, were close to his age. Bartolomé's half sisters were only seven and two. Jacques had become a widower in the same year that Pedro had died. Bartolomé could do well to learn farming and hard work from Jacques. But, Diego knew that Bartolomé would not be content to live out his life in one little village.

His spirit is much like my maternal grandfather, Diego thought. That ancient one had been an *alzardo*, a rebellious one. His name was Tupinar, and he called himself an *Amazigh*, in the language of the old ones. He lived as the people of *Gran Canaria* did before the Spanish came, wild and free. He farmed the high land and herded goats. He made his home in the caves of the precipitous mountains.

Diego knew that Bartolomé would never be content to live the settled life of a farmer. Away from the protection of one's home village and family farm, the world was a dangerous place. Therefore, Diego made certain that the short history lessons, such as the one today, were followed by brisk exercises in weaponry.

Now sixty-six years old, Diego was still quick and strong. His hands were thick with calluses, and weathered into leather. His white hair and beard flowed with every movement. His voice was deep and confident. Twenty-five years in the Spanish Army had conditioned him in the instruction of others. He was well respected in the village of Bencheque, where he had been granted a small parcel of land as a service pension. His neighbors and friends addressed him as Don Diego out of respect. Bartolomé always addressed Diego as *Abuelo* (Grandfather). He said the word with the same respect that a young soldier would say First Sergeant.

Sometimes the exercise was in the use of a walking staff as a weapon. Today, the exercise was to be in the use of two traditional *Isleño* weapons, the *magado* and the *sunta*. The *magado* was a cross between a lance and a pike. Made of fine wood and tipped with an obsidian point, it was not a thrown weapon but used as a thrusting, stabbing weapon very much like a bayonet. After the Spanish colonized the Canary Islands, the obsidian blade was replaced by a steel one.

The *sunta* was a mace-like weapon with a hatchet-sized handle topped with a fist-sized stone. It was normally carried in the belt, until combat seemed imminent. Then it would be hung from the right forearm by a leather loop. When carried this way, a drop of the right hand would allow the *sunta* to be quickly gripped by the handle, ready to strike. These weapons were almost always used together.

Diego's cramped little cottage was much too confining, so they both went out into a small clearing near the trail along the bayou. Bartolomé stood for inspection. The headless handle of a hatchet served for the *sunta*. It hung from his right wrist by a leather loop so that, if he were to drop his right hand, the grip would fall into his palm. The staff that served for a *magado* was a little short, but it would serve. Diego considered the perfect length for a *magado* to be seven feet. At this length, it was short enough to be used with agility yet long enough to keep the bayonet or sword away.

"Remember, the *magado* is never thrown. You must use it as a thrusting weapon. The *sunta* is only used if your opponent is within the *magado*," Diego would admonish every time.

"On your guard," Diego barked as he leveled his own pseudo-*magado*.

Bartolomé caught the butt of his *magado* in his right hand about a half foot from the end, and pressed it to his waist. His left hand gripped the shaft about two and a half feet above his right. This angled the shaft so that the tip was leveled right at Diego's throat. Bartolomé was fourteen years old, yet he was taller than Diego. He stood only two inches short of six feet, and was muscular, the result of a young lifetime of physical labor. His left foot was forward. His weight was mainly on his right. His knees were bent slightly, ready to be shifted quickly as the action would demand.

Diego assumed a similar stance, facing Bartolomé about ten feet away. This resulted in the two shafts crossing a foot or so from the tip. Except for the weapons, they looked to be boxers squared off for a fight. Diego slapped his pseudo-*magado* against Bartolomé's and knocked it aside. Bartolomé quickly brought the shaft back in line.

"Do not allow me to engage your *magado*," Diego said. He then demonstrated how one should react to such a move. Instructing Bartolomé to try to slap his shaft aside, he dropped the tip quickly just enough that Bartolomé's shaft passed over it. Immediately, he returned to the guard position. His shaft was always pointed at Bartolomé. "This is called 'disengage'," Diego said as he again demonstrated by moving his point to avoid contact, yet keeping it pointed at Bartolomé's throat or chest. "Now you do it," he said.

Every time Diego attempted to strike Bartolomé's *magado* away, he would "disengage" and avoid contact. The exercise continued from this simple disengagement to combining the move with "parry," "lunge," "thrust," and "repost."

The parry was an action in response to a thrust or lunge by the opponent. It was accomplished by quickly pushing the right hand down from the hip to a point away from the body and level with the groin. "Protect your balls," Diego would say. Then with a short firm move, the opponent's incoming weapon was directed to one side or the other. It was important that the move be only enough to create a near miss. Too little movement was an obvious error, but too much left one exposed to other attacks and out of position to take advantage of the opponent's miss.

The lunge was accomplished by bringing the right hand up to the chest so that the shaft was level, and stepping forward strongly with the left foot. If the opponent's parry was weak or insufficient, one could drive the point into the enemy's body. The lunge was combined with a disengagement move to avoid an insufficient parry, or a power slap to move a weak parry aside. It was used when the enemy was close enough to be reached without stepping forward with the right foot.

The thrust involved an initial move identical to the lunge. Then the combatant would step forward with the right foot, release the grip of the left hand, and push the shaft forward for the full length of the right arm. Such a move usually followed a lunge that fell short or failed to penetrate the enemy. It was a risky move that left the user vulnerable to counterattack, so it had to be employed carefully.

The repost was an attack that followed a successful parry. As soon as the opponent's lunge or thrust was pushed aside, the combatant would instantly respond with a thrust or lunge at the now exposed enemy. Most victories were accomplished through a repost. Diego drilled Bartolomé in the use of the repost until the reaction was instinctive. "Train until the actions flow without thinking," Diego said. He had observed that, in combat, men would always do what they had been trained to do, even if it was the wrong thing to do. If they had not been sufficiently trained, they would freeze or run away. Courage had confidence as a foundation. When good training built well-founded confidence, courage would follow.

The *sunta* was brought into action when the combatants were too close for the *magado* to be used. It was the weapon of last resort. The opponent was held with the left hand, and bludgeoned with the *sunta* in the right hand. Bartolomé had trained in these techniques and the use of the walking staff in defense with Diego since he was eleven. He was now quite accomplished.

"Enough for today; you are getting too good for me," Diego said proudly as he clasped an arm around Bartolomé's broad shoulders. "Besides, it is getting late. You need to be on your way to your mother's."

Today was Sunday. On every other day of the week, Bartolomé was at his stepfather's small farm near the village of Terre Aux Boeufs, located on a bayou of the same name, upstream from Bencheque.

* * *

Bartolomé didn't mind walking up the trail at night. With his walking staff, he felt he could deal with anything the darkness could present. He made his good-byes around the house and set off for home in the gathering dusk. The walk took about an hour, so it would be full dark just as he arrived home.

The trail home followed the bank of Bayou Terre Aux Boeufs. It was beaten smooth and hard by the hooves of oxen and mules and the feet of the laboring men that towed boats, barges, and sleds up and down the bayou. The waterway was much too narrow for sailing, so navigation was accomplished by rowing, poling, or towing. Towing was the method favored for heavy barges or sailboats. Every bush or shrub between the trail and the water's edge had long been cut away so that the tow ropes could pass unimpeded. The opposite bank did not have such a beaten trail. The downstream trip was with the current and there was no need for a tow.

The setting sun and rising moon provided sufficient light for Bartolomé to make his way. He passed a few travelers, all of whom he knew, and in a few miles, he passed beyond the indistinct boundary of Bencheque, his grandfather's village.

The land along the bayou trail he now traveled had been a wilderness. The air was heavy with smoke from many smoldering piles of brush. The forest was being cleared. A new plantation was being established. This land had been too far from the Mississippi River and downstream from New Orleans to be considered prime farmland until recently. The gossip was that the new land owners were rich Americans, but Bartolomé had never seen them. He could see the tents and lean-tos of the workers; most were Irishmen, contracted to clear the land. The worksite was too isolated to risk using slaves. A slave surrounded by wilderness and separated from his family could not be expected to resist an attempt at freedom.

After he had walked another two miles, he passed into Terre Aux Boeufs, his mother's village. He ceased speaking Spanish to those he met. His greetings changed to French, the language of his mother and the village in which he lived. Though only a few miles apart, Bencheque and Terre Aux Boeufs were very different worlds.

In 1814 Louisiana, a village could be predominately French-speaking, or Spanish, or English, depending upon many things. All the inhabitants of the territory had been Americans for less than a dozen years, as a result of actions far away. Napoleon, the Emperor of France, had acquired Louisiana from Spain through the puppet government he had established there by intimidation. Napoleon sold all of Louisiana to the new United States on an impulse. The Americans were looking to buy New Orleans and wound up with all the Louisiana territories, from the Gulf of Mexico to Canada. None of the citizens of Louisiana were consulted. Most were ignorant of the change in government for a year or more. Rulers do not need, nor do they seek, the peoples' consent to act.

The public ceremonies that announced the change were held in the *Place d'Armes* in front of the St. Louis Cathedral. It consisted of lowering the Spanish flag, the reversion to France having been an open secret, and raising the French flag. Less than a month later, the French flag was struck and replaced by the American flag. In less than thirty days, it was official. All Louisianans were now Americans. A few resented the sudden change. Some welcomed it, particularly the growing American population in New Orleans, but most just continued with their lives as best they could.

"*Enfin* (Finally)," his mother announced as Bartolomé arrived at the back door. "Did that Old Spaniard feed you?" she asked as she glowered at him.

"*Oui, madame*," was all Bartolomé had to say. The answer didn't matter. A "yes" answer was scorned because she had waited to prepare something. A "no" drew the same ire because now there was more work to do. Bartolomé went into the yard, checked on the pigs, and headed to bed. He went up the steps that ascended from the front porch to the boys' room in the attic. It was an Acadian tradition that, as soon as a boy reached the age of thirteen, he was moved from within the house to a dormitory in the attic until he married or moved away. There he would sleep with his brothers and other unmarried male kin, banned from the house as if adolescent boys were not fit company for the rest of the family. In the case of Bartolomé's stepbrothers, it was not a bad idea.

None of the three were cruel or evil, just uncivilized. At first, they tried to lord over Bartolomé. Maurice, who was seventeen, was particularly convinced that he had to demonstrate his dominance. After a few rounds of fisticuffs, which the younger Bartolomé barely lost, the victor was so exhausted by Bartolomé's tenacious resistance and refusal to quit that he soon decided that winning wasn't worth it. Jules and Gabriel, Bartolomé's other two stepbrothers, were twelve and thirteen, and were content to let things be. Oceane, seven, and Inez, two, were Bartolomé's half sisters and they slept in the house proper.

Bartolomé found his way to his section of the loft while his stepbrothers snored. They were sound asleep this early in the night for there was little else to do. They were not permitted to have candles or lanterns in the cramped space. If they did have a source of light, what good would it be? None could read, except Bartolomé, and tomorrow, there was plowing to do.

Bartolomé thought that perhaps a trip to the market in New Orleans to sell some smoked ham to the merchants was possible. It was too early in the year for good vegetables. Everyone raised their own chickens, so eggs rarely fetched enough to bother with. But high quality smoked hams, and Jacques made the best, always sold well.

If he was lucky, he might borrow a book from William Stout. Bartolomé had never been to a formal school. Father Menée, the local priest, would tutor some of the children in reading and writing. Few would go, and those who did, did so infrequently. Bartolomé went every chance he got. He was such an eager student that, by the time he was eight, Father Menée had begun to teach Bartolomé some English as well. William Stout, who worked a stall in the New Orleans market, took a liking to Bartolomé and his desire to learn. For a few extra wild ducks or some other game, Stout would expand Bartolomé's English vocabulary. Sometimes, a small book was available.

Tomorrow, it would be the market, if he could convince his stepfather that his stepbrothers could handle the farm chores and the price of smoked ham was up. Jacques spoke only French. If he brought Bartolomé along, the English- as well as Spanish-speaking shoppers would be included as potential customers.

Jacques had long ago decided that the trips to sell their produce to the market vendors would include Bartolomé. He had noticed that the prices he received were usually much better if he went to the trouble of traveling all the way to the New Orleans market and he had Bartolomé along to barter. He could always sell his produce to one of the *canoteurs* along the bayou who would buy seasonal produce at a reduced price then row up to New Orleans and resell the goods at that market price. The better price at the market appealed to Jacques.

CHAPTER 2

As soon as the sky began to lighten, the entire household was about. Jacques had decided that today he would bring a dozen or more smoked hams to the New Orleans market.

"Bartolomé," Jacques instructed, "go to the smokehouse and pick no less than a dozen hams that are ready for market."

Jules and Gabriel were instructed to begin work on an addition to one of the pig sties. Maurice was sent to the woods to select and cut a tree as fuel for the smokehouse.

"Cut it into manageable sections this time. Stack it to dry in the *t'abri*," Jacques said. Last time, Maurice had cut the logs in lengths that protruded beyond the little lean-to and the wood did not dry properly.

Jacques was going to take the wagon so there would be no horse available for plowing. Once the horse was hitched to the wagon, Jacques drove to the smokehouse, where he and Bartolomé loaded fifteen fine, smoked hams. Four of the hams had aged nearly a year and the rest were freshly smoked.

The trip to New Orleans would take two to three hours, depending on the trail conditions. It was infinitely faster than the ox-drawn sleds that many of the farmers used. The sleds could haul greater weights, but an ox just cannot be rushed. They started up the trail along Bayou Terre Aux Boeufs toward the Mississippi River. The bayou was a distributary of the Mississippi. When the Mississippi was high, the bayou flowed with a rolling current, as it did today. The boat traffic going upstream had been reduced to a single towed barge.

Bartolomé believed that it was the strong current when the river was high, and the narrow bayou, that kept his village so small. It did not help that the bayou met the river downstream from New Orleans. Bringing produce to market by boat against the current was hard work. Then he remembered hearing about the new steamboats. They moved by the power of an engine. He speculated that such boats would be much too large for the narrow bayou. He resolved to see one of these vessels and learn more of the mechanics of steamboats.

The plodding horse was able to outpace the tow mules and there were no ox sleds on the trail. It wasn't very long before they reached the Poche plantation, situated at the intersection of the bayou and the river. The road to the city lay to the right, the bayou to the left. Besides raising sugarcane, Poche permitted the operation of a small swing ferry that would carry passengers across the bayou if they were traveling further down the river trail.

Bartolomé was fascinated by the ferry operation. A barge was moored against the north bank at a plank dock or landing. One end of a heavy rope was fastened on the upstream end of the barge, and the other end to a large tree on the opposite bank where it was permanently fixed. There were several heavy weights along the rope, so it would sink when slackened, to allow the passage of boats in the bayou. When the passengers and freight were aboard, Bacenaux, the ferry master, would cast off from the landing and the current would sweep the ferry downstream.

Because it was anchored to the tree, the ferry would swing in a great arc until it came against the opposite bank, where it was moored to offload. The trip back was a little more arduous. Bacenaux would winch in another line that was attached to the north bank landing to return. The ferry master's skillful use of a large rudder and knowledge of eddies and currents reduced the physical labor enough that it was a one-man operation.

Not far from the ferry landing stood the great brick ovens the plantation used to process the harvested sugarcane. Great cast iron pots, large enough to hold a full grown horse, sat empty in the ovens. There was no harvest underway just now.

The trail became a road along the river. As they passed acres of sugarcane fields, they could see the slaves working among the rows. Slaves were much too expensive to own and maintain for anyone in his village, or his grandfather's. Only the large plantations that filled the land between the villages kept slaves.

Bartolomé's grandfather disapproved of slavery, not that he could have ever afforded one. "It is not the *Isleño* way," he would say. "God gave us free will; why is it that some men think they can take away what God has given?" Not many people in Louisiana agreed with such radical thoughts. Bartolomé had adopted his grandfather's moral objections.

Bartolomé also believed that slavery did not make economic sense. The cost of buying and maintaining a slave workforce required a huge initial investment. Costly slave rebellions would break out and the local militia had to be activated to restore peace. The rebels would damage property and kill citizens. Men of the activated militia were prevented from working their farms or businesses until order had been restored. These men, who were too poor to own slaves of their own, had to interrupt their work and put their lives at hazard hunting down dangerous runaways and rebels. All of this just to prop up the wealthy plantation owner's way of life.

Runaway slaves were a constant source of desperate men who often committed serious crimes. It was not a month ago that a runaway field slave had killed and mutilated a young house slave girl belonging to a prominent New Orleans lady. Everyone was outraged. The militia was called out and the community searched everywhere for the runaway without results. Another angry man was on the loose in Louisiana.

It was less expensive to hire labor, if there were laborers to hire. That was the heart of the enterprise. Laborers were hard to find in a country where every man could claim land for himself. Bartolomé believed that when land became dear and men were deposed to work for others, slavery would perish. He underestimated the power of tradition.

The road along the river often passed a wide, oak-lined corridor that led to a plantation's main house. The house servants, having been long aware of the wagon's approach, would sometimes stop Jacques to see what he was bringing to market. Unlike the rag-clad field hands, the house servants dressed as well, sometimes better, than Bartolomé. Chatting and bartering in French, the servants would examine the wagonload of produce. If what Jacques had to sell was an item that the plantation did not produce, or had in short supply, a sale was made. Fresh produce was grown on every plantation, but sometimes hungry mouths outpaced the crop. The smoked hams that each plantation produced were beginning to run out after a long winter. By the time Jacques and Bartolomé reached the city, they had sold two of the aged hams.

"Every one of the plantations this far up maintains a canal to the bayous that lead to the anchorages in Lakes Pontchartrain and Borgne," Jacques explained. "That way they need not fight a current to bring trade to New Orleans. It is easier to travel through Bayou Sauvage or St. John and arrive in the heart of the city. Some of the larger plantations bring their canals all the way to the river. When the river is high, they open the canal to the river and use the water rushing to the swamp to run a mill."

Bartolomé knew that the waterways into the city from the east were heavily traveled by commerce, legal and otherwise; mostly otherwise. The new plantation being built between Terre Aux Boeufs and Bencheque had begun with Irish day laborers digging a canal that extended from near Bayou Terre Aux Boeufs to a coastal bayou. Every plantation operated a smuggling trade through their own network of tidal waterways that led into one of the coastal bays. Ocean-going ships would anchor in a lake or bay and offload into smaller craft for the trip inland. This commerce, far from the control of the government, supplemented their legal trade.

Before they could see the city, Bartolomé could smell it. That was what struck him most about the city. It stank. All the ditches ran with black water that often had a green scum at the edges. The residents of the smattering of houses on the outskirts of the city would toss refuse and waste out a convenient window or off the side of a porch. Jacques had established a rubbish pile for his little farm far from the house. These city dwellers were not so fastidious.

The housing grew closer together as they approached the fallen and disappearing picket palisade that was called the city rampart. A fortress wall had only been planned, never built. The only sign of a fortification was an earth and timber redoubt known as Fort Saint Charles. Only two guns were mounted on its raised platforms. These cannons faced the river. Any approach from another quarter was not challenged by Fort Saint Charles. The Spanish had recognized long ago that building a fortress city at this site was futile. The low terrain and swampy soils could not support a great wall. Nor could a city in this tropical climate ever survive a siege. Defense of New Orleans rested on a scattering of fortified gun positions along the waterways.

Once they were into the city proper, they found every street covered in horse manure, and gutters running with the contents of last night's chamber pots. In the more affluent parts of the town, outhouses reduced the flow of surface sewerage a little. When overflowing, a man was hired to empty the pit under the outhouse. The city lots were too small to simply move the outhouse to a new pit as was done on the farm. The man would transfer, by hand bucket, the contents of the pit into a barrel on an ox sled. The load was then sledded out to the nearest bayou or isolated ditch past the settled area and dumped. A traveler to the city had to cross a ring of fly-covered filth bordering every road or trail. If it weren't for the money to be made, Bartolomé would just as soon not visit the city. Perhaps it would rain and at least temporarily wash the filth away.

The market was a little cleaner. The merchants kept the horses out of the market area where food was being sold and there were outhouses at the periphery of the main building. When they arrived at the market, Jacques tended to the wagon. The hitching area was crowded with wagons, buggies, and even one fine, team-drawn carriage. While Jacques searched for a hitch, he attempted a few sales to the house servants who were quick to greet a new arrival in order to obtain a first look at his wares. Bartolomé strode off to Stout's stall. William was there, as usual, this time surrounded by copper pots and jerked beef. Every time it was something new.

"Mr. Stout, how goes your day?" Bartolomé asked.

"It goes well, young sir, well indeed," Mr. Stout answered.

Bartolomé explained that he had his stepfather close by with thirteen fine, smoked hams. William quickly offered the use of a small hand cart to fetch the hams to his stall. Horses were not allowed into the market until after dark. William knew Jacques' hams always sold well. They quickly agreed on the usual arrangement. Bartolomé would sell the hams out of the stall and William would get 10 percent of the sales for the use of his stall. Bartolomé returned to Jacques, towing the cart.

"Mister Stout is here and he has agreed to our usual terms," Bartolomé explained. Jacques had tethered the horse at a public post. He helped Bartolomé load the cart and then walked with Bartolomé to confirm the deal with Mr. Stout. Once done, Jacques excused himself and left for other parts of the city. His intent was to find a bolt of cloth, an ax, and, if the dollars held out, a few other items, as well.

Bartolomé enjoyed working in the stall. If he did not recognize the customer, he didn't know which language he would have to be prepared to use. It was a challenge that sharpened his language skills.

"*Goede ochtendmeneer*," said one of his first shoppers. She was a wide faced, smiling lady. This one threw Bartolomé. It wasn't German.

"I'm sorry, madam. I don't know what you said," Bartolomé tried in English. Nothing but a blank stare was the response. French didn't work any better, but Spanish brought a response. The lady was Dutch! Her Spanish was rudimentary, but with the assistance of gestures, a sale was made.

A *femme de couleur* (free woman of color) stopped by. Fully half of the black population of New Orleans were free citizens. The Spanish and French traditions of slavery allowed a slave to buy his or her own freedom. Frequently, a slave was freed in the owner's will as a reward for faithful service. Many other blacks had arrived at New Orleans as free immigrants, the result of the Haitian Revolution and the following turmoil between a series of despotic rebel rulers and harsh colonial governors sent to that sad island by Napoleon.

Bartolomé knew her by reputation. She was Madam Barbeaux, an important *mambo* (priestess) of Voodoo, a religion from West Africa that was common among the Haitians. She wore a simple white dress drawn tight at her slender waist. Her dark hair was tucked beneath a wide straw hat instead of the more popular bonnet. She preferred sandals to shoes, even in the coldest weather. Her complexion was the color of a strong tea. Her eyes were dark brown. When she spoke, she looked unwaveringly into Bartolomé's eyes. Bartolomé could not guess at her age. She seemed ageless and quite attractive. Her height, about four and a half feet, did little to reduce the power and dignity she possessed. She was famed for her knowledge of unusual medications and, some said, incantations. When she walked among the crowd in the market, the shoppers parted before her like the sea before a ship. She also had some very powerful connections.

"Young sir, I am in search of a ham cured and aged with the burning of the *Tchmench* tree," she said. Her French had a strong Haitian accent. She closely examined the one remaining aged ham. Aged hams sold for three times what a simple smoked ham would get. "If you have such a ham, it must have been in the smoke of that tree for at least three full moons."

Bartolomé knew the tree. *Tchmench* was the Chitimacha name. It meant "bloody river," or "river of blood," or "blood by the river." He couldn't remember which. He did remember that it had great, long, sharp thorns. The Americans called it the toothache tree. If one chewed a leaf of the tree, it would numb the mouth.

"I am sorry, madam," he answered. "We have only used water oak in our smokehouse."

She was not visibly disappointed. "If, sir," she replied, "you are able to bring me a ham so aged, it will be well rewarded. Gold, not silver, must be exchanged for the ham. You will know how to find me." She drifted away.

Gold! he thought. Even the smallest gold coin was worth a hundred times what the best hams would bring. Bartolomé had never held a Spanish gold piece. Spanish silver *reales* were the coins that fueled the market. The large silver eight-*reales* coin was universally called a "dollar." The Americans minted a silver dollar that was nearly identical in size to the Spanish eight-*reales* coin or "piece of eight," but not as pure. Gold was rarely seen.

Even though he had not been selling for very long, only two hams remained. Bartolomé sat down to read a book that Mr. Stout had given him. It was *Henry V*, by William Shakespeare. It was the first play he had attempted, and he was engrossed in picturing the action.

"May I examine one of these hams, young sir?" a voice said.

Bartolomé looked up and saw a uniformed nanny. Because she initiated the conversation in English, he rightly guessed that she was an American. She was accompanied by her "young lady." It was the custom that a maturing young lady would accompany her nanny on marketing trips so that she might learn the process.

Bartolomé placed the remaining hams on the stall table so they could be examined closely. While the nanny was examining the ham, he stole a bold look at the young lady.

She wore a blue cotton dress with white lace. The dress hem touched the ground and only a toe of her boot could be seen. She wore full-length gloves, and her head was covered with a bonnet. A lock or two of red hair showed from beneath the edges of the bonnet. Her eyes were green and sparkling. A few freckles adorned her cheeks. Her complexion, what little of it he could see, was a white as milk. It was a cool spring day, so she also had a shawl about her shoulders. He guessed her age at about fourteen or so. He could not make himself look away from her face. Instead of admonishing him for being so brash, she simply smiled and glanced down. The nanny purchased both hams.

She turned to her young lady and said, "I fear that this is all we will be able to buy today. My French is horrible and I do not see any American vendors with vegetables." She then addressed William. "Mr. Stout, do you know of any English-speaking vendors that we may visit?"

"Besides myself, there are none here today, Miss Wren," he said. Miss Wren was a new but frequent visitor to his stall. She was more comfortable with English-speaking vendors. Her struggle to learn French was progressing, but slowly. She could understand what was being said, but when she attempted to speak, the words came so slowly that others would often finish her sentences.

"If I may, madam," Bartolomé said. He was more than a little surprised at himself, but he continued. "You have left me with nothing to sell. I could offer my services as a translator. I could even help you carry your purchases."

Miss Wren looked at him with a disapproving glare. This barefoot and plain cotton-clad farm boy she had never seen before was offering to serve as a translator. She had heard him converse with others in French, and now he was addressing her as if he were an English baron's son.

Before she could say anything, Stout spoke up. "I can vouch for the lad," he said. "His English, as you can see, is fine, his Spanish is excellent, and he was raised in a French household." Mr. Stout could see that a formal introduction was appropriate. "Madam Wren and Mistress Steward, may I introduce you to Master Bartolomé deMelilla."

"Imagine that, Miss Wren," the young lady said. "Three languages! The only thing the sisters will teach me is Latin." Her smile was easy to see from under the bonnet. The sound of her voice was thrilling. Bartolomé felt something strange deep inside.

"Hush, Anna!" Miss Wren said. Then she spoke to Bartolomé. "How much will it cost me for these services?"

"Why, nothing at all, madam. You are a good customer. I look forward to your continuing patronage," he said. He almost bowed, but he decided that might be too much.

"Oh, please do let him help us, Miss Wren," Anna said. She gave her nanny a little tug on the sleeve. "You have known Mr. Stout for some time. What harm could it be?"

"Very well," Miss Wren said as she reluctantly accepted Bartolomé's offer. "I will have you know, young man, that I understand French well enough that I can tell what is being said."

With that, she gave Bartolomé the canvas sack that held the hams and then, directing him to lead, they went to the other stalls where fresh vegetables and other items were on display. Bartolomé knew most of the vendors and the fair market value of the goods. Haggling was minimized.

Bartolomé was burdened with most of the purchases while Miss Wren carried the rest. Anna arranged to walk next to Bartolomé most of the time. They managed a whispered and frequently interrupted conversation. Miss Wren appeared uneasy that her young lady was so forward with this farmhand.

"How do you pronounce your name? Mister Stout spoke it so quickly," Anna said.

"Bar-toe-low-may," he replied. "Day-ma-lee-ya."

"Bartolomé," she said. The sound of her saying his name was intoxicating. "Where are you from, Bartolomé deMelilla?"

"I was born in Terre Aux Boeufs, a village not far from here. My father and grandfather came here long before I was born. They were from the island of *Gran Canaria*," he said.

She looked directly into his eyes as he spoke. She appeared to be genuinely interested in every word.

The shopping was done much too quickly for Bartolomé's liking. Soon, they were at the ladies' buggy and driver, hitched just beyond the "no horses" zone.

"Thank you for your help, young sir," said Miss Wren after he had placed their purchases in the buggy.

"It was my pleasure to be of service, madam and mademoiselle," he said.

"Mister deMelilla, you were of great service. Perhaps it may chance that we might use your help again," Anna said while a shocked Miss Wren looked on.

That was much too forward, Miss Wren thought. *I must have a firm talk with Mistress Anna.*

"I am at your service," Bartolomé said. He decided that he was going to make certain that there would be many more opportunities to serve.

* * *

Bartolomé made his way back to Mister Stout's stall. Mister Stout was closing up for the day.

"Can you tell me more about the ladies?" Bartolomé asked.

Mister Stout knew which ladies he was referring to. "That is Bernard Steward's daughter and her nanny," he replied. "He is the new owner of the mattress works over near where Bayou Pecheur ends near the river."

The mattress works! Bartolomé knew the place. They were always ready to purchase processed Spanish moss to use as stuffing for cushions, mattresses, and the like. The moss fibers were also sold to builders for insulation and as a plaster base. The process of picking the moss, soaking it for six weeks, cleaning it, drying it, and bringing it to the warehouse was barely worth the money.

Bartolomé thought about the process. If he could buy processed moss from people along the bayou for a few bits, then make the trip up the back bayous with a flatboat full of moss, he might turn a profit. He decided that the idea was worth further consideration.

Jacques came to the stall to collect Bartolomé and the day's take. He was very pleased with the cash from the day's sales. He was also bubbling over with excitement from what he has just witnessed on the river. It was the steamboat, *New Orleans*!

"*Quelle vision* (What a sight)! You should have seen it, Bartolomé," he said. "It shot great columns of smoke into the air and no sooner had they cast off than the giant paddlewheels spun around and it raced upstream."

The *New Orleans* was one of Fulton's boats. It had been visiting the city for a few years now. The steamboat was stuffed with cargo and passengers on every run, upstream and down. It was the spring of 1814, and the war between Britain and America was hindering trade along the Atlantic coast. British ships had imposed a nearly continuous blockade and often intercepted international shipments and even hindered trade that was simply between neighboring colonies. Commerce from Europe was often diverted to Louisiana rather than making an attempt to smuggle goods past the British. Here, the war didn't appear to touch the city. In spite of constant rumors of a pending British invasion, it all seemed distant. Fulton's steamboat plied the Mississippi unhindered by the war. Bartolomé hoped that the next time they came into New Orleans he would see the steamboat.

"How often does the steamboat visit, Mister Stout?" Bartolomé asked in English. Mister Stout understood French well enough, but sometimes it took him a long time to put sentences together.

"About once in every ten days," he answered. "Goes all the way to Natchez and back, she does."

If he planned well, Bartolomé was certain he could make it into New Orleans about once a week. As long as he could return home with some silver, it wouldn't be a problem. Jacques had toyed with the idea of allowing Bartolomé to make the trip alone. After all, he was a big lad. And he brought back cash. The problem was supplying enough produce to sell. They would have to discuss the matter on the long ride home.

CHAPTER 3

They traveled down the river road and crossed the last remnants of the old city palisade wall as the lamplighters were beginning their rounds. It would be dark by the time they reached home.

At first, Bartolomé was lost in thought. Jacques was about to ask him why he was so quiet when Bartolomé spoke up.

"Let us stop for a moment at the mattress works at the village where Bayou Pecheur comes to the river," he said. "Mister Stout gave me an idea."

Jacques just shrugged. The mattress works were close to the river road. Several houses and buildings lined both sides of the short, narrow canal that extended Bayou Pecheur right up to the road along the river. The river would only flow down Pecheur when it was at flood stage. Otherwise, boat traffic to the mattress works had to come up the bayou from the east. Cargo arriving on the river side would be offloaded at a landing on the river and carted to the warehouse.

When they arrived at the mattress works, Jacques waited in the wagon while Bartolomé went to the tally window, only a few feet away from the road. It was from this window that the business of delivering supplies, such as cloth, cords, and other raw materials was conducted. The man at the window was a red faced Irishman.

"State your business," was all he said.

"If I were to deliver dried moss to the landing, what would it fetch?" he asked. He tried to appear experienced and business like.

The Irishman smirked. *Just another moss picker*, he thought. *He'll bring in a few pounds of moss and leave with a dollar, maybe.* "The going rate is one bit of silver for ten pounds of quality moss. That is one silver dollar for every eighty pounds. If it ain't dried and cleaned proper, nothing," he said. "If you come to the landing, ask for Moine. He will examine your goods and tell you if there is a deal"

He thanked the Irishman, hoping he wasn't named Steward, and climbed back on the wagon. Jacques asked what was said.

"If I were to tell folks along the bayou that I would pay a bit for twenty pounds of dried moss, how many takers do you think I would have?" he asked.

Jacques thought a while. Youngsters would welcome the opportunity to earn a little silver. Regular moss pickers would like to eliminate the long trip into Bayou Pecheur. Most farmers would have better things to do. "I am not sure," he said. "Several, maybe."

"If I could repair the old *bateau*, I could pass up and down the bayou twice a week or so. When I had the boat full, I could pole up the river to the mattress works and sell the lot at a bit for ten pounds," he said. He had saved about four dollars, so he had enough seed money to buy five hundred pounds.

The *bateau* was a wide skiff that had been used to travel up and down the bayou long ago when the path along the bayou was not wide or well-worn. The boat had been made in Acadia and somehow carried to Terre Aux Boeufs. It had showed up on Jacques' farm after a hurricane, in disrepair, but salvageable.

Jacques thought a while. "I'll rent the boat to you for a dollar a trip and you keep up with your chores," he said.

The next day, the word was passed along in the village that Bartolomé would pay one bit for twenty pounds of processed moss. Almost every household had some moss about for stuffing a sagging mattress, patching a bit of plaster, or weaving a crude rope. The regular pickers had some moss ready, but in small batches that did not justify a trip into town. Three days after the word was out, Bartolomé made his first collection trip. In that one day, he bought five hundred pounds of fine, processed moss. It was as much as the boat would hold.

That evening he asked Jacques if he could depart the next day for New Orleans. Somewhat to Bartolomé's surprise, Jacques agreed.

* * *

Madam Barbeaux stood in an open field of tall grass. She was wearing her thin cotton sleeping gown. She did not recognize the wide, flat field around her. She had grown up on the island of Haiti where the landscape consisted of cane fields or steep hills. The grass here was dry, brown, and dead looking. It rippled in the warm wind with a hissing sound. A tall, armed African warrior appeared and walked up to her. The sun was setting, or maybe rising, directly behind him. She shaded her eyes as she looked up at him. It was the powerful warrior loa (spirit), Ogoun.

He has come into my dream world, she thought. This had never happened to her before. Her contact with the spirits had always been after she had performed an intricate ritual at her altar. On the last waning of the moon, Barbeaux had been granted permission to speak with Ogoun. Ogoun was the loa who gave courage to the just. He was the protector of the innocent. It must be important for a loa to cross over without ceremony or sacrifice.

"Mambo, the one you seek," Ogoun said in Haitian-accented French, "is protected by Loa Kalfu."

This was bad news. It will be difficult for her to accomplish her contract against a protected one.

"Loa Ogoun," she answered, "I have contacted the young man you suggested to me. I am certain he will provide what you have requested."

"Know this, mambo," Ogoun said. "This one that I have chosen is young, but he is strong. You may be able to influence him through the spirit world for a short time only. After that, he will be as a strong wind. None in the spirit world will be able to direct him. Loa Erzulie can help you enter his dreams now, while he is young. When he becomes a man, he will be too strong."

"Ogoun, how will I make my contract against a protected one?" Madam Barbeaux asked as the hot wind blew her hair across her face and molded the thin cotton gown against her body.

"Evil must be confronted by good, greed by alms, vileness by purity, cowardice by courage. When the vile one is struck down, the depths to which he is banished will be as deep as the instrument of his death is pure. The young one who prepares the blood feast offering for you is pure of heart. The meat he prepares will have great power against the evil one."

"After the dry season, the ham will be ready. You must purchase it with pure gold. Go to your altar and offer the ham to Kalfu when I say. He will feast on the offering and be distracted. Only then will the protected one be vulnerable."

* * *

That morning as Bartolomé left, some of the young folks had gathered along the bayou to watch him pass. If he were successful, it meant that they had a source of spending money, so all wished him well. Every youngster had already gathered some fresh moss and placed it in shallow ponds here and there to soak. In six weeks, they could retrieve it and wash away the now rotten bark and twigs, leaving the dark fiber strands that formed the core of the moss, and sell it to Bartolomé for silver. There would be no need for them to make the trip to New Orleans.

Bartolomé's small boat was about sixteen feet long with a four-foot beam. It was powered by two long, heavy oars or a push pole, depending upon the conditions. The bayou was not flowing very fast, so Bartolomé rowed. The oars were chocked so that one rowed standing up and facing forward. He glided along at a comfortable pace. There was little traffic on the bayou. He rowed with dignity and purpose.

"I am the master of my boat," he said aloud. "I am about my business on my own."

When he reached the ferry landing, Bacenaux called out, "Traffic coming through," and dropped the weighted swing line so the boat could pass. Bartolomé swelled with pride.

Once on the river, he had to concentrate on the flow patterns. He stayed close to the bank and avoided the fast currents farther from shore. Often the water would form eddies and back currents. The four hours it took to get to the mattress works passed quickly. He lashed his boat to the Bayou Pecheur landing.

"I am looking for Moine of the mattress works," he announced to the three or four men who were about.

"I am Moine," said a gray-haired black man, "Let me see your goods."

Moine was weathered and bent with age. By his dress, Bartolomé took him to be a free man. His eyes were milky with cataracts, so he had one of the others hand him one of the tightly bound little bundles of moss. He rubbed it with his hands and smelled it.

"This will do," he said. One of the men at the landing pulled a small cart close to the boat and all, except Moine, loaded the bundles onto the cart. It took three trips, but the moss was delivered and weighed. Moine would check a bundle from each load.

"Well, sir, see Mister Getty at the tally window for your pay," Moine said.

Moine returned to the landing where they were expecting a barge from New Orleans, with cloth and bunting. Bartolomé went to the tally window. He was relieved to learn that Mister Getty was the red faced Irishman he had spoken to last week. He had worried that Getty might have been Bernard Steward and the beautiful Mistress Anna Steward's father.

"The tally is 493 pounds, young sir. That comes to six dollars and one bit," Getty said.

"Evidently, the tally rounds off to the benefit of the house," Bartolomé muttered.

Mr. Getty pretended not to hear Bartolomé's complaint as he counted out six silver coins. He then picked up a half of a coin and placed it on the table. He positioned a small hatchet on the half coin and struck it with a hammer. The fragment that was cut off was one eighth of a whole coin.

"Here you go, six and a bit," he said.

Bartolomé wrapped the money in a piece of cloth and placed it in his haversack and went back to his boat.

"Moine, may I keep my boat moored here for a while? I would like to look about," he said.

"Leave the boat, if you wish. Pull it to the side here so it is out of the way. It will not be bothered," Moine said.

Bartolomé did as he was directed. He retrieved his walking staff and set off toward the cluster of buildings. He was looking for someone, but he had to appear as if he were not.

Most of the houses and other buildings were barge plank shacks. People from the upper reaches of the Mississippi would build barges to float their goods down to the port. After all they carried had been offloaded, the barges would be disassembled and the planking sold to build houses. Even the nails were pulled, straightened, and re-sold.

These "river men" would then make the return trip upstream on foot or horseback. This was the most dangerous part of the enterprise, for their pockets fairly burst with bank notes. The most common bank note was the ten dollar note, which had "TEN" on one side and "DIX" on the other. River boatmen often called New Orleans the "Land of Dixie."

Normally, river men would tarry for a while in the city until enough had assembled to form a caravan for the return trip. Unfortunately, staying in the squalid rooms for rent in New Orleans was just as hazardous as traveling the wilderness. Seeking safety in numbers, boatmen would sometimes form great rafts of a dozen or more boats and travel together downriver and caravan back up.

One house on Bayou Pecheur was more substantial than the bargewood buildings that populated the village. It had a high stucco-covered wall all around. Other buildings were crowded about it so that small alleyways were to the left and right. The front wall was set against the dirt road.

A servant came out the door. Bartolomé could see a courtyard through the door as it closed. The servant was a young slave. He was small, frail, and very black.

"*Qui possède cette maison*," he asked the servant. A blank stare was the reply. He tried English. "Whose house is this?"

"This is Master Steward's house. You had better not try begging here. You will be lashed for certain," the servant replied.

Bartolomé felt his face redden. *The fool takes me for a beggar*, he thought. He suddenly assessed himself. He was shoeless. His clothes were worn but clean. At least he wore a white cotton frock over his shirt. There were many about too poor to own even a simple cotton frock. Before he could walk away, the door opened again. Out stepped Anna and Miss Wren!

"Bartolomé," Anna said excitedly. She walked toward him. Miss Wren attempted to grab her by the arm, but Anna expertly slipped by. She walked up to Bartolomé, smiling. "What brings you to Bayou Pecheur?" she asked.

Bartolomé was very conscious of his appearance, but Anna's attitude swept away the clouds. She stood close to him and looked directly into his eyes. He could have touched her hand by slightly reaching out.

"I am here on business, *mademoiselle*," he said. "I have delivered a load of moss to the warehouse." He didn't mention that it was all of six dollars worth.

"Mistress Anna, we must go," said Miss Wren with a frown. The nanny looked as if she was preparing to drag Anna down the street.

"Perhaps we will meet in the market again some time," Anna said as Miss Wren all but pulled her away.

"I would like that," was all he could say.

Then they were gone. *Into the warehouse to see Papa, no doubt*, he thought. He knew where she lived now. He was going to be delivering a lot more moss and dressing better.

Bartolomé walked along the canal until it connected to a small bayou. He wanted to see the conditions he would face if he decided it would be easier to forgo the river and take the eastern route through the slow-flowing coastal canals and bayous. He walked along the bank for a quarter mile. The bayou was little more than a narrow ditch, but it could float his small boat.

By the time he started back, the sun had begun to set. He hadn't planned on walking so far and he worried if his boat would still be there. He reached the Steward's house at dusk. If there were lights on inside, he couldn't tell. The moon was full, so the boat ride home would be easy. He had warned his mother that if the return trip was delayed until dark, he would sleep in the boat at Poche's Ferry. He was going to get a scolding, though.

The street was vacant as he passed the Steward house and headed for an alley between two buildings. Suddenly, two men stepped out of the alley.

One brandished a knife. The other began to work his way in a low creep around behind Bartolomé. Both were quite drunk. Bartolomé came to the guard position with his walking staff.

"Well, boy," the Knife said. "Did you have a nice walk? We saw your pay day. Give it over."

The Knife never saw it coming. The walking stick was pointed at his nose, so when Bartolomé made a strong lunge, the Knife didn't even try to dodge it. The end of the stick caught him square on the bridge of the nose. Blood flew everywhere. The Knife's knees buckled and he grabbed his smashed nose with his free hand.

Bartolomé brought the stick back hard, and with a circling motion, struck the Creeper on the temple. The butt of the walking sick landed with a loud, crunching noise, and the Creeper went down without uttering a sound. He gave the Knife another strong lunge to the middle of the chest. The crack of breaking ribs was followed by a groan as the man hit the ground. All was quiet. Bartolomé picked up the blade the Knife dropped. It was well made, heavy and wide.

"I wonder how many throats were cut by this blade," he said quietly. He tucked it in his belt and hurried off to his boat. He would have to spend the night at Poche's Landing.

Anna was standing at a small, barred window with her hand to her lips. She was about to call out to Bartolomé when the hooligans jumped him. It was over so fast she did not have enough time to recover to call for help. She watched as Bartolomé disappeared into the night. Bartolomé's actions were violent, fast, controlled, and terrifyingly effective. Was it fear she felt, or something else? She resolved that she would speak with Bartolomé again.

* * *

Anna awoke and sat up quickly. She had not slept well. The vision of Bartolomé's street fight would not leave her thoughts. When she did sleep, Bartolomé entered into every dream. When she lay awake, she embraced her pillow and imagined Bartolomé's face. He both frightened and fascinated her in equal measure. There was no doubt. Something very strange was happening to her.

Miss Wren knocked on the bedroom door. "Time to rise," she said in a singing tone.

She acts as if I'm still a child, Anna thought. *I have been fourteen for half a year, and still I'm treated as a child.*

"Anna?" Miss Wren persisted, "Are you up?"

"Yes, Miss Wren," she said as she donned her robe. "Please come in."

With the help of Miss Wren, which was not welcomed, Anna dressed for the day. Her father insisted that the family breakfast together every morning. They always sat in the same order. Bernard sat at the head of the table. Her mother, Grace, occupied the end opposite Bernard. Anna sat on the side, with her back to the kitchen, and her brother, James, was across from Anna on his booster chair.

James was only five and he talked incessantly. "Hush, James," Grace said. "Your father is talking."

"As I was saying," Bernard continued, "there were two ruffians found this morning, not ten paces from our door. They must have been fighting. Both were so injured that the constable could not get a straight answer from either of them."

Anna looked down and pretended to be interested in her breakfast ham. It was a slice from the last of the smoked ham they had purchased from Bartolomé. It seemed like years ago. Bartolomé's smiling face filled her thoughts, followed by thoughts of the fierce fight she had witnessed. She said nothing.

"Will they be arrested?" Grace asked. "I am glad that we have a tall, strong wall around us."

The Steward house was a square-shaped construction, built around a large courtyard. As were most proper homes in the area, it was of Spanish design. The exterior walls of the house, made of two-foot thick oven-baked clay bricks, formed three of the four walls of the compound and were windowless on the ground floor. The fourth wall, also made of oven-baked brick, was against the river-side alley.

Matching cisterns sat in the corners where the house turned to abut the street. There, the roof drains and gutters from the second floor filled them with rainfall. Access to the second floor was provided by two stairways, one at either side of the fourth wall adjacent to an alley. There was a small, iron-barred window near one corner, positioned so that someone standing on the second step from the ground could look out into the alley. It was from this window that Anna had witnessed last night's fight.

The street side base of the square enclosure had an opening that provided access to a pair of large wooden carriage gate doors. A pedestrian doorway had been set in one of the large gates. The second floor of the house continued over the carriageway. The kitchen was little more than an enclosed porch that opened into the dining room on one side and to the outdoor oven on the other.

"I cannot say, Grace," Bernard answered. "The constable thinks one may die of his injuries, so there is no telling. He also suspects that the pair may have been involved in the attack on John Too. They have been hauled off to the city to see if Mister Too can identify them."

Anna remembered the story of how John Too arrived at New Orleans. He appeared at the Hall Bank with three gold coins, and speaking the kind of English heard on British ships manned by pressed sailors. The bank officer who established the account just could not understand the Chinese name. Exasperated, the Asian depositor asked the banker, "What name you?"

"My friends call me 'John'," the banker replied.

"Then I am 'John Too'," the newly christened John Too said.

John Too had been accosted and robbed on the road to New Orleans some days ago. He had been severely injured in the attack, but he was recovering.

"What shall you do today, Bernard?" Grace asked. She always addressed her husband by his first name.

"I must solve the problem we are having with materials. There has been a great demand for mattresses and construction materials. The city is growing and it is hard to find enough treated moss. I certainly don't want to resort to straw or the like," he said. "Anna, are you going with Miss Wren to the market today?"

"No, Father. Today I must go to the convent for my lessons. That shall take all day," she answered. It was all she said.

Grace noticed that Anna seemed preoccupied. She was usually more talkative at breakfast. Lately, the farm boy in the market was all she chatted about. Today, Anna would only answer when spoken to. Something was definitely bothering her.

What was that boy's name? Grace thought. It didn't come to her. Miss Wren had mentioned him once when Della was nearby.

"Dat boy jus' a *coonée*," she had said.

Della was the cook and kitchen maid. Bernard had purchased her locally. Her English was good, so she served as liaison between the English-speaking staff that Bernard had moved down from Boston and the local staff he acquired in New Orleans. Grace was to learn later that *coonée* was Creole slang. It roughly translated as "country bumpkin."

Once Bernard is out of the house, Grace thought, *Mistress Anna and I are going to have a talk.*

* * *

At Poche's Landing, Bartolomé was up and about before the sun. The first streaks of light were enough for him to be on his way. He had not slept well. The vision of the knife-wielding man would loom out of his dreams only to be replaced by a blood covered, moaning wreck of a man at his feet.

After the fight at Bayou Pecheur, Bartolomé had walked down to the landing and launched the boat for the trip home. He cast off and was preparing to begin rowing downstream when a fit of the shakes came over him. He had to sit in the boat shaking for a few minutes until they passed. All that training with his grandfather had actually paid off. Everything happened so fast that all he had time to do was react. Now, when it was well over, he shook. He wondered if he were a coward.

Today, the trip downstream was easy and relaxing. By the time he reached his village, he was feeling much better. He could see his mother waiting by the bank of the bayou as he rowed into sight. He regretted that he was a cause of concern, but he had said that he might camp at Poche's Ferry.

"*Enfin,*" his mother said as he pulled to the bank. "Maurice passed by Poche's Ferry at eight last night, and you were not there."

Enfin must be her favorite word, Bartolomé thought. "He must have just missed me," he answered. "I have over six Spanish dollars for yesterday's trip."

He did admit to himself that of that six, three were reimbursement for the money paid to the moss collectors and one was due to Jacques for the rental of the boat, which left two as profit. Two dollars for a little rowing was not bad. It was less than the hams would bring on a single trip, but there was little invested.

"*Mais rien*, I was worried," his mother said. Her tone was not angry. It reflected love and concern. Bartolomé instantly regretted being the cause of any grief for his mother.

Bartolomé reminded Aimée of his father, Pedro. She still mourned his death, still loved Pedro, even after remarrying, and bearing Jacques two beautiful daughters. Pedro was big, powerful, strong, and gentle. Simply the memory of his deep blue eyes could almost bring her to tears. Fever took the man from her. Bartolomé seemed, sometimes, to be the ghost of Pedro. The thought unnerved her. Perhaps that was why she rarely showed any affection to Bartolomé. When she did, he was simply not accustomed to it.

"We are glad to see you home," Jacques said as Bartolomé stepped up on the porch. "Now go with Maurice to help collect wood for the smokehouse."

Maurice hadn't cut enough wood on his last trip so another expedition was in order. The two trudged off together, with an ax and a hatchet between them.

"That is a big one," Maurice said as he gestured to the knife that Bartolomé had tucked in his belt.

"I picked it up in a dark alley," Bartolomé replied. "Someone dropped it there."

Bartolomé took the knife out of his belt and handed it to Maurice to examine. It had a large, heavy blade about eight inches long, and was razor sharp on the cutting edge.

"It is almost a sword," Maurice said as he handed it back. "How could someone have lost that?"

"It may have been too heavy for him," Bartolomé said as he tucked the knife back into his belt.

They walked along a small trail that was raised a few inches above the wooded lowland. Bayou Terre Aux Boeufs flowed from the Mississippi River forming a portion of a great bird's foot delta. When the river was high and water diverted down the bayou, it would often overflow the banks, building up the land along the bayou on either side of the waterway with sediment. As they walked deeper into the woods, the land fell away from the bayou into a low swamp. Water oak grew all about the trail once they were far from the village.

They came to a storm-felled oak tree that must have been three feet in diameter. It had been down for some time and had dried quite a bit. It was enough to fill the needs of the smokehouse for some time.

"*Perfectionner*," Maurice said. "We will not have to store it long before it will be available for use."

The smoking process used both green and cured wood. The heavy dried wood was the fuel that kept the fire going. Green wood would be added in small portions if a more flavorful smoke was needed. Sometimes, hot coals from the brick oven where meals were cooked could be added to the pit for the smokehouse. This expedition would provide fuel for the home as well.

Maurice began trimming the branches with the ax. Many of the branches were large enough to cut into logs. The tree trunk was much too large to tackle today. They would have to return with wedges to split off properly sized portions.

Bartolomé went off with the hatchet to select saplings of the proper size to make a *travois*. The construction of a *travois* required two poles of twelve-foot lengths and four to five poles in three-foot lengths. The butt of the longer poles would be trimmed at an angle so that the tips could slide easily along the muddy trail. Cross braces were lashed at intervals, starting a foot from the butt and ending three feet or so from the tip. The lashings were made from strips of bark or, if available, a heavy, flexible vine.

Any load could be tied on the cross-bracing. By standing in the space between the pole tips, one could pull a heavy load along the trail. The leverage advantage of the long poles meant that the butt tips on the ground carried the greater weight. The muddy soil offered little resistance to the tapered wood as the device was pulled along. If an animal such as a horse or an ox did the pulling, the poles of the *travois* would be much longer, the cross bracing wider and the lashings made of rope. Wagons were of little use in narrow, winding, muddy trails.

Maurice was near enough to be heard chopping away as Bartolomé felled both runners and cross braces. He began stripping bark with the large knife for the *travois* bindings. He made two fine *travois* and had enough bindings left over to secure the loads. Then he saw it.

The *Tchmench* tree was the largest he had ever seen. It was at least twelve inches in diameter, and covered with long, sharp thorns on the trunk and branches. Each thorn had a long center spike and several side spikes that jutted out from the base. Some of the thorns were nearly a foot long. It was going to take a long time to harvest wood from this tree. The work had to be carefully planned. The thought of Madam Barbeaux's offer pushed any trepidation aside. He was going to get enough wood from this tree to age a ham for three months.

Bartolomé returned with the two *travois* to where Maurice was working. They loaded one of the *travois* with what Maurice had already cut. Together, they cut enough to fill the second *travois*.

"After we bring these loads in, I will return for some more," Bartolomé proposed.

"Why?" asked Maurice. "There is enough now for some time. The *t'abri* will be full."

"I have a special order for an aged ham using the wood of a certain tree," Bartolomé explained. "I have found the tree nearby."

"Fine," Maurice said, "as long as you do not expect me to help."

It was not unusual for someone to ask for a ham smoked in a specific wood, such as pecan or hickory. Maurice didn't think about it anymore. It didn't involve more work for him, so he didn't care.

They trudged along the trail, each pulling a loaded *travois*. They would occasionally stop to repair a binding or simply catch their breath. The day was half gone when they arrived at the farm. Together, they unloaded the *travois* and filled every available space in the lean-to. What didn't fit in the lean-to was stored at the oven wood bin.

"I'm going back to work on the other tree," Bartolomé announced. "I won't need a *travois* because I have a lot of work to do to prepare the tree."

Maurice shrugged his shoulders. He didn't care what extra work Bartolomé had to do as long as he could stay out of it. Bartolomé headed back with only the hatchet and that sword of a knife.

"Where is he going?" Jacques asked as he walked up to where Maurice was disassembling the *travois*. The wood would be used as green fuel. Nothing was ever wasted.

"He had a special wood request," Maurice answered. They both looked back toward where Bartolomé had gone.

"It will be months before we do any serious smoking," Jacques said. "Summer is nearly here. What we have now is for our house and we will not butcher any pigs until late fall. He knows that."

The new spring piglets needed to grow. There were simply no animals to spare.

CHAPTER 4

Bartolomé arrived at the *Tchmench* tree with about three hours of working time left. First, he lopped the thorn spikes off the trunk with the hatchet. He had to take care with every stroke not to contact other spines while attempting to strike one off. After a few minutes of work, he had cleaned the trunk, with only a few wounds to his hand and arm. The thorns inflicted a burning puncture wound that bled profusely. He had removed all the thorns within reach. He would need to fell the tree to remove the rest of the thorns. That task he left for another day.

On the way back, Bartolomé felt quite tired, and he stopped often to rest. At one point, he lopped off a few palmetto fronds and made a little bed on the muddy trail. He lay on the fronds to rest, and when he was half asleep, he heard a noise in the brush. *A deer*, he thought, *has caught wind of me.*

He barely moved his head to look up the trail. It was a wild hog! Bartolomé pulled his hatchet. A wild hog was a serious danger. The pig, alarmed by the movement, stopped what he was doing and glared at Bartolomé. Bartolomé quietly positioned himself. First, he rose to his knees, and then managed a crouch. He had the hatchet in his right hand and the knife in the other.

The pig stomped a fore-hoof, grunted, then dashed into the thicket. Bartolomé could hear it for a while. Then all was silent again. The action seemed to revive him. He went to where the pig had been rooting around. He could see what remained of a large snake the pig had been feeding on. There was sign of pig activity all around. A wallow had been created in the mud under a large oak tree with a thick canopy. The branches spread over the muddy wallow, creating a sheltered area. There were many trails in and out. Bartolomé finished the trip home warily, but without further incident.

That evening at supper, Bartolomé ate very little. He felt very tired and sore.

"You seem very listless, Bartolomé," his mother said. "Are you ill?"

"No, I think not," he answered. "I think I have worked too hard cutting firewood. I will feel better after I have had some sleep."

With that, he excused himself, went out on the porch, and slowly climbed the outside stairs to his bed. His lips seemed to tingle as he lay down, and he fell into a sound sleep. When his stepbrothers tumbled into the room, he didn't even stir.

"Look at him," Maurice said. "A little work with an ax and he's beat."

* * *

Madam Barbeaux was standing beside the trail near the *Tchmench* tree. She was barefoot and wearing a long, thin, cotton nightgown. Her thick, black hair was pulled back into a bun. The wind blew her gown tightly against her body until every detail was accentuated. She walked around the *Tchmench* tree as Bartolomé watched from the trail. She picked up one of the long thorns and examined the sharp tip.

"Tu ha hecho bien (You have done well)," she said to Bartolomé. "This tree will serve my needs, young sir." She was speaking in *Isleño*-accented Spanish, not the heavy Haitian French she had used when they met in the market.

"I think it made me ill," Bartolomé said weakly.

"If the thorns pierce your skin, rub your wounds with the leaves of the tree," she answered. "After a while, you need not worry with it, for you will become immune to its sting. Use the thorns in the smoking fire as well. I will send the animal to you when you are ready."

She moved close to Bartolomé. He could feel her body against him. There was the smell of rum on her breath.

"If you finish this task for me, your reward will be gold," she said as she stood on her toes, looking up at him from against his chest. "It will be gold and my friendship."

Her dark eyes looked deep into his. He felt as if she were reading his thoughts. She began to kiss him.

* * *

Bartolomé, Bartolomé!"

Someone was calling his name. He recognized Gabriel's voice.

"Bartolomé, wake up!" Gabriel shouted as he shook Bartolomé out of his deep sleep. "Father wants you up and down to breakfast. There's work to do."

Bartolomé stumbled down the stairs to the porch. He was shaken by how real the dream seemed. Everyone was gathered at the breakfast table talking about plans for the day. There was always something to do for everyone. Mending, planting, weeding, and countless other chores provided work for every hand.

"If you are going to fill a special order, you cannot allow it to interfere with your chores, Bartolomé," Jacques admonished. "Where are you going to get the meat for this order? I have no pigs to spare."

"I know where there is a wild pig about. He is over two hundred pounds and will do just nicely," Bartolomé replied. He then changed the subject. "Once summer's here, there will be little cash to be made at the market. With your permission, I should go to Bayou Pecheur to see if more can be made on the moss or if I can find a buyer for garden produce."

Jacques knew that Bartolomé was right about the market. In the summer, activity in New Orleans slowed to a crawl. Vegetables and other greens spoiled quickly and rarely survived the long trip in any condition to sell. Few ships docked and commerce stagnated. Citizens with any resources left for their summer houses on the gulf coast, the north shore of Lake Pontchartrain, or other places to escape the heat and the feared yellow fever. Spain still controlled those areas, but the citizens of New Orleans traveled to their summer homes as they always had when Spain controlled all of Louisiana. It was as if nothing had really changed. Louisiana's borders with Spanish Florida were rarely garrisoned.

Transporting vegetables to Bayou Pecheur might prove profitable. It was closer to the farm and the people there were fishermen or mattress workers or tradesmen. A few had their own gardens, but there might be enough people willing to buy fresh produce. The money that Bartolomé had made selling moss in just one trip was promising.

"After chores, Bartolomé will make a trip to Bayou Pecheur," Jacques decided. Bartolomé would be only fifteen years old in June, but he had shown an ability to create business that Jacques appreciated. Jacques had decided that next fall, when the city markets become active again, Bartolomé could go alone to conduct the family's business.

After the pigs were fed, sties mended, and the gardens tended, Bartolomé was excused to begin the twelve-mile walk to Bayou Pecheur. Using the stout walking stick, Bartolomé could make the trip in less than two hours. The only time they used a wagon or a boat was to haul a heavy load. Walking was how one got around, unless one was rich enough to own a riding horse or a buggy. Team-drawn carriages were exclusively for the very wealthy.

* * *

It was afternoon by the time he arrived at Bayou Pecheur. He walked along the river road nervously, half expecting the two hooligans he had fought a few days ago to be about and spoiling for revenge. Moine was at the landing, but few other hands were there. Already the summer lull was beginning.

"How goes your day, Moine," Bartolomé said.

"I ain't dead and I ain't in jail," Moine replied. Bartolomé soon learned that that was Moine's standard reply.

"Tell me, Moine," Bartolomé said as he leaned on his walking staff, "are there folks about who might be interested in produce or such this summer?"

"Yes, a few. Best talk to Mr. Getty," Moine replied. "He could set you onto some that's had poor luck with their gardens."

He found Mr. Getty at the tally window. He was helpful, and even offered a little, open shelter to Bartolomé to set out produce whenever he wanted, for a fee.

"But," Mr. Getty said, "what we really need is a more reliable source of moss."

"How much could you use?" Bartolomé asked.

"Two thousand pounds a day for starters," Mr. Getty said. "It is the lack of material that keeps our sales low. Between building in the city and our furniture needs, we quickly use all we can get."

"I might be able to help, but that is a lot of moss," Bartolomé replied.

Bartolomé left Mr. Getty at the tally window. He then began the business that had really brought him to Bayou Pecheur. He walked along between a few buildings until he reached the alley where the fight had been. He stood there for a moment, but there was no sign of the skirmish.

"Bartolomé," someone whispered. He recognized the voice. It was Anna.

Bartolomé looked about. There was a small, barred window in the strong wall around the Steward house. He saw Anna's fingers as she waved at him through the bars. He rushed to the window. It was slightly above his head, but he could see Anna well enough. All else was forgotten.

"Anna," he said in a hushed tone. "I am very pleased to see you again." He surmised that she was standing on a bench or chair, for her beautiful face filled the little window.

"And I to see you, Bartolomé," she replied. It never failed to thrill him to hear her say his name. "Why are you here today?"

"I could say that it was to do some business," he said, "but in truth, I hoped to speak with you."

She could not believe that this man, and she considered Bartolomé a man, was interested in talking with her. He was a man of the world. Conducting business, free to go where he pleased, and afraid of nothing. She feared him. She admired him. And she was drawn to him.

"It was business, I am certain," she said. "I heard Father say how much they need the moss you supply."

"Little wonder," he said. He didn't want to talk about moss, but until something else came up, it would have to do. "They need to stop requiring the moss to be processed. There is a small pond just off Bayou Pecheur not half a mile downstream that is shallow when the river is not high. What needs to be done is buy the moss raw and process it themselves. Everyone with a *pirogue* would collect moss if they didn't need to prepare it and haul it here to sell it." A *pirogue* was a small, shallow draft boat made from a single cypress log. Anyone who did anything in the cypress swamps and estuaries had at least one *pirogue*.

"You should mention that to Father's tally man," she suggested.

"I will do that today," he said. There was an awkward silence. *Oh please, God*, he thought, *give me words.*

"I've been learning Spanish," Anna said suddenly, much to Bartolomé's relief. "One of the sisters at the convent is teaching me. I like it much better than Latin."

"Perhaps I could help you, as well," Bartolomé said.

"Oh, could you?" Anna said. "I would so like that."

He began with a few everyday phrases, first in English, then in Spanish. Anna knew quite a few of them. They chatted back and forth through the window for a little while.

"*Cuántos años tienes* (How old are you)?" Anna asked. She was pretending to practice Spanish, when in reality she wanted to learn more about Bartolomé.

"*Catorce*. I will be fifteen on the fifteenth of June," he answered.

The answer surprised her. She thought he was much older!

He is only a few months older than I, and yet, to all he meets, he is a man, she thought. Her admiration for Bartolomé increased. A deeper feeling was there, as well. She had witnessed how dangerous he could be. Was it fear? She could not tell. She only knew that she had never felt this way before.

"Of the three languages you speak, Bartolomé," Anna asked, "which is your favorite?"

Bartolomé thought about it for a long while. He had never considered the idea of a favorite language. He spoke what was needed for each situation.

"It is not a matter of favorite," he said. "Each language has its strengths. English is the language of precision. If I want to describe something or direct someone, English allows me to be very clear in my intensions. It is the language of business. French is the language of leisure and indulgence. If I want to tell a joke or sing, French is best. Spanish is the language of honor and devotion. If I want to express fidelity and devotion, Spanish is the only language that will do it properly. Promises should only be made in Spanish."

"And to whom have you expressed devotion, Bartolomé?" Anna asked. She was a little afraid of the answer she might hear.

"My grandfather," he said without hesitation. "He has helped me in many ways."

"Anna, what are you doing?" Miss Wren called out from across the courtyard.

"I am just looking out," Anna said.

"Well, come away from that window. It is time for supper," Miss Wren said as she went back inside.

"Please stop by to talk with me when you can, Bartolomé. I shall think of some way that we can meet that does not require a wall between us," Anna said. Then she was gone.

Bartolomé stood for a while, staring at the now vacant window. He had never felt so wonderful in his life.

She asked if I would talk to her again, he thought. "Anna, *nada me parará* (nothing will stop me)," he said aloud to the iron-barred window.

* * *

He headed off down the alley. He tried to develop a plan that would provide the opportunity for regular conversations with Anna. He toyed with offering his services as a Spanish language tutor, but rejected the idea.

Miss Wren would spot my true feeling right away, he thought. *I could never sit and chat with Anna and hide my love.* He admitted it to himself. "Love" was what had him.

He began the trek home. On the way, he passed the tally window. As always, Mr. Getty was sitting there. Bartolomé wondered if Mr. Getty ever left the tally window.

Surely, the man must sleep, he thought, *or answer a call of nature.*

Mr. Getty looked up from his paper work as Bartolomé came to the window. He waited for Bartolomé to speak.

"Sir," Bartolomé said. "I have been thinking about your dilemma."

"And what that be?" Mr. Getty asked.

"The need for a large quantity of moss," Bartolomé replied. He leaned on his walking staff. "Well," he said, "if you were to contract with the Rodriguez plantation for the use of the small pond on their land along the bayou, you could soak, clean, and dry raw moss. I could deliver as much raw moss as you can use."

"You could never bring me two thousand pounds a day," Mr. Getty said.

"I wouldn't do it by myself. I could contract with trappers and farmers from all about to bring the moss to waterways where others could load barges to be brought here. Every man would make money. I would make a little on each load." Bartolomé said. He waited for a reply.

"I don't think you can do it, but I'll ask Mr. Steward," he said.

"Please do that. If he agrees, just give me a few days to spread the word." Bartolomé said. Bringing in raw moss didn't interrupt a trapper's or a farmer's normal chores like having to not only collect the moss, but soak it for six weeks and dry it, as well. He was certain he could get enough.

The walk home was the most pleasant stroll Bartolomé had ever experienced. The air was fresh and clean. The sky was clear and a darkening to twilight blue. The world was wonderful. If this idea of his worked out, he could see Anna every day!

The next day at breakfast, Anna was her cheerful self again. She didn't mention how wonderful she considered the linguistic skills of that farm boy.

Grace noticed it. *Perhaps she's finished with brooding over that farm hand*, she thought. She had not had a chance to talk to Anna about her infatuation with the boy. Now that it seemed over, she let it go.

Bernard came in and took his seat. "Good news, Grace," he said. "Mr. Getty has had a fine idea. We will offer to lease a pond nearby on the Rodriguez land to soak and dry raw moss ourselves. Mr. Getty is certain that he can obtain raw moss in much greater quantities than processed. I still need to work out the costs."

Anna could not believe what she heard. Bartolomé's idea was going to be attempted. If it worked, she was going to figure out a way that they could visit regularly. So what if Mr. Getty got the credit.

"What has you so amused, Anna?" Grace said. She could not help but notice Anna's expression.

"Nothing really, Mother," Anna replied. "James was making faces."

* * *

Madam Barbeaux was exhausted from a long night's work. She had been communicating with certain spirits which required deep concentration.

Loa Legba had been reluctant to permit Barbeaux to contact Loa Erzulie. None of the spirits can be contacted unless Legba or the evil Kalfu grants permission. Barbeaux decided that she had to bribe Legba with rum.

In her prayer room, she had an altar with two candles. She placed a small bowl between the candles and ritualistically filled the bowl with rum. First, she would drink a little rum and then say, "Old one, open the window so that I may speak with the beautiful Erzulie." Then she would pour a little rum in the bowl and blow across it. The process was repeated three times before she fell into a trance and Legba opened the window to the other world.

Barbeaux looked around. She was standing on a narrow trail crowded by tall ferns. Erzulie came to her along the trail, carrying a large, straw basket on her head. She was dressed in a long, colorful cloth that wrapped around her and tucked in at the breasts. She stopped, removed the basket from her head, and placed it next to her at her feet. It was covered and appeared to be light. She removed the tightly twisted towel that had formed a cushion for the basket from the top of her head. Her hair fell free in long, raven black waves that reached below her waist.

"Mambo, why do you wish to speak with me?" Erzulie asked.

"Beautiful Lady, carry me across into another's dream world. I must instruct one who does my bidding," Barbeaux said. "For this, I shall sacrifice a silver comb for your long hair"

Erzulie smiled and removed the cover from the straw basket. She tilted it forward toward Madam Barbeaux. "Peer within, mambo," she said.

Barbeaux placed her hands on the rim of the tightly woven straw. She glanced at Erzulie, and looked into the basket.

Madam Barbeaux could see Bartolomé standing near a *Tchmench* tree. He was bleeding from his hands and arms. Instantly, she was standing at the *Tchmench* tree with Bartolomé. She moved very close to him and concentrated. His hands were bloody and he looked at her with a confused squint in his eyes. She knew not to speak. Speaking aloud would do no good, or it might bring her out of her trance and the spell would fail. Instead, she looked into his eyes and concentrated on how pleased she was with his progress.

Bartolomé turned his hands palm up and looked at his wounds. *You must use the leaves to counteract the poison in the thorns,* she thought. Madam Barbeaux concentrated on what she wanted him to do. He looked back into her eyes and she knew that he would do what he had promised.

Suddenly, Bartolomé turned away. Someone was calling him and the spell was broken. Madam Barbeaux awoke on the floor in front of her altar. She was tired, but pleased. She would obtain the specially aged ham that she needed.

CHAPTER 5

W ord was sent to Bartolomé that Mr. Getty was prepared to buy the raw moss just as they had discussed. The price would be one dollar for every two hundred and fifty pounds delivered to the Rodriguez pond. This was about one-half mile down Bayou Pecheur from the mattress works. A millrace canal that served the Rodriguez plantation skirted the pond and connected to Bayou Pecheur some miles from the Mississippi River. Bayou Pecheur flowed into Bayou Bienvenue, which emptied into Lake Borgne.

Bartolomé realized that the best way to bring a great quantity of moss to the pond was to come in from the east instead of fighting the river current with a barge. Several collection routes could be made from many different waterways through thick cypress forests that were heavy with moss. The collection route would terminate at the pond. He had only two problems. He needed a barge and he needed seed money.

The barge had to be about twenty-five feet wide; any wider and it would be hard to navigate through the bayous and canals. Sixty feet long would do. Barges of those dimensions were common along the back canals, bayous, bays, and lakes, where they were known as "lighters." Many ships preferred to anchor in the coastal waters of Lake Borgne and offload their cargo onto these lighters to be poled or rowed into the city or plantations. This required them to have their cargo handled more often than sailing directly to the river docks, but it saved about eighty miles of sailing up an unpredictable river. Ships with cargo that was unsuitable for lighters had no choice but to make the long tack up current.

One man who operated a fleet of lighters was John Too. His office was near Congo Square in New Orleans. Mr. Too was also known to invest in an enterprise if it promised a profit. Bartolomé decided that he would try Mr. Too first.

Congo Square was an open area near the upper end of Bayou Sauvage, not more than five miles upriver from the mattress works. Slaves and free blacks would congregate in the square on Sundays to dance and practice Voodoo religious rituals when they could. Local authorities would rarely interfere.

It didn't take Bartolomé long to find Mr. Too's place. The sign on the door said "Too Drayage." Bartolomé stepped off the street into a small hallway that was lined on both sides with benches. When a merchant ship was anchored in the lake, laborers would fill the hall, clamoring to be assigned to lighters. Based upon the type of goods to be offloaded, the size of the lighter and crew would be determined by Mr. Too, and workers would be assigned accordingly. The ship would then be loaded with material destined for Europe or the Caribbean on the return trip of the lighters.

Inside the hall and across from the entrance was a tally window, not unlike the one at the mattress works. Bartolomé half expected to find Mr. Getty sitting on the other side. Instead, an Asian gentleman looked up from his desk. It was Mr. Too, himself. Bartolomé had expected a clerk that he would have to convince to allow an audience. Mr. Too literally lived at the office. He had a small apartment above the hall. A narrow stairway led down to the tally room.

"Mr. Too, I am Bartolomé deMelilla. I have a business proposition that I would like to discuss with you," Bartolomé said. He tried to appear accustomed to discussing business.

Mr. Too studied him for a moment. Bartolomé couldn't tell if Mr. Too was amused or interested. Suddenly, Mr. Too stood up and said, "Wait there. I come round."

Mr. Too disappeared from the window. After a few seconds, a doorway opened into the hall and Mr. Too hurried through. Again, he examined Bartolomé. Bartolomé felt quite uncomfortable. He stood there for a moment, and then leaned against his walking staff. Mr. Too showed special interest in the great knife that was tucked in Bartolomé's belt.

Perhaps, I should have not brought the knife, he thought. In truth, he had forgotten it was there.

"You young," Mr. Too finally said. It wasn't a question. "You carry walking staff all time?"

"Yes, sir," Bartolomé answered. "I have far to walk."

"All time big knife, yes?" Mr. Too said, gesturing at the blade.

"Though it is new to me," Bartolomé said, "I have become accustomed to it."

"Tell me your proposition," Mr. Too said as he sat on one of the long benches.

Bartolomé collected himself. He began his rehearsed presentation. "I have contracted to haul raw moss for the mattress works on Bayou Pecheur. For this, I would need a small barge, say twenty-five feet by sixty feet, and a loaded draft of three feet. It needs to be small enough to be handled by two or three men. I will have trappers, pickers, and others bring any moss that they have collected in the swamp to a canal or bayou where this barge will pick it up. I will pay the pickers a dollar for every five hundred pounds. It should take two or three days to make a collection trip. The mattress works will pay me a dollar for every two hundred and fifty pounds I deliver."

"Little barge, no problem," Mr. Too said. "It will carry forty thousand pounds of freight and draw only three feet. I can rent to you for ten dollar a week."

"Mr. Too," Bartolomé admitted sheepishly, "I don't have enough money to pay you in advance."

Mr. Too smiled. Then he said, "I tell you story. Last year, John Too is walking to city. Two men jump out from hiding. Before John Too know what happen, he down on ground. Men beat him. One man hold big knife to his throat. Tell John Too give money. John Too give."

Bartolomé straightened out. *He's recognized the knife*, he thought. Bartolomé didn't know what to do.

"Last month," Too continued, "constable bring me to see two men in jail. Ask me if I know them. I say 'Yes, these two beat me. Take my money.' Then the constable say, 'These men say they robbed by man with big stick.' How much you need, Mr. deMelilla?"

Bartolomé was surprised by the abrupt end to Mr. Too's story.

"A hundred dollars would do nicely. It will be enough to buy the raw moss, pay two deck hands, and rent the barge." Bartolomé said. He tried to act as if he was accustomed to such high finance. He had never seen one hundred dollars in one place and the thought of barging twenty tons of moss made his head swim.

"Barge in Bayou Sauvage. I have it brought to Bayou Pecheur. I send man with you to work barge. You pay me for barge, two dollar interest on loan, and pay man later, when you sell to Mr. Steward at mattress works," Mr. Too said.

"I'll need to pass the word to the trappers and others along the route. I will return in three days for the barge," Bartolomé said. "And thank you, Mr. Too." Bartolomé was amazed that he had actually done it. Now there was work to do.

* * *

Bartolomé left Mr. Too's office worried. He had made a deal to bring the moss to the Rodriguez Pond, made a deal to obtain the barge and a deck hand, and obtained financing. Was it going to work? He headed off to Bayou Pecheur. First, he would stop to see Mr. Getty. Then, he would see if he could manage a little visit with Anna before setting off down Bayou Pecheur and beyond to pass the word.

Mr. Getty was standing outside the tally window talking to another man when Bartolomé arrived. "Here is the young man who is going to deliver the raw moss to the Rodriguez Pond." Mr. Getty said as Bartolomé walked up.

The man standing with Mr. Getty was well dressed, and appeared to be in his fifties. He had a full beard with only a sprinkling of gray.

"Mr. deMelilla, I would like you to meet Mr. Bernard Steward. He is the owner of this business," Mr. Getty said when Bartolomé was near enough.

They assessed each other as they shook hands.

He is young, but he has a firm handshake and a confident way about him, Bernard thought. He fancied himself a good judge of character.

This is Anna's father! He is a prosperous business man. Bartolomé's mind raced. *What could she possibly see in a poor dirt farmer like me?* Bartolomé was more determined than ever to make a go of the enterprise he had hatched.

"Mr. Getty tells me that you can deliver a ton of raw moss a day," Mr. Steward said in a questioning manner. "Between our production and the building demands in the city, that may not be enough."

"It will not be in a steady stream of a ton a day, Mr. Steward. My first run will be on the fifteenth. The raw moss will be placed in the Rodriguez Pond to cure for six weeks. As the first haul is curing, I will add later deliveries on a regular basis. Once you begin to recover and process the initial batch in six weeks, you will be able to recover and dry as much as you need daily from then on," Bartolomé said confidently. He hoped that he could come close to the plan he set out.

Just then, Anna and Grace Steward appeared. Bartolomé was so intent on impressing Mr. Steward that he didn't notice them until Mr. Steward spoke up.

"Excuse me, gentlemen," Mr. Steward said as he turned to speak to his wife and daughter. "What is it, Grace?" he said. He appeared to be less than pleased that she had interrupted the conversation.

Anna and Bartolomé exchanged a silent, but heartfelt greeting.

She is more beautiful every time I see her, Bartolomé thought.

Anna had been watching Bartolomé and her father discussing business as she and her mother approached the men. She noticed that Bartolomé was dressed a little better. His trousers and shirt were still plain white cotton, as was his frock, but very clean. He was wearing shoes instead of being barefoot, even though it was June. Leaning on the sturdy walking staff with his ever-present haversack hanging at his side, he was the very picture of a rugged tradesman and experienced man. The feeling it gave her was inexplicable. It felt like pride.

"I came to see if you would like to come home for noon," Grace said to her husband. "We are having something new for you to try. I did not intend to interrupt business, gentlemen. Forgive me."

"Yes, of course." Bernard replied. "But where are my manners? You know Mr. Getty, of course. I would like you to meet our newest moss procurer, Mr. deMelilla. This is my wife, Grace, and my daughter, Anna. My youngest, James, is at home with the nanny."

"Mr. deMelilla, a pleasure." Grace said as she extended her hand, palm down.

Bartolomé took her hand by the fingertips and made a slight bow. "The pleasure is mine, madam," he said. Then, with a nod to Anna, he simply said, "Mistress Anna."

"Hello, Bartolomé," Anna said. "I am glad to see that you are well."

Bernard was startled that his daughter obviously knew deMelilla. Mr. Getty had not mentioned the lad's first name. He was not as startled as his wife.

Bartolomé! Grace thought. *That's the name of the linguistic farm boy!* Yet, the young man that she saw now, though not rich, was no country bumpkin. He was tall, strong, confident, and well mannered.

"I was fortunate enough to assist your daughter and her nanny in the market some weeks ago. I was their translator as they visited vendors who did not have a command of English. I am flattered that Mistress Anna remembers me," Bartolomé explained with a smile. He dared not mention that there may have been other communications, particularly clandestine conversations through a barred window.

"Mr. Bartolomé speaks three languages quite fluently, Father," Anna said. "His command of each language is with the accent of a native speaker. Sister Teresa tells me that this is very rare." She tried to look at Bartolomé without revealing her admiration. She failed. It was very obvious to Anna's mother that there was an emotional attachment developing between them.

"That must be of great use here in New Orleans," Bernard said. "It seems that every third man speaks no English at all. That is very different than what we were accustomed to in Maryland."

Anna had given Bartolomé a family history during one of their meetings. Although from the northeast, where Protestants were in the majority, the Stewards were from Catholic Maryland. The family had moved to New Orleans for business opportunities and to avoid the harassment of the British. Lately, rumors had begun to fly that the British might be coming to New Orleans.

"We must be on our way," Grace said. "Please pardon us, gentlemen. Come, Anna." Mother and daughter hurried off to the Steward house. Bartolomé watched until they rounded the corner of the building.

"Well, sir," Bernard said, "I will have Moine at the pond on the evening of the fifteenth. He will have a scale, and when the delivery is done, come to the front to be tallied in."

"I will have a scale on the barge," Bartolomé said. "Now I must pass the word to the potential pickers. Please excuse me."

Bernard watched Bartolomé as he strode off along the bank of Bayou Pecheur. He took long strides as the walking staff shot out ahead. He seemed to pull the trail to him as he went.

I will have to talk to Grace about Anna befriending foreigners, Bernard thought.

* * *

It didn't take Bartolomé long to contact several trappers, fishermen, and other settlers along Bayou Pecheur who were interested in picking moss. Most had done it before from time to time, but the prospect of not having to process it was appealing. It was summer time, so most would have been idle. It was a good chance to pick up some hard coinage. Bartolomé explained the route that the collection barge would take and the time that it could be expected to arrive at certain landmarks. It was dark by the time Bartolomé arrived at home. There was not so much to answer for now. His long trips held a promise of profit that would be shared with the household. Jacques had decided long ago that some of the missed chores Bartolomé usually performed could be spread among the three brothers. The family needed the money.

The next day, Bartolomé was up early. His mother gave him a few biscuits, which he wolfed down. As he placed enough jerked meat and hardtack in his haversack to provide for the day, the rest of the house was beginning to stir.

"I need to finish collecting the wood for that special order," Bartolomé told his mother. "It shall take me most of the day, but I should be finished before dark." He paused long enough to tell Jacques what his plans were. Jacques had no objection.

"Why do you need so much rope?" Jacques asked. Bartolomé had several feet of strong rope slung over his shoulder.

"I have to make a snare for the wild pig," was the reply.

"A snare?" Maurice had just arrived at the table. "Nobody can snare a pig. It is not a rabbit. A pig might weigh two hundred and fifty pounds or more! How are you going to snare that?"

"If I fail," Bartolomé said, "then you may laugh; not before."

As Bartolomé strode off to the trail, he could hear Maurice recounting to the rest of the family how only a fool would try to snare a wild pig. It made his ears burn.

He had not gone very far along the wooded path before he encountered a water moccasin blocking the trail. A big moccasin will not flee from man or beast. Instead, it will coil on the trail and dare anything to come near, as did this one. The stout walking staff made short work of the snake.

Bait to quell caution, Bartolomé thought. A plan was forming. When he reached the area where he had encountered the wild pig, he went to the oak tree that formed the canopy over the hog wallow. He tossed one end of the rope over a limb and tied it off so the free end lay in the pig-trodden area. He then dropped the dead snake near the end of the rope. After that, he continued on to the *Tchmench* tree. After several hours of hard work, he had a good load of wood and thorns. These he loaded onto a *travois* he had made, and he began the trip home.

He stopped frequently and searched along the trail. Finally, he found another snake. This he killed and tossed on the *travois*. As he approached the wallow, he made more noise than was necessary. The first snake had been accepted by the wild hog while he had been working on the *Tchmench* tree. He tossed the second near the end of the hanging rope, and finished the trip home. He had tomorrow to finish cutting the rest of the *Tchmench* tree and begin to build the snare. After that, he had to meet the barge at Bayou Pecheur, where Mr. Too had promised to have it ready with a deck hand. The rest of that day was to be dedicated to shipping moss.

"Did you snare any wild hogs?" Maurice asked while at breakfast the next day. His tone was full of ridicule.

"Yes, but it was too small," Bartolomé replied. "I let it go. Maybe I will do better today."

This brought a good laugh from everyone, except Maurice.

* * *

This time, when Bartolomé reached the wallow, he did more than simply drop a dead snake. He went to the fast end of the rope that hung over the branch and made a small sling in the line. This he pulled up to the bottom of the branch. He secured the sling to a branch with another, thinner rope, using a slip knot that he had smeared with wax. He placed a heavy log, maybe fifty pounds or so, in the sling. The bulk of the weight was borne by the stout branch. The slip knot simply prevented the load from rolling off its perch. Then he left to finish the *Tchmench* tree. On the return trip, he re-baited the area. The wild hog had been there. He added another heavy log to the sling.

Paciencia, he thought. *Patience wins the prize.*

His plan was to feed the wild hog with snakes at the bottom of the rope. This favorite food would cause the pig to become accustomed to the rope and Bartolomé's scent. Each trip, he would add a log to the sling, until it was heavy enough to do the job. Then he would set the trap.

The day arrived for the first expedition of collecting moss. Bartolomé was up before dawn. It was his birthday, a fact that he had forgotten. He had some bread for breakfast and was on his way. He wanted to reach the barge at Bayou Pecheur at first light. He had many miles to pole a large barge, with the help of Ferdinand, the hand Mr. Too had sent to help.

Bartolomé arrived at the barge just after full sunrise. Ferdinand was there and they set off at once. The decking on the sides of the barge was about two feet wide and ran the full length of the vessel, from stem to stern. The rest of the barge was open to the bottom. Empty, it drew less than a foot of water. Bartolomé carried a long pole as he walked along the deck on one side, and Ferdinand did the same on the other. When they reached the stem, both would press one end of their poles into the water bottom and walk to the stern, pushing on the pole. For every step to the rear, the barge glided forward. When they reached the stern, each gave a final shove. The barge would glide along while they walked to the stem again. Progress was surprisingly fast.

Bartolomé was relieved to see that there were several pickers at the first designated meeting place. The first haul was fifteen hundred pounds of tightly bound raw moss. By the time they reached the last station, the barge was piled high with bundles of moss. The stack was eight feet high measuring from the bottom of the hold, and towered five feet above the walking deck. In total, he had accumulated twelve and a half tons of moss. The barge still rode high in the water and glided along easily.

The return to the Rodriguez Pond was as easy as the trip out. Moine was waiting, as promised. Together, they tallied the load and placed the bundles in the pond. After soaking for six to seven weeks, the soft exterior on the moss strands would fall away, leaving a strong, black fiber. The fibers could be woven into rope, used to insulate walls, or used to stuff pillows or mattresses. By making such a trip every three days or so, there would be a steady supply of the fibers.

After securing the barge, they walked the mile or so to the mattress works. Bartolomé did a little mental inventory. He had spent fifty dollars paying the pickers. He paid Ferdinand two dollars for the day's work. Of the forty-eight dollars in his haversack, he owed Mr. Too twelve dollars for the rent of the barge and interest. That was an outlay of sixty-four dollars.

Mr. Getty was at the tally window, as always, when Bartolomé and Moine arrived. Ferdinand had continued on to New Orleans.

"Here ya go," Mr. Getty said as handed Bartolomé a hundred dollar bank note drawn on the Hall Bank in New Orleans. Bartolomé had turned a profit of thirty-four dollars for a day's work!

"By the way," Mr. Getty continued as Bartolomé examine the bank note. "Mr. Steward said to tell you that he won't be need'n you to bring in any more moss."

Bartolomé was stunned! "I don't think I heard you, Mr. Getty. Could you say that again?"

"Look, lad," he said. He resented having been forced to deliver the news. "Mr. Steward reckoned that he could send folks that work here out with barges to get the moss. No need to pay a middle man."

Bartolomé walked off without saying another word. The thought of such a betrayal burned. Worst of all, how would he arrange to see Anna? He would not have considered the venture had it not been for the need to see Anna. The walk home took longer than usual. He was more determined than ever to meet with Anna regularly. He arrived home just as dark was settling in.

Jacques was delighted when Bartolomé gave him seventeen silver dollars. He had promised to split his earnings with the family.

"Why the long face?" Jacques asked. "Look at all this silver. We all might go into the shipping business."

Truth is," Bartolomé replied, "that's the last of it. Steward has cut me out of the trade."

Jacques looked as disappointed as Bartolomé felt.

Maurice walked up as Bartolomé was explaining the betrayal to Jacques.

Finally, Bartolomé sighed and said, "Tomorrow, I will visit Mr. Too to settle with him, and then I'll return to finish that special order. And snare a hog." He looked directly at Maurice as he spoke. Maurice pretended not to hear.

Everyone at the supper table was happy and congratulated Bartolomé on his birthday and his profitable endeavor. This did much to lift his spirits. He said his good nights and headed out to go up to his bed. Behind him, he could hear his mother describing what she was going to get the family with this bit of extra cash. Even so, he was weary and fell asleep quickly.

* * *

Bartolomé could smell rum. The scent was very strong. He opened his eyes. Madam Barbeaux was sitting next to him on the bed. She was wearing that same sheer cotton nightgown.

"*Es tu prepare* (Are you ready)?" she asked. Again, she was speaking Spanish with an *Isleño's* accent. "Ogoun is interested in you. He has promised to help. *El Comedor Serpiente* is strong and cunning. But, he is greedy. Ogoun will send him to you. *El Comedor Serpiente* is a favorite of the evil loa, Kalfu. Kalfu has caused much suffering. Kalfu is our enemy. You must be careful."

She then lay on her side next to Bartolomé and put her arm around him. There was a scent in her hair. He could feel her warm body pressing against his side.

* * *

Bartolomé was suddenly awake. The room was dark. It was still night, but dawn was near. The brothers remained sound asleep as Bartolomé dressed and went down the stairs to the porch. Jacques was on his way back from the *t'cabine* (outhouse).

"Good morning, Bartolomé," Jacques said as he took a seat on one of the chairs on the porch. "What are your plans for today now that the shipping business has withered?" Jacques was truly disappointed that Bartolomé's venture failed and he was trying to cheer the boy a little.

"I think I shall bring that wild pig in today," Bartolomé said with a smile.

Jacques was relieved to see that Bartolomé did not dwell on his recent setback. "I do not know how you plan to do so. Snaring a wild hog is something that I have never heard done," Jacques observed. "If anyone can do it, you can."

Bartolomé hadn't realized that his stepfather held him in such high regard. That simple statement of encouragement was well received. "Thank you, Father," Bartolomé replied. He had never called Jacques "Father" before.

Jacques rose from the chair and put a hand on Bartolomé's shoulder. "You must be careful," was all he said. He returned to the chair and looked toward the sunrise so that Bartolomé could not see the tear in his eye.

Bartolomé left the porch and went to the tool shed. He got the ax instead of the hatchet that he had taken on every other trip to the wallow. His mind was racing as he went along the trail. The dreams of Madam Barbeaux seemed so real. *El Comedor Serpiente* (The Snake Eater), could only have meant the wild pig that Bartolomé had been baiting into complacency.

He stopped at promising locations to poke around the brush along the trail with his walking staff. *Where are the snakes when you really need one,* he thought. He poked around a promising brier clump and was about to move on when he saw a large moccasin curled in a palmetto. He had to prod it down onto the trail, where it coiled and threatened to strike. After several attempts, Bartolomé pinned the snake's head to the ground with his walking staff and lopped off the head with the ax. The snake was very large. Bartolomé carried it slung over one shoulder like a length of chain. The headless corpse writhed and twisted about as it hung down his back. The actions of the snake heightened Bartolomé's senses and his excitement as he approached the wallow. He half expected the pig to be there ready to attack. Instead, all was quiet. The snare rope and trap weight were all as he had left them.

He climbed up to the great limb where the snare rope crossed and pulled up another large log to lash to the bundle. He estimated that he now had over five hundred pounds of weight teetering on the broad branch. A single slip knot was all that prevented the load from rolling off and falling free. He had placed a small stick in the loop of the slip knot to prevent an accidental tug from setting the weights free. He had coiled the running end of the trip line on the wide branch. This, he tossed to the ground. He then returned to the ground and made a lasso in the free end of the weighted rope and secured the smaller line from the slip knot to a spot on the lasso. He spread the lasso and covered it with small leaves and other debris. He was careful to prop the sides of the lasso up off the ground. He then stepped back and examined his work.

I hope pigs can't count, he thought. There were now two ropes draping down from the tree canopy. The large, stout one, with a heavy load on the other end, had been there for several days. The smaller line, the one that led to the slip knot, was new. He placed the corpse of the snake on the ground in the center of the camouflaged lasso. One more climb up to the counterweight to remove the stick from the loop of the slip knot and the trap was set.

He climbed down for the last time and, after another quick look around, he continued up the trail to where the *Tchmench* tree had been. He began to make another *travois*.

Old Snake Eater is accustomed to me working here, he thought, *so there is no need to be quiet.*

He finished the *travois*. He paused for a moment. He did not hear anything out of place. Instead of simply waiting, Bartolomé began to chop on another tree so that it sounded like he was working. Everything must seem normal. After a few blows on the tree, he would stop and listen. Finally, he heard a loud commotion from the direction of the wallow. Something had tripped the snare!

CHAPTER 6

B artolomé hurried up the trail toward the wallow. He worked hard to resist the urge to run. He needed to see what the situation was before he acted. As he approached the turn in the trail that led to the wallow, he could hear the pig squealing loudly. There was the sound of brush being shaken and he was certain he could hear the ground being stomped. He placed his trusty walking staff on the ground and grasped the ax in both hands. *Someone is going to die*, Bartolomé said to himself as he stepped into the open.

The snare had worked! A wild pig hung by one rear foot. The heavy counter load was enough to lift the three hundred pound animal. But the load was on the ground. The rope was too long and the weight had landed before the pig was completely clear of the ground. The animal's front hooves could gain enough traction to make a small run. Each rush would end as the counterweight lifted slightly off the ground and pulled the pig back. If this went on much longer, the weights would eventually fall out of the sling and the pig would be free. Bartolomé had to act quickly.

The instant it saw Bartolomé, the pig made a wild rush at him. Bartolomé jumped back and the pig was restrained just before it could get to him. Bartolomé noted where the rush ended. The pig momentarily stopped its frantic rushes and glared at Bartolomé.

It is now planning the next move, Bartolomé thought. He could sense that the animal was aware that the man was responsible for its predicament. It was thinking, searching for some way to get free to attack. Both knew that this was going to end in death. Bartolomé also began to appraise the situation. The pig was huge. It was hairy, black, and coated with mud. It had four long, froth-covered tusks that protruded from the corners of its mouth. The tusks made a loud noise with every snap of the powerful jaws. The coarse hairs on the heavy, humped back stood out like quills. Its eyes were filled with hate, not fear.

Bartolomé could sense that another rush was being planned, so he positioned himself to meet the attack. He stood where the last run had ended and grasped the ax so that he could strike with the back of the blade. He had no hope of cutting through the armored hide of the beast. His best chance was to render it unconscious with a blow to the skull. He had slaughtered many a domestic pig in this manner, but those animals were held in a stock, not rushing about and wielding tusks.

It came straight at him. Bartolomé stepped aside and swung the ax hard at a spot where he guessed the pig's head would pause as the rope ended its run. The great head reached out with a loud snap, the rope tightened, and there was a pause, for just an instant. Bartolomé could see the animal's eyes as it recognized its mistake. In that brief moment, it was powerless to act. The back of the ax caught the pig on the skull just above the eyes, with a loud thud.

Dazed, the animal slid back as it was pulled by the counterweight. Its front hooves left two long grooves in the mud. It shook its head and tried to focus its eyes on Bartolomé. Before the pig could recover, Bartolomé ran forward and delivered another hard blow. This was enough to render the beast unconscious. Bartolomé dropped the ax and drew his knife. He grabbed the stunned animal by the chin, lifted the head, and cut its throat. It bled in great spurts until the huge heart stopped beating. It·was dead at last. Yet, even dead, it hung menacingly and seemed to stare at Bartolomé.

Bartolomé sat down in the mud of the wallow. He had done it. No one had ever snared a wild pig before. He had done it. Now the shakes came. His whole body trembled until he nearly dropped the bloody knife.

Why does this happen? he asked himself. *All the danger is passed. There is no time for this foolishness.*

After a little while, he had calmed enough to cut the carcass down and field-dress the pig. Normally, the entrails and other organs were saved and used when a pig was butchered. As Jacques was fond of saying, *"Tout le cochon est bon."* Today, it was hot and no boiling pot or helpers were available, so Bartolomé would harvest what he could. He brought the *travois* into the clearing and loaded as much of the carcass as he could take. He did not skin it, as the thick hide would help protect the meat during the rough trip home. The rest of the animal, including the fearsome head, he left behind. Scavengers would quickly devour all of what was left.

* * *

Jules and Gabriel were working near the tree line when Bartolomé appeared, pulling the burdened *travois*. Gabriel looked up from his work and exclaimed, "My God, he's done it! Look, Jules. He's done it."

Both rushed to Bartolomé to see the prize. They took turns slapping Bartolomé on the back and examining the black, hairy carcass.

"You walk in front," Gabriel said to Bartolomé. "Jules and I can pull the *travois* to the house."

Bartolomé retrieved his walking staff from the *travois*. He had lashed it, the ax, and the recovered rope from the snare over the prize. His muscles ached and he was glad to walk unburdened for a while. As they began to approach the house, they caught sight of Maurice working near one of the sties.

"Maurice, come see," Jules called out. "He's done it!"

Maurice ceased working on the pen and ran over to the small procession.

"Look at the size of the thing," Maurice said. Domestic pigs were rarely allowed to grow to this great size. The mass of the thing, even headless and field dressed, was impressive. Even Maurice slapped Bartolomé on the back.

"I thought the old man was insane," Maurice said, referring to his father. "I saw him preparing the fire for the smokehouse. I asked him, why start the smokehouse when there was no meat to hang. He said, 'Bartolomé will bring a pig today.' I think *mais jamais* (that will never happen)."

Maurice took a corner of the *travois* from Jules, who then ran ahead to tell the rest of the house what had happened. It was not long before Jules disappeared up the path to the house.

"Will you sell all this meat?" Gabriel asked.

"No. I have promised a single smoked and aged ham. The rest will be ours," Bartolomé replied. "We can smoke some, feast on some today, and age what is left."

That pleased Gabriel. He had always heard that wild pig tasted much better than domestic. Now he was going to find out for himself.

By the time they reached the smokehouse, Jacques and Bartolomé's mother were there, along with the little sisters and several neighbors. Jules was running through the small village, spreading the news of Bartolomé's great feat.

Aimée, holding Inez on her hip, with Oceane by her side, approached the small crowd that had gathered as if she were approaching a coiled serpent. All hands were busy unloading the travois and skinning the carcass to prepare the meat for cooking. Some was to be roasted today, but most was destined for the smokehouse.

"Brother Bartolomé, how did you kill it?" Oceane asked. She looked at him with wide and dark eyes. She always addressed her siblings with the title "brother" or "sister." No one knew how she came to this habit; it was just how Oceane was. Bartolomé, taller than anyone in the family, possessed an air of competence that made him a giant in her eyes.

"*T'Yeux Noirs*, I struck it on the head with an ax," Bartolomé replied. No one but Bartolomé addressed Oceane as "Little Black Eyes." They would often play a game wherein Oceane would ask a direct question and Bartolomé would answer with a single, direct, unembellished answer.

"Why did it let you?" she asked.

"It had reached the end of its rope," he replied.

"Did it hurt?" she continued.

"No, I didn't feel anything," was the reply.

"How shall we eat all this meat?" Oceane was smaller than one quarter of the load on the *travois*.

"One bite at a time," Bartolomé said.

The conversation continued in this manner for a few exchanges.

Eventually, others were able to draw out the entire story. For the rest of the day, as Jacques and his sons butchered the meat and prepared the various cuts, groups of curious villagers stopped by. Bartolomé had to repeat the tale so many times that he began to develop a script.

"I had been baiting the snare for days with snakes that I had killed," Bartolomé would begin, whenever enough had gathered to warrant a retelling of his exploit. After about the tenth telling, he suddenly thought of his grandfather and how each of the old man's tales would began with a special phrase. Now here he was, fifteen years old, and he had a tale of his own. He wondered if he would develop as many as his grandfather.

Jacques had chambered off a small section of the smokehouse so that whatever was hung there received smoke from a selected portion of the burn pit. He hung a large ham in this quarantined section to begin the smoking and aging process. Jacques had no experience with the *Tchmench* wood and he didn't want to expose meat in the rest of the smokehouse to an unknown flavoring.

The tenderloins were destined for roasting that very evening. The family planned to share the feast with the many neighbors who would arrive throughout the evening. Each visitor would bring a dish or a bottle of wine to share with all. The successful hunt had become an impromptu party involving the entire village that would last well into the night.

For many months to come, the woods around Terre Aux Boeufs were festooned with every kind of trap or snare imaginable. No one ever caught a wild pig or any other animal of note. Occasionally, an adventurous boy or two would be bruised. Finally, the mothers of the village issued a kind of decree wherein all the youngsters were forbidden to set any traps or snares larger than a rabbit box.

* * *

The day after the great feast, Bartolomé decided that he would go into New Orleans to insure that his "client" intended to keep the terms of the special order. Before leaving, he tended to the smokehouse. Jacques had situated the house well, and the smudge pit was safely above the surrounding land. The *Tchmench* wood smelled sickly sweet as it smoldered. Two or three times a day, Bartolomé or Jacques would add a single sharp spine which would smoke heavily, but rarely flared into flame. It was the time of year where frequent rains could be expected. Some of the storms could be quite violent, so the smokehouse needed to be cared for often to maintain the smoldering fire and correct temperature. If a hurricane should strike, it could ruin the process.

The true purpose of Bartolomé's trip into New Orleans was to contrive a visit with Anna. He knew that Madam Barbeaux would be good to her word. Propelled by his sturdy walking staff, and the prospect of Anna, Bartolomé was nearing Bayou Pecheur before ten in the morning. He avoided the main buildings and tally window, and worked his way around to the alley next to the Steward house. He paused in the alley, uncertain of what to do. He noticed the young slave boy he had spoken with some days ago passing near the alley on some errand.

"Good morning," Bartolomé said as the boy passed him.

The boy was startled and then he recognized Bartolomé from their earlier encounter. "Don't be mess'n round here," the boy said as he made as fierce a frown as he could muster. "They be woop'n beggars."

"I'm no beggar," Bartolomé said with a smile. He held out an eighth of a dollar in his hand, "How would you like to earn this bit of silver?"

The boy looked about to be certain no one was watching, and then he ducked into the alley for a closer look. A bit could buy many wonderful things as long as he could hide it from his task masters.

"What you be want'n Shortstep to do?" he said. He was curious but very suspicious. He had once heard of a houseboy who let a burglar in, for a silver dollar. The houseboy had showed up drunk on the rum that the dollar bought. Unable to explain how he earned enough to buy rum, the truth came out and the houseboy was hanged.

Bartolomé correctly surmised that "Shortstep" was the boy's name, at least in the Steward household. "I have a note for Mistress Anna," Bartolomé said. "Deliver it to her, and I will give you this silver bit."

"Shortstep can do that," he quickly replied. "Give them both to me."

"Do not be so quick to think me a fool, Shortstep. First the note, and if you succeed, I will give you the silver bit." Bartolomé said.

Shortstep thought it over for a moment. "Give me the note. Shortstep be right back for the bit," the boy said as he extended a clean and smooth black hand. The lack of dirt and calluses marked him as a houseboy.

Bartolomé handed him the note. "I will know by nightfall if you have been successful. Return here after dark and the silver bit will be under this corner of the wall." Bartolomé indicated a spot where a seam in the wall met the ground.

"How can I be sure," Shortstep said with a squint.

"What have you got to lose?" Bartolomé said.

Shortstep took the note and, with a shrug, hurried off to finish the interrupted chore.

Bartolomé was not so foolish as to trust a houseboy. For all he knew, Shortstep would turn the note over to anyone in the house and it could eventually fall into Mr. Steward's hands. In consideration of this eventuality, he simply wrote, *"Hierro llorar en seis."* If intercepted, it would make no sense. If Anna were discovered with it, she could say it was part of her lesson. Only Anna would know that *hierro llorar* (weeping iron) referred to the iron-barred window that looked onto the alley. During one of their small love chats disguised as Spanish lessons, Anna had noticed that the cool evening breeze from the river had cause condensation to collect on the iron bars of the window.

"Look, the iron bars are crying," she said. "How do you say 'weeping iron' in Spanish?"

"Hierro llorar," Bartolomé had told her. It was a memory that he had placed deep into his heart.

With any luck, Shortstep would pass the note, Anna would remember her comment, decipher the message, and guess that six was the time to meet. Bartolomé would be back from his meeting with Madam Barbeaux at six.

Bartolomé walked back up the alley toward the upriver side of the village of Bayou Pecheur. He paused for a second near the window of weeping iron on the off chance that Anna might sight him. He heard no sound from the walled household, so he pushed on to New Orleans and Madam Barbeaux.

* * *

New Orleans was relatively inactive now that full summer was here. The market was poorly attended by both vendors and shoppers. Bartolomé had learned that Madam Barbeaux lived in a small house on Rampart Street, where she would receive "clients" and hold such religious services as were required of a mambo.

He approached the house just after noon. As he did so, he watched as a veiled lady exited the house and entered a fine, team-drawn carriage. A footman helped her across a plank that bridged the small wood-lined roadside ditch and aboard the carriage. He gently closed the carriage door before returning to the platform where he rode at the rear of the carriage. The driver whipped the team and the carriage sped away. The rich carriage was out of place in this part of the city.

Most of the houses in New Orleans had doorways that opened directly onto a walkway called a *banquette* that bordered the narrow streets. The more affluent areas had sidewalks of brick, but here the walkways were wood. Wide, rough-hewn planks bridged the ditches at street corners and in front of some of the houses. Raised just high enough to be above the filthy street, the walkways dodged around the steps that descended from the doorways. These doorways opened into the beautiful courtyards of the wealthy houses. Far in the rear of the courtyard would be a large cistern to collect rainwater for cooking and drinking. Sometimes there would be a deep well to bring in water for washing and other non-potable uses. There would be a stable as well, with an entrance to the street. Behind the stable, or through it, would be the "convenience." Sometimes it was a simple outhouse; sometimes it connected to a drain that ran to a ditch or bayou.

Bartolomé ascended the steps to Madam Barbeaux's house and searched the door for a knocker or bell. Just before he gave up and knocked on the door with his bare knuckles, he decided that the small handle that extended from the center of the door was some kind of bell. He gave it a small pull and then a push. Nothing happened. He then gave it a twist and it rang out.

In the case of Madam Barbeaux, the doorway did not open into a courtyard. When Madam Barbeaux opened the door, Bartolomé could see a sitting room behind her. He knew that if you continued through the house, a door would open into a yard where would be a cistern and a garden.

"Young sir," she said with a smile. She spoke with the heavily Haitian-accented French she used when they had first conversed. "I am happy to see you. Come in and tell me the news that you have."

Madam Barbeaux stepped back and gestured for Bartolomé to enter. He stepped across the threshold and she closed the door behind him. Light filtered in from the windows. The glass panes were open, but there was fine netting covering the openings. Two candles burned on a bare table against one wall. A small white cup was between them. A few chairs were also in the room, arranged in little rows facing the table. One wall was covered with many rows of shelves cluttered with items, some of which were unrecognizable to Bartolomé.

"Please, sit," Madam Barbeaux insisted. She was wearing a white cotton dress and was barefoot. Her hair was drawn up tight behind her head in a bun. Bartolomé took the chair indicated. It was on the row nearest the table. Madam Barbeaux pulled her dress up to her knees and sat cross-legged on the floor before him. Bartolomé was startled by her boldness.

"Madam," he started, "I have come to inquire if you are still interested in acquiring a ham aged in the smoke of a *Tchmench* tree."

She showed little reaction. "You know that I am," she said.

"I can provide you with one," he continued. "I have already begun the aging process. It will be ready by September."

"That is well," She said. "Could you age it until December? Three months is a minimum. Six months is ideal."

"I have enough wood to do that," he said. "If I need more, I will gather it."

"Do you have the thorns as well?" she asked. "It is important to add the thorns to the fire."

It took a moment for Bartolomé to realize that it was only in his dreams that the suggestion of including the thorns had been raised.

"*He hecho así*," Bartolomé answered.

"Young sir," she said," I do not speak Spanish."

"I have done so," Bartolomé repeated in French.

"If you can age this ham until the last week of November or first week of December," she said, "I will pay you two gold Spanish doubloons. If you can introduce a *Tchmench* thorn to the fire daily, I will add a fine gold chain."

"I am already doing these things," he said. "I will bring you the ham after November has passed but before the first week of December is gone."

"If you do this thing, I will pay you the gold," she said as she stood up. She then went to the table and retrieved the small cup. She took a sip and then offered the cup to Bartolomé. "A toast to our contract," she said.

Bartolomé accepted the cup and took a sip. It was rum. He felt the warm liquid pass down his throat. He handed the cup back. Madam Barbeaux smiled and looked into Bartolomé's eyes. The meeting was concluded.

Bartolomé turned to leave, but he paused at the door. "I will see you come December, madam. Farewell until then."

Madam Barbeaux only smiled and hoisted the cup. Bartolomé descended the steps to the walkway. When he turned to see if she had any more words to say, he saw that Madam Barbeaux had silently closed the door.

The small sip of rum was pleasing to Bartolomé as he moved along Rampart Street with long strides. His walking staff made a thumping noise on the wooden walkway as he hurried along. First, he had to see Mr. Too and settle accounts. Then he would continue on to Bayou Pecheur, and Anna, by six.

* * *

It was a short walk to John Too's place of business. There must have been a ship at anchor in one of the bays, for there were several men milling about the entrance to the Chinaman's Hall, as the drayage office was known locally. There was some grumbling when Bartolomé tried to enter the hall.

"Slow down, ya bugger," one grizzled bargeman said. "Ya must wait ya turn. And you are a stranger, as well." The barge-working community was small and a newcomer was not welcomed, even in the cool months when there was more than enough work to do. Now that it was summer, paying jobs were sparse. The speaker was stout and weatherworn, with a long gray beard. He rolled his *r*'s and was obviously a Scotsman.

"I am not here for a job, sir," Bartolomé replied calmly. "I have other business with Mr. Too." He did not demand that the man step aside, but his body language left no doubt that "step aside" was included.

"I best not see ya working a barge," the man threatened. Then he stepped aside with a mocking gesture for Bartolomé to pass.

As Bartolomé warily opened the door, he was prepared for any possible action. The disgruntled Scotsman did nothing. The hiring hall was filled with pipe smoke, whiskey smell, and ragged men in weathered clothes.

All but a few were barefoot. All conversation ceased the instant Bartolomé stepped in. Ferdinand, the man that Too had sent with the moss barge, was there.

"*Oiga*, Bartolomé," Ferdinand called out. He waved to Bartolomé, to be seen through the crowd. Bartolomé waded over to Ferdinand and greeted him in Spanish. During the long trip collecting moss, they had conversed in Spanish, and Bartolomé was not certain if Ferdinand was fluent in any other language. The fact that a known bargeman recognized Bartolomé changed the attitude of the men awaiting assignment, and the hall began to fill with general conversation.

Ferdinand wanted to know if Bartolomé had another barge to move. When he learned that none was to be had, he switched to English. "Too bad that you do not have any freight to barge today," Ferdinand said loudly enough for others in the hall to hear. "Perhaps another time. Do not forget your friend."

Bartolomé was certain that if he had come with a need for bargemen, the conversation would have continued in Spanish. He promised Ferdinand that he would not be forgotten, and continued to the job window. This time, he did not have to push through the throng. The bargemen made way for Bartolomé now that they were put on notice that he did not seek a job, but might bring jobs.

Mr. Too was not at the window, but Bartolomé could see him seated at a desk off to one side of the little cubicle.

"Mr. Too," Bartolomé said just loud enough to gain Mr. Too's attention. When Mr. Too saw that it was Bartolomé who had called out, he quickly came to the window.

"Mr. Bartolomé," he said. It sounded more like "Bottle may," but Bartolomé never attempted to correct the pronunciation. English-speakers seemed to have difficulty with the name. Mr. Too was far from an English-speaker. He could just barely make himself understood in the language.

"Please to go to door. I let in," Mr. Too said and disappeared.

Bartolomé went to the door in the hall that Mr. Too had used to enter the hall the first time they met. Mr. Too cracked the door to make certain that it was Bartolomé on the other side. He then opened it just enough for Bartolomé to enter, then closed it behind him as if the crowd in the hall were a strong wind that needed to be kept out.

"I am here to settle our accounts," Bartolomé said as he retrieved a packet from his haversack. "I have here the hundred dollar repayment, the interest on the loan, rent for the barge, and pay for the bargeman." He placed the packet in Mr. Too's hand. The remainder of the profit, seventeen silver dollars, he kept tightly wrapped in cloth in the haversack. Any coins carried in a haversack were always wrapped so they did not make any sound. It was not wise to go about New Orleans with coins jingling in your clothing.

"Come with me," Mr. Too said. He led Bartolomé into a small annex to the office. He placed the packet in a desk drawer without even opening the folds of the makeshift envelope. Indicating for Bartolomé to sit on a small stool near the desk, Mr. Too sat in the large-backed chair at the desk. It seemed to swallow the small man. Mr. Too folded his hands. "I learn that you no have contract with Steward now," he said sadly. "Be no discouraged. Many tries at business fail."

"That is so," Bartolomé said. "I have other enterprises afoot." He tried to sound as if he was wise in the ways of the world. The fact that Steward's betrayal burned deeply was something he did not want to be known.

Mr. Too thought a while. Then, as if a decision had been made, he slowly said, "Perhaps, a possibility I may have job to offer. It make some travel. You young. No wife. Maybe you take?"

"That would depend upon the job," Bartolomé replied. There was no way he was going to take a position that would separate him from Anna for any length of time.

"Yes, of course," Mr. Too said. "We talk another time. When I know for certain I need someone for job."

Mr. Too led Bartolomé back to the job hall and held the door for his exit as if he expected the crowd to rush the opening. When Bartolomé exited to the street, the crowd there was much less hostile. Evidently, the news that the stranger was a shipper had reached the street. The Scotsman was gone. Bartolomé set off for Bayou Pecheur. He had ample time to reach the Steward house.

CHAPTER 7

When he arrived at the road into the cluster of buildings containing the Steward house, he paused for a moment. He made a special effort to suppress the urge to rush forward. Instead, he carefully surveyed the scene. He pulled a small, brass compass from his haversack. It included a folding vane that, when unfolded, acted as a sun dial. He turned the dial until it was properly aligned with the compass needle and read the time. It was half past five or so. There was time to make a careful approach to the alley.

He did not know if his message had reached Anna. Shortstep could have easily told his master of the attempted contact in hope for a greater reward than a silver bit. If a trap were being set for him, he was determined to find out before it could be sprung. He passed up and down the neighboring alleys and streets. He paused often. There were few people about and what little activity there was seemed normal. He remembered how he had tricked *El Comedor Serpiente* by noisily chopping away to make everything appear normal.

It was nearing six o'clock, and Bartolomé positioned himself at the entrance to the alley where he could be seen by someone peering out of the small, barred window. It was almost precisely the same spot he had fought off the foolish drunken robbers a lifetime ago.

There was movement at the window and a glimpse of red hair. He glanced behind him and then to the left and right. Nothing unusual was to be seen. He rushed forward and reached the window just as Anna's face appeared behind the iron bars.

"Bartolomé," she whispered, *"Son usted allí?"*

"Soy yo," he answered. Bartolomé pulled up a small crate that was near the window, to act as a step. He grasped the bars and she placed her hands on his. This had always been the limit of their physical contact. On the rare occasions that they met in public, they dared not even shake hands. Forced restraint made these brief meetings sweeter for them both. They continued their conversation in Spanish, as much as Anna could muster. They reverted to English when necessary, although Anna proved to be a quick study.

"I had heard that Father dismissed you and now has his employees collecting the moss," she said sadly. "It was not that your service was lacking. It was because of me. Mother made it clear to me that I am not to see you."

"It matters not," he answered. "I took on the task only to be near you."

"What shall we do?" Anna said, nearly in tears.

"I will find a way," he answered. Anna's tears vanished and her face seemed to radiate.

"Was Shortstep discreet?" he asked.

"Yes, but I fear we cannot use him as a contact. He risked much just in passing the note to me," she said. "Look. In the corner of the window here, the iron frame is loose. We could place small, folded notes here that would never be found unless one pulls back on the frame."

"Write only in Spanish if you can. I will do the same," he said. "We shall both word our messages so that they will appear to be language lessons. If that fails, I will discover another way. If you do not hear from me from time to time, do not think I have forgotten you. I may have to accept a position that will require my absence for a while. If that happens, I will tell you."

Anna hoped that the prospects for the new position would not materialize, and said so. She steered the conversation to the war with England. All of New Orleans was buzzing with speculation that the city might be invaded. The militia drills were performed with more martial effort and less drunken rowdiness than usual. Many of the businessmen had together pledged to form their own militia regiment. Others, like Anna's father, did not participate. Jacques, Bartolomé's stepfather, had been put on notice that the local militia was going to increase training to twice a month.

"Will you be ordered to the militia?" Anna asked.

"When I am seventeen, it will be expected of me to join," he answered. "And I will."

Anna knew little of Bartolomé's regular exercises with his grandfather. He was much better trained in the combat arms at fifteen than most of the men that formed the local militias. Aside from firing a lead ball, there was little difference between the bayonet and the *magado* as employed in hand to hand combat. In this regard, the *magado* was superior because of its greater length.

Bartolomé had witnessed many a drill. Militia training consisted of lock-step marching, volley, and countermarching. The militia officers read from a manual and then marched the men about, depending upon that officer's interpretation of the instructions. Loading in ranks was an elaborate set of commands that usually consisted of two or three words each. The last word of the set was emphasized to cause the solder to act.

"Load ARMS," and the soldier would bring the lock of the musket to his front.

"Open PANS," and the priming pan would be opened.

"Handle CARTRIDGE," and a paper-rolled cartridge containing powder and lead ball would be withdrawn from the cartridge box and held in the right hand.

"Tear CARTRIDGE," and the soldier would tear open the powder end of the cartridge with his teeth.

"PRIME," and a small amount of powder would be tapped from the cartridge into the priming pan. The old-timers would order, "Prime your LOCK," or just "LOCK."

"Shut PAN," and the pan would be closed.

"LOAD," and the remaining powder from the cartridge would be poured down the barrel of the musket, followed by the lead ball wrapped in the paper.

"Draw RAMROD," and the rod would be withdrawn from the bottom of the musket.

"Ram down CARTRIDGE," and the ball would be forced to the bottom of the barrel until it sits tightly against the powder.

"Return RAMROD," and the rod would be returned to its place under the barrel.

"Shoulder ARMS," and the musket would be placed on the left shoulder.

"Make READY," and the weapon would be removed from the shoulder and cocked.

"PRESENT," and the musket would be pointed toward the enemy.

"FIRE," and the musket was discharged.

The officers contended that a well trained soldier could fire three rounds in one minute. Bartolomé couldn't see how that was possible and he never witnessed a drill where even two rounds per minute were accomplished.

Every day's exercise ended with an imitation volley followed by a charge with fixed bayonets. Little attention was paid to how one actually fought with the bayonet. It was assumed that the enemy would be in flight; otherwise, the officers would not have ordered a charge.

Bartolomé and Anna continued to talk for a few more minutes, until Miss Wren called for Anna to come in to eat. Their parting was made with promises of future contact using the hidden note drop.

Bartolomé returned the crate to where he found it, lest someone notice its location under the window and guess at the function it had served there. He then placed a silver bit where he had promised Shortstep it would be. He was not about to risk an unhappy courier informing the household of the rendezvous.

* * *

He left the alley by the back way. Before every move around a turn or at a corner, Bartolomé would stop and examine his surroundings. Often there were villagers about, so he had to disguise his actions and not appear overly alert. His grandfather had often warned him to remain aware of his surroundings. "Do not go about like a horse with blinders, seeing only what is directly before you," Grandfather would say. "Observe the world all about you."

Once he was free of the cluster of buildings, he hurried along the road toward home. The sugarcane fields that bordered the road were tall, and harvest would start in a few months. Sugarcane is a two year crop, but the crops were rotated so that half the fields were harvested every year. Harvest time was a big event. When the harvest came, the roads were jammed with oxen sleds, wagons, laborers, and travelers, slowing the progress of pedestrians and riders alike.

After the harvest came the arduous work of reducing the cane to sugar. The cane was crushed and then boiled in large kettles. Using long-handled ladles, slaves would skim the surface to collect the floating, sugar-laden residue. This residue was carried hot in the ladle to another kettle where it was rendered further. The process was repeated along a line of half a dozen kettles or more, until the sugar separated into a glutinous mass that was scraped from the hot sides of the last kettle.

It was dangerous work, as the ladles were large and unwieldy, the kettles boiling hot, and the line of slaves had to snake around the roaring fires. The English labeled this process the Jamaican Train. Slaves who did the work called it *La Danse Jamaïcaine* (the Jamaican Dance). Burns were so common that a scarred leg or foot decorated nearly every sugar plantation field slave.

Bartolomé strode along the left-center of the road through the tall cane. Walking near the far edge of the road exposed one to an ambush from persons hidden in the cane rows. The same general rule held for walking in the city, particularly after dark. Bartolomé always walked so that the nearest buildings were to his left. Being right-handed, he could repel attacks from his left with greater dexterity. He also kept as far from the buildings as the conditions allowed. This provided the greatest response time to an ambush from an alley or doorway. His grandfather had taught him well.

Bartolomé heard some rustling in a cane row ahead and to his left. He brought his walking staff to the guard position and listened. There was another rustle in the cane row. He kept his eyes on the origin of the sound and began to move to his right when he suddenly realized that he was fixing his attention on the sound and had blocked out the rest of the world. He stepped back to the center of the road and began to scan in every direction. There was another rustle. Bartolomé backed up the road a few paces and stepped into a cane row. He knelt upon one knee and waited.

There was something very wrong here. The rustling in the cane was too loud to be anything other than intentional. It wasn't any animal. The sound emanated from the same location every time. It was as if whoever was causing it wanted to be heard. Bartolomé waited, his senses on high alert. The sun had set and the trail was lit in an orange-colored twilight. After some time, a young black man came out of the cane where the rustling had been.

"Where'd he go?" the man said.

Another man, older and larger, suddenly appeared from the cane opposite where his accomplice had hidden.

"Shuddap," was all the other said. They spoke in crudely accented English.

Bartolomé surmised that the two were runaway slaves. He realized that he had almost fallen for the trap. While one kept his attention with small movements on the left side of the road, the other man would wait until the victim had moved into striking distance. If Bartolomé had continued to advance, circling away from the sound and concentrating his vision on that area, he would have moved closer to the bigger man. His back would have been to the attacker and his attention elsewhere. Bartolomé vowed to never again be so easily distracted.

The two men stood in the road. They talked quietly as they looked back toward the city. It wouldn't take them long to realize that their intended victim didn't just disappear.

"He in the cane," the older man said, finally. "Go back where you was."

"It getting dark," the younger man protested.

"Go," the older man ordered.

As the men turned to reenter their hiding places, Bartolomé rushed from hiding with a loud yell. The older man had his back to Bartolomé, and before he could turn around, Bartolomé punched him square in the small of the back with the end of the walking staff. This sent the man sprawling head first into the cane row. Bartolomé wheeled around to deal with the younger man, only to see him fleeing up the road toward the city as fast as he could run. Bartolomé turned again to confront the older man. The second assailant was running away through the narrow cane row.

Pursuit is only wise when you know where you are going, Bartolomé thought. He had almost forgotten his grandfather's admonition to never develop blinders, particularly when threatened. "Seeing what is all around is better than a shield," he said aloud, quoting from one of his many lessons. As he resumed his walk, the shakes came again. This time they were milder and passed quickly.

The remainder of the walk home, though in the dark, was uneventful. The family was gathered on the porch, having just finished the evening meal, when Bartolomé arrived home. The excitement of the recent days was beginning to wane.

"You need to keep better hours," Jacques commented as Bartolomé finished off a fine cut of meat from the wild pig. "Summer is on us now and there is much to do at the farm."

"I will tend to my chores, sir," Bartolomé replied. "I do wish, with your permission, to go into the city from time to time. Mr. Too may have a position for me."

"That will be fine," Jacques said. "Tomorrow is Sunday, and you need to visit your grandfather. He has sent for you."

It had been some time since Bartolomé made the trip down to Bencheque. It was very unusual for his grandfather to send for him.

* * *

Madam Barbeaux stood in the doorway of a round, hide-roofed hut. Loa Ogoun was frowning at her as he squatted near a fire in the center of the hut floor.

"Mambo, you are impatient," he chided.

"Loa Ogoun, he was so near; I had to attempt it."

"Mambo, you must heed me," Ogoun said. He was clearly disappointed. "Kalfu warned him. Kalfu knew that the young warrior would have prevailed if they had fought in the road. Did you not perceive how the man fled into the cane? Kalfu advised the man to retreat and hide in the cane and kill the warrior from ambush. The young one, wiser than you, did not follow. Do as I instruct, and you may yet meet your contract."

"Yes, Loa Ogoun," Madam Barbeaux said as she bowed. A hot wind blew from the hut and Barbeaux was again at her altar.

* * *

The next day, Bartolomé set off for Bencheque. He walked with his family until they reached the church. The villagers usually congregated near the door to the church to visit before going in to Mass. Bartolomé had to repeat his "I had been baiting the snare for days" story one more time for the gathered congregation. He was certain that everyone had already heard the story, but he wasn't able to get away until the church bell rang and Mass started.

He arrived at his grandfather's house well before noon. He was surprised to see most of his Spanish uncles, aunts, and cousins on the porch or about the house.

"We are happy to see you here," Aunt Maria said. Aunt Maria was the sister of Bartolomé's father and the eldest surviving child of Diego deMelilla. "My father is quite ill and he has been asking for you," she said. Her tone was somber.

The other uncles and aunts present spoke in subdued tones. Diego deMelilla had eight children who had survived to adulthood. He was twice a widower and had four adopted children, as well. Most of his large extended family had gathered together at the house. Bartolomé was filled with trepidation as he was escorted by Aunt Maria into his grandfather's room.

"Maria, please allow me to talk to Bartolomé alone," he said. His voice was weak. It filled Bartolomé with dread. He had never known his grandfather to be anything but strong and robust. Aunt Maria withdrew with a bow. Bartolomé turned to hear what his grandfather had to say.

"What is her name?" he said after they were alone.

Bartolomé was startled. "Whose name, Grandfather?" he said.

"The name of the young lady who has kept you away for so many days," his grandfather said with a smile. "You missed three training sessions in a row. A lady must be involved."

Bartolomé blushed deeply. It made his grandfather laugh to see how well he had guessed at the cause of Bartolomé's truancy.

"First, tell me of your capture of the great, wild hog. Then tell me about the lady," grandfather said. All of Bencheque was alive with the tale of young deMelilla's feat. "Your Aunt Maria would say, 'Don Diego's blood-lines show through,' whenever the event was discussed."

"I had been baiting the snare for days . . ." Bartolomé began. He repeated the story in much greater detail for his grandfather's benefit. Many times, he paused to explain how he had applied the lessons learned at this house to the taking of the beast. He could see his grandfather fill with pride during the tale. Finally, it was done.

"Again I ask, what is her name?" his grandfather said. This time Bartolomé could see that there was no way to avoid the question.

"Anna Steward," Bartolomé said. He felt warmth flow over him as he said her name.

"Is she Catholic?" Grandfather asked. The surname was suspicious.

"Yes, Grandfather," Bartolomé replied. "Her family moved here from Catholic Maryland. She has begun to learn Spanish." He added the phrase last with pride. Grandfather never spoke anything but Spanish. Bartolomé often thought that the old man could speak French, but he had never heard him do so.

"I know that she is beautiful and wise," grandfather replied. "Beautiful, for that is how you see her. Wise, because you would never find a fool to be beautiful."

Bartolomé waited as his grandfather repositioned himself with a groan. "No one can tell me what it is that ails me. It is not the fever, nor cholera. I cannot make water without terrible pain," Grandfather said. "But enough of that; reach under the bed and bring out what you find."

Bartolomé did as he was told. What he found was a *magado* and a *sunta*.

The *magado* had a sturdy shaft, much like his walking staff. It was about seven feet long and an inch and a half in diameter. The wood was worn, and cured into an almost iron-like hardness. It was tipped with a fine, narrow, steel blade that ended in a needle-like point. The blade was razor sharp on both sides all the way to the tip. A small curved depression, known as a "blood trough," ran the length of the blade. The few nicks on the shaft had been sanded down and oiled. It was a weapon that had seen some work.

The mace-like *sunta* had a handle of wood as well-worn as the *magado*. A leather wrist strap passed through the grip on the weapon. It was topped with a stone ball that was slightly larger that a man's fist. The dark stone was as hard as flint and had a hole drilled through the center, through which the handle passed. The handle was shaped to be larger than the hole at one end so that the stone wedged firmly in place.

"These are yours," Grandfather said. "Carry them with pride. I have nothing else to give you. My land and other goods will go to my children. These alone I have marked for you."

They visited for some time until Aunt Maria interrupted. "Father," she said firmly. "You need to rest. Bartolomé will see you again soon."

"Rest is on the way," the old man replied. Then he turned to Bartolomé. "Go now. Practice daily," he said. Bartolomé could see that he was weaker than ever. He kissed the old man on the cheek and left. He would never speak with his grandfather again. Don Diego deMelilla died two days later.

CHAPTER 8

Bartolomé looked about carefully. He was moving through the back alleys of Bayou Pecheur. It appeared to anyone who glanced his way that he was just passing through on his way to New Orleans. He strode past the Steward house, turned down the alley along its tall walls, and stepped out onto the road that led to the city. He went around a bend in the trail that was out of sight of the house. There, he stopped and studied the path he had taken. When he was satisfied that he could retrace his steps without being observed, he returned to the alley and the barred window. He pushed on the iron frame, revealing a scrap of paper. He retrieved the note and quickly returned to the bend in the trail on the path to New Orleans.

The scrap of paper was a note from Anna. It was in Spanish. Usually, the note provided a rendezvous time. Anna and Bartolomé had been able to meet at the barred window once a week or so for the last few months. They never seemed to tire of their private time. Today, it was to be different.

"I am watched as I write. Miss Wren sits with me when I do my lessons," the note said. Anna had to write in this cryptic manner so that if the note were discovered it would appear to be part of her Spanish lesson. She was telling Bartolomé that the nanny would sit with her when she was in the courtyard. She could no longer trust that they could continue with their private time. Bartolomé reflected for a moment on how he was going to contrive another means of seeing Anna. There was more on the note.

The note ended with, "The market has many vegetables."

It was Tuesday, November eight, 1814. The city had begun to return to life in mid-September as the oppressive summer slowly faded into fall. Things didn't really begin to bustle until November, when hurricanes, yellow fever, and cholera were less likely. The market was once again a busy place, and would stay so until the following June. This year was particularly busy. Rumors of an impending British attack were rampant. American regular troops and local militia, some from states far away, hurried in and out of town and across southeast Louisiana.

He read the note again. Anna had mentioned that Miss Wren preferred to do the marketing on Tuesdays and Fridays. Today was Tuesday, but Bartolomé had pressing business, so today's opportunity had passed. Bartolomé knew that he could accompany Jacques to the market on Friday. Anna would be there. He took a small pencil from his haversack and wrote on the "lesson" paper.

"*Viernes*," was all he wrote. He did his best to imitate Anna's handwriting, but his forgery would not pass a careful examination. Bartolomé returned the note to the window frame and continued on to New Orleans. Mister Too had sent word that he wanted to talk to Bartolomé.

Mister Too's hiring hall was active. There was no long waiting line. Men entered and were almost immediately given an assignment or received their pay. Bartolomé waited only a short while until it was his turn to step to the widow where Mister Too conducted his business.

"Bartolomé," he said with a wide smile. "Go to door. I let in."

This time when Mister Too opened the door that connected the inner offices to the hiring hall, he opened it wide and ushered in Bartolomé.

Now that there was plenty of work to do, there was no need to worry about unruly bargemen forcing their way into the inner office. Mister Too never kept much coinage about. Most of the bargemen were paid in bank drafts.

"You are aware that the British have attacked Mobile," Mister Too said in a subdued voice as if the wall had ears.

Bartolomé was aware of the situation. Spain, an American ally during the Revolution of 1776, had suffered an invasion by Napoleon's forces. The French dictator was attempting to take all of Europe. The Bourbon King of Spain had been deposed and a relative of Napoleon installed. The following guerrilla war found Spaniards loyal to the monarchy allied with Britain for the first time since the Crusades.

The political situation in New Orleans was chaotic. French-speaking Creole aristocrats admired Napoleon to the point of worship. The Spanish population hated Napoleon because of the conquest of Spain and the sale of Louisiana to America. The Americans distrusted the native Louisianans and rightly considered the population to be filled with spies for France or Spain. Most of the city leaders, if given the chance, would readily surrender New Orleans to the invading British to prevent the destruction of their city. Anna had told Bartolomé of overhearing her father report that several legislative leaders in New England were pressing for a return to the British Empire. America as a nation seemed doomed.

"They were driven off by the American Army," Bartolomé replied.

Mobile was Spanish territory, but with Spain absorbed in a guerilla war against France, her garrisons along the gulf coast were under-manned and on their own. The Americans, under General Jackson, simply moved into Mobile. The British did the same at Pensacola. The feeble Spanish defenders could do nothing to stop either force.

"That is so," Mister Too said. "Claiborne is a fool. Unless there is a miracle, New Orleans will fall before the year is out."

Bartolomé was not particularly shocked by Mister Too's assessment of the Louisiana governor. Claiborne was bureaucratic and contemptuous of the people of Louisiana. As with most men of limited intellect who have been placed in a position of authority, Claiborne was, above everything else, profoundly arrogant.

"I tell you thing that no other know," Mister Too continued, his voice almost a whisper. "If British take New Orleans, John Too dead man. My true name Hue Ne Noch. Noch master of own coastal trading junk in

Western Sea. One day, a British warship sailed up to Noch. With one volley from guns, sink my ship. The British pulled Noch from sea and say, 'Choose. Join this ship, be deck hand, or go back into sea.' For many years, Noch slave. Noch taught English by end of lash. Every time ship reach port, Noch shackled below with other slaves. One such time, Noch slip shackles and escape. Noch killed British officer before he could raise alarm, and swam ashore. Noch was in Mobile. That five years ago. Now Noch gone. All time, forever gone. John Too here."

Killing a British officer was an offense that would not be forgotten, even if it were five years ago. Bartolomé could tell that Mister Too was not going to fall into British hands again. He could flee inland, but all he owned was here. Mister Too was going to resist.

"I need man I trust. Bring message to master of *La Diligent*," Mister Too said, handing a paper to Bartolomé. The paper was folded and sealed with wax. Mister Too did not have to say who the master of the *La Diligent* was.

"How am I to find Jean Lafitte?" Bartolomé asked. "Claiborne has sent a regiment to capture him."

"Lafitte could crush that little force any time. He not want war with America. He will help, but Claiborne not see that," Mister Too explained. "Will you take note?"

"Tell me where to bring it," Bartolomé said, "and I will tell you if I can do it."

"And you keep this trip secret? You not read note?" Mister Too said.

"You have my word that no one shall learn from me that this trip was made and I will not read the note," Bartolomé replied.

Mister Too seemed satisfied. "Many think Lafitte in Texas hiding from Claiborne. I not ask you go Texas. Instead, go Poche's Ferry. There find rowboat tied at point where bayou meets river. Oars will have red tips. Red tips very important. If Bacenaux asks you what you are doing, tell him John Too sold boat to you." Mister Too paused and looked hard at Bartolomé. He continued. "Cross river. Look for red cloth tied high on tree. Tie boat to tree. Wait. A man will come to you. He ask who you are. You say 'Chinaman sent me;' just those words, no more. Man bring you to Lafitte." Mister Too finished with, "You do this?"

Bartolomé said, "I will do this thing." He took the note from Mister Too's hand and placed it in his haversack. He would have just enough time to reach Poche's Ferry and cross the river before dark. After that, he didn't guess, or ask, how much further he had to travel.

"Captain Lafitte will say if he has reply for John Too," Mister Too said. "For this thing, I will pay you four dollars."

That was a respectable sum for just carrying a message. It was plain to see that this was more than just a courier service. This position required trust and involved some danger. Captain Jean Lafitte was well liked among the plantation owners and upper-class population in and around New Orleans. His smuggling business, in which they all participated, was profitable and provided affordable goods from around the world. He was a good man to know. Bartolomé had never met Lafitte, but he had seen him in and about New Orleans.

* * *

Mister Too led Bartolomé back to the hiring hall. Bartolomé left without any more discussion. He hurried along, employing his stout walking staff to strengthen his stride. He was rushing toward a goal and looked it. That's when he suddenly slowed down.

I'm carrying a message to a fugitive. Hurrying along like this makes me stand out like a dog on a scent, he thought. He slowed to his typically strong pace and concentrated on his surroundings. As he passed Bayou Pecheur, he resisted the urge to check Anna's message drop and continued along the trail nearest the river.

In less than an hour, he arrived at Poche's Ferry. The boat with the red tipped oars was moored to a small post and pulled slightly up onto the river bank. The boat had open water style oarlocks so that the boatman rowed with his back to his destination. The *bateau* that Bartolomé was accustomed to had raised oarlocks so that the rower faced his destination. It was intended for use in narrow bayous and sheltered waters.

What a strange way to row a boat, he thought. *It is much better if a man can see where he is headed.*

Bartolomé looked about. Bacenaux was nowhere to be seen. The river was unusually low, and a wide sand bar separated Bayou Terre Aux Boeufs from the river. Foot traffic that wished to continue downstream along the Mississippi simply crossed the bayou bottom on the sand bar. He untied the mooring line and placed it and his walking staff in the bow of the boat. He was preparing to push it off the bank when he heard a rough voice.

"Vous quels sont faisant? (What are you doing)," the voice said. It was Bacenaux. When Bartolomé turned to answer, Bacenaux recognized him as a local, though he didn't know Bartolomé by name.

"I have bought this boat from Mister Too," Bartolomé said.

Bacenaux straightened up with a strange look on his face. "Of course," he said. With that, he turned around and went back to the small shack that was both ferry landing and home.

Bartolomé pushed off and boarded the boat. He tried a few pulls on the oars. He then oriented the boat until it was pointed slightly upstream of what appeared to be the shortest distance across the river. This was to account for the moderate current that would bring him downstream. He then aligned two points on the near shore and began to row in earnest. He reasoned that it would be simpler to keep the boat on the proper heading if he didn't have to keep looking over his shoulder to see ahead. This seemed to work, more or less, until mid-stream where it became difficult to see details on either bank.

Once he finally arrived at the west bank of the river, he decided that he was quite a distance downstream from his intended destination. He kept to the shallows along the west bank and rowed upstream, alert for any sign of red cloth in the tree tops. Just when he was about to try going downstream, he saw it. High in the branches of a tall tree several feet from the water's edge, there was a wide, red sash tied around the trunk. A casual observer would not have seen it.

He pulled to the bank. Stepping out of the boat, Bartolomé grasped the gunnels and forced the boat up onto the shore. He then tied the mooring line to the tree, retrieved his walking staff, and sat on the bow. He held the staff with both hands. The butt was on the ground between his feet. He rested his chin on his arms and waited. After a while, he began to doze.

Alerted by movement in the brush, Bartolomé looked up without moving his head. It was getting dark. A figure appeared from the brush and walked directly to him. Bartolomé sat up without saying a word, and examined the visitor. He was a short but wide man. His shirt was opened down the front and his undershirt was tattered. He wore the wide, short trousers favored by seafaring men. His beard was woven into four long braids, each ending in a gold ring. A large cutlass was wedged in his belt. His face was a mosaic of tattoos and scars. His head was bare. He stopped directly in front of Bartolomé and rested his hand on the cutlass.

"Chinaman sent me," Bartolomé said in English.

The tattooed face glared at Bartolomé for a while. Suddenly, the man said, *"Allons* (Let's go)," and headed into the brush.

Bartolomé leaped up to follow. He had to walk fast to keep pace with the burly sailor. The trail they followed was not well worn. Bartolomé could see places where the brush had just recently been hacked down to clear a path. They were walking upstream and quartering away from the river so that after a few minutes travel time they were in deep woods.

Twilight had faded into full darkness. They traveled without any light but the moon. Slowly, Bartolomé could see some lamp lights ahead. They stepped out onto a wide roadway leading to a large plantation house. Bartolomé knew that the river lay at the other end of the path. He surmised, rightly, that they had cut through the woods to avoid detection. Had they walked up the smooth, wide shore line or the river road, anyone afloat could have seen them.

The guide went around the house to the back. He turned to Bartolomé. "Place the staff and knife here," he said, indicating a spot near a garden gate. "I will bring you to the captain."

There were several men gathered on the rear porch. They were talking, smoking, and drinking as if they had just finished an evening meal. The large porch was ringed by oil lamps. Bartolomé saw that there were eight men in all. He could also hear ladies chatting from within the house. A dinner party was concluding which, as was the custom, required that the ladies withdraw into the house to visit while the men talked business and politics on the porch.

The sailor spoke up. "He's been sent by the Chinaman," he said, in French, as he stepped aside to usher Bartolomé forward.

All the men were well dressed, everyone a wealthy aristocrat. The man who had been talking to the others as Bartolomé and his guide walked up turned around when the sailor spoke. Bartolomé recognized him instantly. It was Captain Jean Lafitte.

CHAPTER 9

"Message for you, captain," Bartolomé said as he reached into his haversack. Out of the corner of his eye, he saw the sailor stiffen and drop his hand to the cutlass.

He forgot to search my haversack when he had me drop my weapons, Bartolomé though.

Bartolomé slowly drew the sealed message from his haversack and held it out for Lafitte. Lafitte looked at Bartolomé for a moment and then took the paper.

"What does Too have on his mind?" Lafitte said as he examined the sealed paper.

"I do not know, captain," Bartolomé said.

"What is your name?" Lafitte said.

"Bartolomé deMelilla," Bartolomé said.

A Spaniard, Lafitte thought. *Why would Too send me a French-speaking Spaniard?*

"Dede," Lafitte called out. A house slave came out onto the porch.

"Yes, captain?" she said.

"Take this man down to the oven and feed him," Lafitte said.

Dede led Bartolomé down the porch steps and to the large oven where the heavy baking was done for the plantation. There were several tables and stools about. Directing Bartolomé to sit, Dede spooned a large serving of a steaming rice dish that Dede called jambalaya onto a tin plate. Bartolomé knew it as *paella*. It was what the servants ate, not the fine cuisine that the gentlemen on the porch had enjoyed. Still, Bartolomé had been on the move quite a bit lately, and he was tired of the biscuits and jerked beef that he carried in his haversack. He devoured the *paella*. Dede had also given him a cup of wine to enjoy with his meal. She left him to eat.

After some time, Dede returned. "The captain wants to see you now," she said. They both returned to the porch. Lafitte was alone.

"Leave us," he said to Dede. When she was well inside the house, he turned to Bartolomé. "Do not return to Mister Too's place until you are sent for," he said. "Continue with your normal activities. Roundtree will bring you back to the boat. Return it to Poche's Ferry," Lafitte said. He then went into the house.

He is certainly a man accustomed to giving commands, Bartolomé thought. *He talks to me as if I am in his employ.*

Roundtree, the sailor who had guided Bartolomé to the house, reappeared. They retrieved Bartolomé's gear and returned to the moored boat by a different path than they had taken on the way in.

Bartolomé placed his walking staff in the bow of the boat. When he turned to untie the mooring line, he saw that Roundtree was gone.

The trip back across the river, in full dark, was something that Bartolomé hoped he would never have to do again. He had to judge his direction by keeping the moon in the same location to his right as he rowed. He developed a routine. Ten strong pulls on the oars, then pause to check the position of the moon and look left and right. Then row some more.

Finally, he was able to discern the dark shadow of a shore line. The gentle lapping of waves along the shore line alerted him just before he ran aground. Standing up, Bartolomé looked about. The best that he could tell, he was downstream from Poche's Ferry. After a little rest, he rowed upstream, keeping to the shallows. It was not long at all before he was at the bayou junction. He ran the boat onto the shore and tied it to the same post where he had found it. It seemed like days, not hours, since he had cast off.

Bacenaux came out holding an oil lamp. The sky was beginning to cloud up. Moon and star light would soon be gone. "I have a lamp for your walk home, young Troyles," he said.

He thinks that I'm Jacques' son, Bartolomé thought. He didn't correct Bacenaux.

"Thank you, sir," Bartolomé said. "I will return the lamp to you Friday when we pass here on our way to the market."

"When it is convenient for you," Bacenaux replied, and retreated into his shack.

It struck Bartolomé that the man seemed almost fearful of him. The lamp was welcome, for the night sky was overcast, and it seemed darker than ever. He walked along the familiar trail with the small circle of light swaying around him. Before long, he was home. When he reached the foot of the steps leading up to the boys' loft, he put out the lamp and placed it on the corner of the porch. He quietly went up the steps and managed to find his bed without waking his stepbrothers. He knew from their snores that they were all in.

* * *

Bartolomé lay down and had just closed his eyes when he heard someone calling him.

"Get up," Maurice called from the bottom of the steps. "There is a lot of work to do."

Bartolomé came down to the porch. The whole family was up, fed, and ready to begin the day's chores. There was no mention of the late hour of his return from the meeting with Mister Too. Everyone knew that Mister Too had asked Bartolomé to come to his office.

"What kind of position did Mister Too offer?" Aimée asked. She simply spoke what everyone else was thinking. Bartolomé's forays have been bringing silver into the household and that was welcomed. That was why Jacques and Aimée tolerated the occasionally odd hours that Bartolomé kept.

"It was not a position he had to offer yesterday," Bartolomé answered. "It was a chore. He will pay me four dollars."

"Will pay?" Maurice asked. "Did you not collect your pay before the chore was done?"

"He trusted me with over a hundred dollars; I can trust him to pay me four," Bartolomé replied. He was a little miffed by Maurice's tone. "Today and tomorrow, we have much to do for Friday if we will bring produce to the market." He added, in thought, *and meet with Anna.*

Friday morning arrived. Jacques had hitched up the horse to the wagon and all hands loaded up the harvest that had been collected through late in the day Thursday. Soon the wagon was full of cabbage, garlic, and the best onions any of them had ever seen. There were a few freshly smoked hams added to the load. The family had held a *boucherie* in October. A *boucherie* was a community gathering of family, friends, and neighbors, when the men killed select pigs and everyone participated in cleaning and preparing the meat.

"Where is your special order?" Maurice asked.

"It is promised for the first week in December," Bartolomé answered. "It is to be aged until then."

"Aged it is," Maurice said.

The smoke from the *Tchmench* wood and thorns was well tended. Despite several heavy rains, the smokehouse fires smoldered, and a family member added a thorn and a fragment of *Tchmench* wood to the pit every day. Oceane had helped with these smokehouse chores. She particularly enjoyed adding a great thorn to the fire. The thorns would often sparkle before smoldering and then issue a cloud of red smoke.

Jacques and Bartolomé set off to the market. The rest of the family had gathered at the gate, and they waved as they creaked up the road along Bayou Terre Aux Boeufs.

Bacenaux saw them coming up the road. He stood by the ferry landing waiting for them to pass. The river was up and the ferry was needed again to cross the bayou. They stopped when they drew up to the landing.

"Here is the lamp you loaned me," Bartolomé said as he handed the lamp down to Bacenaux. "I thank you for your kindness."

"It was nothing," the man said. Out of habit, he gave the lamp a shake and then smiled when he realized that it had been filled. It had been only half full when he loaned it to Bartolomé. This was a sign of respect. A haughty gentleman or plantation master would have used up the fuel and, if he returned the lamp at all, not given a moment's thought to filling it and saving the lender the cost of the oil.

When they passed Bayou Pecheur, Bartolomé didn't even glance at the Steward house. It really didn't matter, for the river road passed too far from the house to really see anything. The iron-barred window could only be seen from the alley. Bartolomé was certain that Anna and Miss Wren would not yet be on their way to the market.

William Stout was at his usual stall. The same arrangements were made. This time it took several trips with the hand truck to empty the wagon. Produce was piled high on the sectioned table. Each slot contained a different vegetable. The hams were on one end. The rest of the stock was tucked away behind a curtain at the rear of the stall to re-supply the table as sales were made.

The market was jammed. Word had reached New Orleans that General Jackson had attacked the British at Pensacola, and shoppers were buying more than usual. Although it was a Spanish possession, the British had armed the fort there with Redcoats. They had forced the handful of Spanish defenders out and treated the fort as if it were their own. Jackson attacked and routed the British to their ships. Every citizen had become a military expert. The speculation varied from, "The British are abandoning the gulf. First they are forced out of Mobile, now Pensacola," to "The British are definitely coming to New Orleans for they have been denied the other ports on the gulf."

Bartolomé didn't know what the British intended, but he remembered one of his grandfather's lessons. "Do not speculate and prepare for what you *think* an enemy will do. Prepare for what an enemy *can* do." Grandfather had often said, "If you think he will strike here, a strike anywhere else will be a surprise." The concept was obvious to Bartolomé. Everyone talked of war. Bartolomé thought of Anna.

About midday, he saw Anna. She was accompanied by Miss Wren, her nanny and chaperone. When Anna was certain that Miss Wren was distracted, she gave a little wave of her fingers to Bartolomé. Now that he was sure she knew he was there and was aware of him, he slipped behind the stock curtain. He made certain that Anna saw the move. He waited. Mister Stout and Jacques were busy with shoppers.

Bartolomé heard Miss Wren when she approached the stall. She called for Mister Stout. "The onions are particularly beautiful today, Mister Stout," she said.

"Yes, madam," Mister Stout answered. "Jacques Troyles, here, is the finest farmer to be found."

"Miss Wren," It was Anna speaking. Bartolomé was delighted to hear her voice again. "May I sit near the stall here and read? I am so very tired. You can see me from most any place if I sit here and read," Anna pleaded.

Miss Wren gave a look around. The stall was near the end of the market where a brick wall formed a corner.

"I think it shall be fine if you do so. Here, keep these with you," Miss Wren said as she handed a sack of vegetables to Anna. "I will not go far," Miss Wren said. She gave the area a good look and then moved to another stall.

Anna placed the sack at her feet and jumped up onto a tall stool near the curtain that hid Bartolomé. *"Puedes óigame?* (Can you hear me?)," Anna said without turning. She held the book up so that no one could see that she was talking.

"Your Spanish is very good," Bartolomé replied. "It is hard to see you so close and not hold you."

Anna's eyes closed as Bartolomé said this. "You are holding me now, Bartolomé," she said softly. Then she sighed deeply. "Do you think the British will come? What will we do?"

The British were notoriously cruel. Bartolomé's mother often told of how her mother was driven out of Nova Scotia with a baby in her arms and one on the way. Bartolomé's maternal grandfather had been hanged because he refused to renounce Catholicism. Louisiana was full of people whose family members had suffered at the hands of the British. The Irishman, Mister Getty, once referred to the Union Jack as "the Butcher's Apron."

"Whether the British come or not," Bartolomé said, "does not depend upon what I think. We must be ready for them because they can come."

"Father says he will make passage on the steamboat and go up to Natchez," Anna said.

"That is wise. He has a family to protect. But someday, someone must face them," Bartolomé said grimly.

"I don't want to think about it anymore," she said. Then she pretended to be happy. "My birthday is coming. I will be fifteen on December third."

"I shall get you something special," Bartolomé said.

"I just want you safe," she replied. Bartolomé could see the tears forming in her eyes. All this talk of war was beginning to wear on her.

Just then, she sat up straight. "I can see Miss Wren is finished and she will be coming soon," she said. She held out her hand to Bartolomé behind the curtain. "Good-bye for now."

"I will be at the weeping iron at midnight on your birthday," he said. Then he took her hand and kissed it softly. Anna seemed to tremble. She withdrew her hand and, hidden by the book, kissed the spot that Bartolomé's lips had touched. Bartolomé felt a rush sweep over his body. He stepped back further behind the curtain as Miss Wren arrived. He could see Anna slip down from the tall stool and leave with Miss Wren.

Bartolomé leaned back, almost falling on a pile of onions. He turned to go around the curtain to the stall only to find himself face-to-face with Jacques.

Jacques was smiling broadly. Bartolomé didn't know how long Jacques had been there. Fortunately, the conversation had been in Spanish and some English. Jacques could speak very little of either. It didn't matter, though. They could have been speaking Greek. Jacques could see that Bartolomé and Anna were in love. He didn't know how much had passed between them and he didn't care.

"There is more danger there, boy," Jacques said, "than you ever faced in that wild hog." He laughed and gave Bartolomé a hard slap on the back.

She scares me more than the wild hog, Bartolomé thought.

"The third day of December, I am to make the delivery on that special aged ham," he said as if the mention of the pig had reminded him.

* * *

Mister Too had sent a message, along with four dollars, to Bartolomé. The message said that he should come to the hiring hall when it was convenient, to discuss a possible position. Bartolomé was able to manage time near the end of November to go to the hiring hall. Although this was the month that usually saw the greatest activity in shipping, the hall was not as active as it should have been. Bartolomé learned the reason after Mister Too brought him to the rear office.

"The ships from Cuba no come. Ships from Caribbean no come. All turned back by British," Mister Too said. He explained the intelligence he had acquired to Bartolomé.

The few ships that evaded the British brought reports of increased military activity. A second British fleet had arrived in Jamaica, comprised of warships and many transports. These could only be troop transports. The British had taken more than a regiment of Jamaican soldiers into the ships, as well. Captain Lafitte had rejected, after pretending to seriously consider, a British offer that invited the pirates to join with the British in the siege of New Orleans. The British foolishly thought he would be interested in destroying his best customer. The finest intelligence concerning the British activity came from Lafitte. He maintained a small fleet of swift sloops throughout the gulf that continually supplied him with information on ship movements. Piracy, as practiced by the Lafitte consortium, did not rely on chance to capture the fattest ships.

The message that Bartolomé had delivered to Lafitte was from Louisiana lawyer, Edward Livingston. It was concerning the efforts that Livingston was making on behalf of Lafitte to broker a pardon in return for siding with the United States in the upcoming battle. Livingston was both an old friend of General Jackson and Lafitte's lawyer.

"When next you in city?" Mister Too asked.

"I shall definitely be here on the third of December," Bartolomé said.

"Come see me then," Mister Too said. "We know much more."

The rest of November seemed to drag by. There was enough work around the farm to keep all hands busy. But still, to Bartolomé, time seemed to be suspended. It was as if the third of December would never come. But come it did.

The second of December was, by lucky chance, a Friday. Bartolomé and Jacques were at the market when Anna and Miss Wren appeared. There was no opportunity for any sort of clandestine conversation between the lovers this time. When they were both in the market, they had sometimes been able to contrive a means to isolate several moments to converse. Today's encounter was brief, but it served to confirm the midnight meeting that Bartolomé had promised for the next night. Communications were complicated by Jacques' amused spying and Miss Wren's devotion to duty. There were only brief instances when signs or lip reading could pass between them.

"I must return tomorrow," Bartolomé told Jacques as they were returning to Bayou Terre Aux Boeufs. "I am to deliver that special order."

"There is much to do before I can let you go," Jacques said. "Soon the weather will become cold and we cannot let it catch us unprepared."

"Then I will go in the afternoon and return late," Bartolomé replied. "If the hour is too late, I will stay at Mister Too's drayage and return Sunday morning." It fell right. Anna could easily leave her room at midnight to meet Bartolomé at the window. The lateness of his departure to New Orleans gave him a plausible reason to return the next day.

* * *

The next day, Bartolomé tackled his chores vigorously. Even so, it was well after two in the afternoon before he finished. He went to the smokehouse to collect the aged ham. The last of the *Tchmench* wood had been used. The rest of the smokehouse was full of ham, venison, and beef in the process of being smoked or jerked. The ham promised for Madam Barbeaux had been segregated from the rest so that the *Tchmench* smoke would not be diluted with the smoke used to cure the rest of the meats.

He cut the ham down and placed it in a large cloth sack that had a broad shoulder strap. Once outside the smokehouse, Bartolomé opened the sack to inspect the ham. The color was striking. Most aged hams were very dark brown or black. This ham was bright red. It glistened as if it were wet. He replaced the ham, slung the sack over his back, and set off for New Orleans. He calculated that he would reach Madam Barbeaux's house at five o'clock.

On the way, he risked a visit to Anna's message drop. After confirming that he was unseen, he checked the drop. There was a small note. He placed the note in his haversack and hurried on.

Once safely out of sight of the house, he opened the note. *"Todo es bien,"* it read. *All is well*, Bartolomé thought. The rendezvous was on as planned. Tonight he would meet Anna at the weeping iron.

The December sun was low in the sky when Bartolomé walked up to Madam Barbeaux's door. He ascended the few steps and, before he touched the handle to the bell, Madam Barbeaux opened the door.

"Young sir," she said with a broad smile, "I am very pleased to see that you have come. Come in."

Bartolomé entered the house. It was as before. The front room looked more like a small chapel than a residence. Madam Barbeaux hurried around, lighting several candles until the room was quite bright.

"Please show me what you have brought," she said.

Bartolomé opened the sack and brought out the ham. It weighed about twenty pounds. He worried that the blood red color might be a problem.

"It is beautiful," she said. "I can tell that you have followed my instructions."

She then produced a knife from beneath her skirt and sliced off a small bit of meat from the tip of the ham and tasted it. She closed her eyes and made a faint noise, almost a hum.

"It is perfect," she said. "There has been the hand of a virgin feeding the fire. How . . ." she stopped herself. There is no need to ask him how he knew that the hand of a virgin feeding the fire made it perfect. He didn't know. It was the influence of Ogoun.

"Here is the payment I promised," she said as she handed Bartolomé two Spanish gold doubloons. "And I add this."

She placed a fine gold chain in Bartolomé's hand. It was intricately woven so that the links overlapped. It glistened with every movement. It was a bracelet with a cleverly contrived clasp that allowed it to be easily closed, but securely fastened. Releasing the clasp required both hands so that once fastened on the wrist, it could not be removed by the wearer alone.

Bartolomé wrapped the gold coins in a small bit of cloth and placed them in his haversack. He wrapped the bracelet separately, in another bit of cloth, and placed it in a small pocket within the haversack.

"Madam, I thank you," he said. "If you should ever need a special item again, please call on me." He walked to the door and Madam Barbeaux let him out. She watched from the steps as he walked up the street and out of sight.

"You may be assured that I will call upon you again," she said aloud, though there were none to hear.

Once inside, Madam Barbeaux went to the little altar. *How wise Loa Ogoun was to send me to Bartolomé,* she thought. *I shall pray to the loa and tell him of the success of his plan. He has let it be known to me that this young gentleman has the soul of a warrior.*

She then brought the ham to a closet she had prepared for it and placed it on a meat hook. She returned to the altar and placed a bowl of rum between the candles. She began the chant that would summon Loa Legba and ask for permission to enter the spirit world to converse with Ogoun.

CHAPTER 10

artolomé strode along the wooden walkway. He would visit Mister Too on his way to Bayou Pecheur. He suddenly realized that the street was beginning to become crowded with people, all headed in the same direction and talking excitedly. Finally, he asked a man, obviously an American, what was going on.

"We are on our way to hear General Jackson. He has come to defend New Orleans. He will address the citizens of New Orleans in the *Place D'Armes*," he said. "He has many American regulars with him, and more on the way." The man scurried off with the throng.

Bartolomé had some time to spare. His business with Mister Too would not take long and he did not have to be at Bayou Pecheur until midnight. He decided he would see what this General Jackson was about and went off toward the center of town.

When he arrived, Jackson was concluding his speech. "Thus I have sent forces to every avenue of approach. When the accursed invaders show themselves, we will repulse them with the might of free men. I call upon every man to stand with me and defend this land. I pledge to drive our enemies into the sea, or perish in the effort."

The cheers and huzzahs drowned out most of what was being said. Bartolomé was disappointed that he did not hear more, but he did have the opportunity to observe General Jackson when he passed near him. The man was tall and very thin. He often paused to cough into a handkerchief that he carried at the ready in his left hand. Yet, there was no doubt that this was an impressive, influential leader.

The crowd was slow to disperse. Instead, men gathered in small groups to talk. Most vowed to join in the defense of the city in one way or another. General Jackson had activated the militia and assigned different units to different sectors to act as an early warning. Everyone was convinced that the British were coming. It was simply a matter of when and where. Most agreed that the most likely attack would be up the coast road from the direction of Mobile. There were no deepwater ports nearer that could handle the troop transports. A push up the Mississippi River was a second possibility, but the invasion fleet would have to endure cannon fire from several forts and shore batteries.

Bartolomé decided that speculating on the possibilities was not helpful. He would wait until more was known, not that what he decided would have any effect on anything. He headed for the hiring hall to see Mister Too.

The hall was empty and the door locked. Bartolomé knocked loudly and waited. After a minute, the peephole opened and he saw an eye. Then he heard Mister Too say, "Bartolomé! Very good." The door opened to reveal Mister Too in his finest militia uniform. "Come in, Bartolomé, come in," he said with a sweep of his hand.

"I see that you have joined a militia, Mister Too," Bartolomé noted.

"Yes, private militia. Mostly men in shipping business," Mister Too said with pride. "We go Spanish fort on Bayou St. John. British may come that way."

"Would you not be of greater service conveying information to the Americans?" Bartolomé asked.

"No need now," Mister Too said. "General Jackson get news first hand. I fight if British come St. John. I win. I die. Same–same to me." Mister Too was as happy as Bartolomé had ever seen him. There was a small garrison at the Spanish fort as well as other small redoubts spread throughout the delta. It was one of Jackson's main problems. He could not concentrate his forces until he knew where the British would strike. Then it would be a race to get enough men and munitions to the right place to put up a defense.

"What can I do for you?" Bartolomé asked. It was Mister Too who had requested he drop by.

"I have this for you to keep for me. I die, you bring to Hall Bank. Give to John Ruston. I live, you give back to me." Mister Too said. His lighthearted attitude suddenly changed to a deadly serious one. He handed Bartolomé a packet of paper tied with a string.

"I will do this, sir," Bartolomé said as he accepted the packet.

"I go now Spanish fort," Mister Too said. Night had fallen, but Mister Too only needed to walk a short way to Bayou St. John and then it was an easy boat ride to the fort. "It late now. You stay here tonight. Go home tomorrow."

Bartolomé was surprised by the offer, but it did give him a chance to time his visit with Anna.

"I thank you, sir," Bartolomé said. "I will stay a while, but I should be gone much before dawn."

"Good. Good," Mister Too said. "I go." He pumped Bartolomé's hand and, with a slap on the back, he was on his way.

Bartolomé watched him as he scurried off toward Bayou St. John. His excitement bordered on joy. Then he was gone.

Bartolomé placed the packet in his haversack. He wondered what it was, but he was not temped to open the packet. He knew that this was a personal favor for Mister Too. No mention was made of payment. He closed the front door. There was a single oil lamp burning in the hall. Bartolomé took it off the hook and made his way to the back office. Mister Too had a large clock on the wall. It was seven PM. Bartolomé sat on the chair and rested his eyes for a moment.

* * *

Ogoun stood next to a *Tchmench* tree. "You have done well, mambo," he said. Madam Barbeaux found herself sitting on the severed head of a tusked boar, her bare feet in the blood-soaked mud. "This one is strong. *El Comedor Serpiente* was a favorite of Kalfu, yet this warrior took the animal. A weak mind can be led. This one cannot be made to follow. He is like a strong wind. You must be as a sailing master."

Ogoun came closer to Barbeaux. She could feel the hairs on the cowhide shield that he carried. "What is it that a sailing master must do, mambo?" he said.

"Loa Ogoun," she answered, "a sailing master does not tell the wind where to blow. The master trims his sails so that the wind carries his vessel where he wants to go."

"That is so!" Ogoun shouted. "To do what must be done, trim your sails. Observe the winds. Set your course where the winds are most favorable and you will arrive at your destination."

Then Ogoun was gone. Madam Barbeaux was sitting on the floor of her chapel. The bell in the door rang. Barbeaux went to the door and opened it. There was a team-drawn carriage in the street. The carriage footman had rung the bell. He turned and descended the house steps to the carriage door. He opened it and assisted a veiled lady in black down from the carriage and across the plank to the walkway. He then gently helped her up the steps into Madam Barbeaux's house.

* * *

Bartolomé opened his eyes and looked at the clock on Too's wall. It was half past ten! He jumped up! If he had missed the rendezvous with Anna, he never would have forgiven himself. As it was, he had enough time to reach Bayou Pecheur. He collected his things, checking to be certain nothing was left behind. He would not be able to re-enter the hall once he left by the back door. He felt the bracelet safe in the side pocket, the gold coins, and the paper. He then made his way out the back door.

The streets were very quiet. If martial law had been declared, he would have to avoid any patrols. He strode off with his walking staff at the guard position, alert for the slightest sound or movement. He arrived at the turn in the trail near the Steward house where he could see the walled compound and the entrance to the alley. He made it to be eleven thirty or so. From this vantage point, the house looked dark. He decided that it would be best to pass through the alley once before midnight. It would not be wise to rush down like a buck in rut.

The pass through the alley showed it to be clear. He moved the small crate he had been using as a step to its place beneath the window. He withdrew to a location at the entrance to the alley where there were five or six large vertical planks leaning against a wall. When he stood against the wall next to the planks, he was practically invisible. From this location, he could clearly see the barred window. He waited. Every sense was alert. Not the slightest sound, shadow, or smell escaped his notice. A rat appeared and scampered along the base of the wall until it ran into the side of Bartolomé's shoe. Then it detoured around his shoes and the lumber, and disappeared.

Just then, Bartolomé heard the sound of something moving in the courtyard of the Steward house. The alley was dark, but the night was clear and the moon was high. Bartolomé could see reasonably well. A figure appeared at the window. Delicate, white fingers grasped the bars. He heard Anna whisper, "*Estas allí* (Are you there)?"

He rushed to the window and stepped up onto the crate. "*Sí, aquí,*" he said. Then he grasped her fingers and kissed her fingertips. Anna sighed in relief.

"I was so afraid that you could not come," she said. "Father said that martial law had been declared and that there would be a curfew. Patrols would arrest anyone about without a good reason."

"I did not see so much as a single guard on my way out of the city," he said. The news of possible patrols and martial law would alter the trail Bartolomé used to return to Bayou Terre Aux Boeufs.

He retrieved the bracelet from his haversack. He could not wait any longer to give it to Anna. "This I present to you on the anniversary of your birth," he said as he placed the cloth-wrapped bracelet in her hand. Anna accepted the offering with a quizzical smile. When she opened it, she gasped so loudly Bartolomé feared it might alert the house.

"I cannot accept something so valuable," she said, "and so personal." It was the kind of gift a man, a rich man, would give to his wife, maybe his fiancée. Even in the faint moonlight, Anna could see that this was a wonderful work of craftsmanship.

"You must accept it. It is given from my love. Do not deny my love," he said.

Anna's Spanish was good enough to understand more than the simple translation into English that she made in her mind. Those words could not be translated into English and keep the deep meaning that was there.

"How could I wear such a beautiful bracelet without the world taking notice? How could I explain it?" Anna asked.

"Wear it on your ankle," Bartolomé said. "No one will ever know it is there but you."

Anna felt a sudden thrill. Polite society did not allow a person to mention such an intimate body part as an ankle. She was surprised that the concept of wearing this beautiful gift as an anklet made her feel so wonderfully wicked.

"Let me show you how the clasp works. It can be closed with one hand, but it requires two hands to open it," he said as he demonstrated it. He placed it on her wrist and then removed it.

"I will accept your gift," she said. Her eyes, sparkling in the darkness, said much more. At that moment, Bartolomé knew that Anna was his. There could never be anyone else for him.

There was a noise from within the house.

"Someone is up," Anna said. "We must part." She cast a hasty glance toward the house and disappeared from the window. Just when Bartolomé thought that she had rushed off, Anna reappeared.

"The fit is perfect," she said with an embarrassed smile.

There was another noise. The lovers bid each other good-bye and Anna reluctantly retreated from the window.

* * *

Bartolomé stepped down from the crate and leaned against the wall. He waited a while to see if there was any disturbance. All was quiet. He strode off for home, keeping to the shadows and pausing frequently.

Stopping at the corner of the last building at the edge of the little fishing village, he heard the sound of a small group of men coming up the road.

They did not carry a lamp or light of any kind. Bartolomé could see a tree line and the moonlit waters of the Mississippi River, but nothing else. He stepped back into the alley and waited. A file of seven men appeared from the darkness of the tree line. It was a militia patrol. The file moved noisily along the road. The men spoke to each other in French as they plodded along. They passed Bartolomé's hiding spot without so much as a glance in his direction.

New Orleans is in serious jeopardy, Bartolomé thought, *if she is to depend on men with this level of military discipline.*

He continued down the river. He stayed off the road and chose, instead, to walk along the riverside edge of the tree line. The river was low, so the way was smooth. The tree line hid him from the road and the shadow of the trees hid him from anyone on the river.

When he arrived at Poche's Ferry, he turned to follow the bayou. The ferry was moored on the far bank, and Bacenaux's shed was quiet. The time must have been two or so in the morning. The trail along the bayou was dark and the bank was steep. Bartolomé could not walk the water's edge here as he had done on the river. When he finally reached his village, he allowed himself to relax. Any patrol here would be made up of men he knew and he could explain being about at this hour.

Reaching his house, he ascended the stairs quietly and entered the boys' bedroom. Going to his bunk, he noticed that Jules and Gabriel were sound asleep, but Maurice was not there. Bartolomé was exhausted. He placed his knife, walking staff, haversack, and outer clothing between his bed and the wall. No sooner had he lain down than he was asleep.

* * *

Morning arrived instantly. Jules and Gabriel were up and chatting just as the eastern horizon began to lighten.

"Bartolomé, it is about time you were up," Jules said as soon as Bartolomé opened his eyes. "Papa and Maurice have been called out for the militia. We are the only ones here for Mama and the girls." Jules' words had a worried tone to them.

Bartolomé could see that both of the boys were very apprehensive about what lay ahead. "Then we better get about the business of taking care of them," Bartolomé said with greater confidence than he felt.

They all dressed and went down to the porch to see what was in store. Aimée and her daughters were up and preparing breakfast. It was strange not to see Jacques at the table. His chair and Maurice's were leaning against the table.

"We know what chores are to be done, Mama," Gabriel said. Then he began to eat his breakfast and said no more. He was on the verge of tears and feared that if he said any more, he could not hold them back.

Bartolomé took the cloth-wrapped gold coins from his haversack and gave them to his mother. "The family's share of my special order," he said.

Aimée opened the cloth. When she saw the two Spanish gold doubloons, she quickly sat down. The last time she had held a gold doubloon was on her wedding day to Bartolomé's father. It was her dowry. Now her son has given her twice that sum. *Damn this war,* she thought. *Just when this family is doing well, Jacques is pulled away from us.*

Jacques and Maurice had been posted to a small redoubt down Bayou Terre Aux Boeufs where Bayou La Loutre branched off to the east. The redoubt was more of a wooden stockade than a serious battlement. Situated at a turn on the bank of Bayou Terre Aux Boeufs, it had lines of fire down the center of both bayous. Two small deck guns, only two-pounders, had been mounted on makeshift carriages. One was trained down Bayou Terre Aux Boeufs and the other down Bayou La Loutre. The redoubt was not far from the village of Bencheque. It was just across the bayou from the house where Don Diego had died, but it might as well have been in China. Jacques and Maurice could not help when it came to the work needed to keep the farm going.

Bartolomé and his stepbrothers were reasonably able to adjust to the fact that they had to do without Jacques and Maurice. Winter was setting in. The nights came early and cold. Some days, the clear skies would provide a pleasant day; other times, a cold rain persisted for days. Two weeks had passed before Bartolomé was able to contrive a way to visit Bayou Pecheur. When he returned, he was heartbroken. There was a note in the frame.

"Father has decided that we shall all go to Louisville," it read. Anna's beautiful script was in English. Obviously, she no longer feared discovery. The house was boarded and vacant. Bernard Steward had taken all of his "property" with him as well, so there was no one to care for the house.

* * *

The days now seemed to be even drearier to Bartolomé than could be accounted for by the weather. Aimée noticed her son's melancholy, but she could not draw from him any cause. He insisted that he was just tired from the extra work.

Almost daily now, messengers would pass through the village bringing news of the situation. All plantation owners were ordered to block their back canals so an invader could not come in by water. Aimée was able to send word to the redoubt at Bencheque that they were faring well.

Jacques and Maurice replied with messages of their own. One of the militia sergeants could write. The men dictated a letter to say they were faring well and were in need of nothing. Maurice reported that he was particularly disappointed to discover that military work was boring and tedious. When he wasn't training on how to load the little cannons, he was digging trenches or hauling garbage. They did not even patrol. The local fishermen were up and down both waterways, so any movement into the bayous would be instantly discovered. Bartolomé read the letter to the family several times before Aimée stored it away in a small box.

The sun set on the twenty-second of December to a cold night. December twenty-third dawned as bleak and dreary as ever. Bartolomé awoke to some commotion along the road. Dressing quickly, he rushed down to see what it was all about.

Though it was dawn, a group of villagers were clustered on the road. As Bartolomé walked up, one turned to him. "It has happened," he said. "The British have landed at the Villere plantation. More troops are coming in every minute." The man was panicked. He ran down the road to spread the news.

Bartolomé turned around to see his mother standing on the porch. She held a towel to her face. Fear showed through. The British had come again to molest and rob her family, just as they had her parents and grandparents.

Bartolomé went to her and took her hand. "We must decide what to do," he said. "They will turn toward New Orleans, but scavenging parties will be sent about to obtain food for their army. They may come as far as here. We must load all we can into the wagon and go to Bencheque. That will be too far from the city for the British to bother with."

"Unless they take the city," Aimée said. "Then the bastards will come to every home and . . ." She didn't finish the sentence. They both retreated into the house and put everyone to work.

Before noon, the horse was hitched and the wagon loaded. It was piled high with cured hams, jerked beef, and farm tools. The breeding sow was tied to the wagon frame. Jules was at the reins. Bartolomé didn't climb up with the rest of the family.

"Come," Aimée said. "Get up on the wagon."

"No, Mother," Bartolomé said. "I will serve this family best if I can help prevent the fall of New Orleans. A warrior serves his family best when he can keep the enemy far from their door." He was quoting Diego.

Aimée could only say, "*Vaya con Dios.*"

Bartolomé had never heard his mother speak Spanish before. It may be that "Go with God" was the limit of her vocabulary. He watched the wagon join the caravan of refugees going down the road to Bencheque. If the city fell, there would be no hope for them. He went into the house and retrieved his *magado* and *sunta*. He left his waking staff on the porch and used the *magado* in its stead. The *sunta,* he tucked into his belt opposite the knife he had acquired what seemed like a lifetime ago. He slung a bedroll across his back that contained a blanket and a change of clothes.

He began the trek to New Orleans. He was going to join General Jackson's forces, if they still existed. Or die in the attempt.

* * *

By the time Bartolomé reached Poche's Ferry, the steady stream of refugees heading down the bayou had ceased. Bacenaux's shed was vacant and the door wide open. The rowboat with the red oar tips was gone. Bartolomé believed that if he moved further up the river he would begin to encounter the perimeter guards for the British camp. He had two choices. He could travel away from the river and try to pass the British camp in the swamp. If he went that way, it was certain that he would have to swim several canals. It would be full dark by then, which would assist any attempt to pass through British lines. The other choice would be to travel up the bank of the river and try to pass the British by swimming in the river. The nights had been very cold, sometimes freezing, so the idea of swimming was not very pleasant.

He decided to go to the swamp. As he passed the rear of Bacenaux's shed, he saw the tip of a *pirogue* sticking out from under the shed. A third choice was now available. He could cross the river and go upstream along the west bank far out of range of the British. He pulled the *pirogue* out from under the shed. It was in good condition and well formed. There was also a paddle in the boat. He decided that if he left Bacenaux a note, it would do no good. The man probably couldn't read, and Bartolomé had neither paper nor pencil. With a vow to return the boat when he could, Bartolomé pulled it to the river and set off for the west bank.

Once out in the river, he could see a ship in the fading light, far upstream. It was anchored near the west bank and just opposite the Rodriguez Canal. He crossed to the west bank and began the trip upstream in the shallows where the currents were mild. As he neared the point opposite the Villere plantation, he could see men in red uniforms along the levee of the east bank. It was dusk and he could not see much more than the men silhouetted on the levee. Some pointed in his direction, but he would be able to keep about a thousand yards from them, well out of range of any fire arm. If they had a cannon they could have skipped a six-pound ball that far, but it would have been a waste of powder and shot.

After some time, he began to draw close to the ship that he had spotted when he first crossed the river. He was nearly to the ship before he could make out her name on the stern. It was the *USS Carolina*. Several men on the ship came to the stern and one swung a deck gun in his direction.

"State your business," one of the sailors shouted in English.

"I am from Terre Aux Boeufs," Bartolomé shouted back. "I have come to join General Jackson."

"Come to the gangway," the sailor said. He pointed to a stairway suspended from a spar that ended in a small landing at the water.

Bartolomé paddled to the landing, and securing the *pirogue*. He climbed onto the landing and up the stairs. He was met at the top by an officer. "I am Captain Henley. Tell me what you saw of the British as you passed their camp," he said.

"I did not see much for I kept to the west bank and out of range. It was growing dark," Bartolomé replied.

"How many guns did you see?" Captain Henley continued.

"None, sir," Bartolomé replied. "At least there were none on the levee, nor on the river side of the levee. If they had any further inland, I cannot say."

"What experience do you have aboard a ship?" the captain asked.

"None, sir," he replied. "This is the first time I have ever been aboard a ship."

Captain Henley looked a little disappointed. This strong young man could be of some use if only he knew a handsaw from a marlin spike.

"Be on your way," he said. Bartolomé was ushered down to the platform.

Bartolomé returned to the *pirogue* and set off for the point where the Rodriguez Canal met the river. He could see widespread activity on the bank as he approached. He did not know the time, but it was dusk and the cold air caused a puff of mist with every breath. He landed and pulled the *pirogue* far up the bank. When he reached the top of the shallow levee, he saw that an army was on the move. A long column of soldiers, American regulars, was passing by. He saw the regimental banners of the Seventh and then the Forty-fourth Infantry. A Tennessee militia unit was in the mix, along with a local private militia unit he did not recognize.

One of the local militia sergeants ran over to Bartolomé. It was William Stout, the man who ran the market stall that Jacques and Bartolomé rented on consignment.

"Bartolomé," he shouted. "How did you pass the British lines?"

"I came by *pirogue*," Bartolomé explained, "up the river."

"We are going to attack the British this very night," Sergeant Stout said. "Fall in beside me. We are in dire need of messengers who can speak French and English. We will put you to service." Stout then rushed back to his post beside the marching militia pulling Bartolomé by the arm.

Bartolomé placed the *magado* at shoulder arms and began to march behind Sergeant Stout, trying his best to keep the pace. After a mile or so, an officer on horseback came alongside Bartolomé.

"Who are you, lad?" the officer said. Somehow, among all the mixture of uniforms and militia, this officer had noticed that Bartolomé was a new addition. Stout's militia unit had checkered frocks. Bartolomé's white cotton frock stood out.

"I am a messenger for Sergeant Stout," Bartolomé said. He didn't even know the identity of the militia he had just joined.

"Sergeant Stout," the officer called out, "join us." Stout fell back the one or two paces it took to march alongside the mounted officer and Bartolomé.

"This man tells me he is your messenger," the officer said, leaning down so he could talk without shouting.

"Yes, sir," Stout said. "I've know the lad many years. He is fluent in English, French, and Spanish. He was born and raised here. He knows every trail and bayou."

"Well, he's my messenger now," the officer said. Then, turning to Bartolomé he said, "I am Major Tatum, aid to General Jackson. Come with me."

The major rode ahead with Bartolomé jogging along behind the horse. They passed a narrow neck of land where the Rodriguez Canal ended at the river. Then they turned away from the river. It was not long before they came upon a cluster of mounted officers.

"General, I have obtained a messenger familiar with the lands and languages," Major Tatum said. The man he was addressing turned around. It was General Jackson.

"Excellent, major," he said. "We have gathered together all that can be marshaled for this attack. I have sent General Carroll's regiment toward the city as a reserve. We will attack now. Please advance with the mounted scouts and send word when you have encountered the British force."

General Jackson then turned to Bartolomé. "What is your name, messenger?" he said.

"I am Bartolomé deMelilla," Bartolomé replied.

"I'll never remember that," the General said. "Today you are 'Dago.' Stay with this command, Dago. We will need you."

CHAPTER 11

By the time the army of regulars and militia were assembled into an orderly formation, it was past six in the evening. A general advance was ordered. The battle line marched forward for several hundred yards, crossing sugarcane fields that had been harvested in November.

Soon, firing could be heard in the distance ahead. No big guns, just scattered musketry. The army was nearing the De La Ronde plantation when an officer rode up to the command.

"Sir," the officer said with a salute, "we have made contact a thousand yards from here. We engaged a formation of no more than two hundred Redcoats. The reconnaissance force has retired to a defensive position to await the army."

"We all now await the signal from the *Carolina* that she is in place," Jackson said. He then ordered the army into a line of battle and sat back on his horse as relaxed as if this were a rabbit hunt. Bartolomé was amazed at the calm demeanor of the man. Most everyone else was wide-eyed and rushing about.

The skies off to the right front of the army brightened with orange flashes. After a moment, the heavy report of cannon fire could be heard and felt. It was the *Carolina* firing on the British camp.

"There is our signal, gentlemen," General Jackson said. "You may begin the attack. May the hand of Providence be your guide." Then he turned to Bartolomé. "Dago, see that officer?" he said as he pointed with his sword. "That is Colonel Ross. Go to him now and say that you are my messenger and a translator. He will make use of you."

The army surged forward in the darkness. Bartolomé reported to Colonel Ross, who was in command of the Louisiana militia units in the field.

"Stay with me," the colonel said. "When I send you with a message, deliver in it both English and French, for in the heat of battle, men hear only their native tongue."

Bartolomé marched along behind the colonel's horse. He could not see much. The rear of the long, dark battle line stretched beyond his view in the darkness. The orange flashes from the *Carolina* continued. The time between the flash of a broadside and the sound of the cannonade grew shorter. They were closing the distance between the army and the British camp. Suddenly, the mist before the battle line burst into a bright orange billowing cloud. The sound of a thousand muskets being fired in volley was something Bartolomé had never experienced. He had heard his grandfather describe the sound as a *"crujido* (rattle)." That description seemed to fit, for no single shot could be heard, just a roaring rattle of noise. The smoke drifted back and obscured all but the nearest ranks.

Bartolomé could hear one of the officers giving orders to the ranks just to his front. The long list of loading commands he had heard when he watched militia drills was not used. Instead, the officer shouted, "PRESENT WHEN READY. LOCK AND LOAD." The solders in the ranks primed their locks, loaded the powder and ball, and then pointed their muskets at the enemy. When enough in the ranks were presenting, the officer ordered "Fire," and then "LOCK AND LOAD."

There was another volley and then another. The militia was firing at the rate of three volleys a minute. The field guns that had accompanied the army in the advance added a cannonade to the army's musketry. Still, as far as Bartolomé could tell, the British had not returned fire.

To his left, Bartolomé could see the two regiments of American regulars in a battle line. They fired a volley and advanced. This occurred all along the line until the whole world seemed to be orange balls of light and smoke. Return volleys could now be heard, scattered and disorganized.

The army advanced from position to position in a steady and determined pace. Great care was given that each unit was well aware of its neighboring formation. As the battle continued, gaps began to develop. A portion of a militia unit lost contact, and confusion began to mount.

Bartolomé had to run behind Colonel Ross as he rode back and forth issuing orders to his command. Now, when the army advanced, they would step over the bodies of the British who had been killed or severely wounded in the attack. Some were in uniform and some were without coats. Most had been stripped of their boots and muskets, taken by members of the Louisiana militia in need of proper arms and footwear.

Bartolomé did not have time to closely examine the carnage for he was busy making certain that, when Colonel Ross needed him to translate, which was often, he was there. Aside from the bodies, Bartolomé saw very little of the battle from his station at the colonel's flank. It was all smoke, noise, and confusion. Finally, there was a pause in the advance. Musket volleys could be heard far beyond the battle area. No one could explain why firing would be taking place so far from the American ranks.

"Messenger," the colonel shouted to Bartolomé. "Return to the general and tell him we have bloodied the scum, but if we advance much further, we shall be in jeopardy of fire from the *Carolina* or our own men." Smoke had rendered the darkness total and impenetrable.

Bartolomé rushed off to the rear. He ran all the way with his *magado* at the guard. When he reached the general's command corps, he delivered the message. General Jackson waited a while and then said, "We shall begin a slow withdrawal and retire to the Rodriguez Canal. There we will build a defense." He sent messages to each of the commanders to that effect. Bartolomé delivered the message to Colonel Ross. The whole army began to retire in stages so that none were left exposed if the British mounted a counterattack.

* * *

As the force began to gather at the Rodriguez Canal, the sun began to rise, and Bartolomé realized he had not slept for two days. The whole army, along with civilian volunteers and even slaves, began the task of casting up defensive works in the face of an enemy that may attack at any time. No one was spared the task of digging and hauling mud or splitting pales. Free citizen and slave worked side by side in the muddy canal bottom. The small neck of land at the head of the Rodriguez Canal was removed so that the river flooded the land through which the British must advance.

Bartolomé had been dispatched to a battery being constructed next to the river. Called Battery Number One, it was a small redoubt situated so the cannons of the battery could fire along the front of the defensive lines as well as along the river shoreline. Bartolomé's job was to carry messages from the general's command on the east bank to a similar defensive line being prepared on the west bank. A contingent of Marines commanded by Lieutenant Bellevue along with Sergeant Stout's militia unit provided infantry support for the redoubt.

Progress was slow, but after a few days, a formidable defensive position began to take shape. The *Carolina*, unable to move upstream because of the strong current and unfavorable winds, had been sunk. Some of her guns had been salvaged and added to the ramparts.

There were almost daily actions by the artillery and the *USS Louisiana*, another Navy ship anchored in the river. They fired volley after volley on the British troops as the Redcoats attempted to move toward the Rodriguez Canal. In return, the British fired many rockets, the majority of which flew overhead or burst in the fields in front of the ramparts.

During lulls in the firing, all hands labored to improve their little redoubt and add placement for a new cannon and even a mortar. One of the guns and some of the crew added to Battery Number One had been salvaged from the *Carolina*. Bartolomé was kept busy translating, for most of the militia spoke only French, the Marines and sailors spoke only English, and several of the mortar crew spoke only Spanish.

Bartolomé shared a shelter with one of the Marines and came to know quite well all the men serving Battery Number One. During a lull in the firing, Marine Sergeant Doyle became quite interested in the *magado* that Bartolomé carried.

"What's that lance you have, Dago," he said when the opportunity for conversation arose. Bartolomé explained that it was a *magado*, not a lance, and that it had been his grandfather's.

"My grandfather fought the British many times under Governor General Gálvez, and he never lost a battle," Bartolomé told Sergeant Doyle with more than a little pride.

"Sounds like bragging to me," Doyle said. "Show me how you use it."

Although Doyle insisted that Bartolomé could demonstrate by attacking with the *magado*, Bartolomé finally managed to convince the sergeant to allow him to substitute a cannon ram for the *magado*.

"Well then, attack, Dago," Sergeant Doyle said. "When I take that stick from you, I'll whip your arse with it."

Bartolomé assumed the guard position. Doyle made a swiping move with his hands as if to brush the ram aside or grab it. Before he could react, Bartolomé delivered a stout punch to Doyle's chest. Had he wielded the *magado* instead of the blunt ram, Doyle would have been run through.

"I was not ready, Dago," Doyle said, rubbing his sore chest.

The other Marines had gathered around. They began to urge Doyle on. One called out, "Don't let that Dago make a fool of you."

Doyle's ears turned red. "I'll deal with you later, McFee. Shuddap."

Two more attempts to take the ram from Bartolomé resulted in two more welts on the sergeant's chest.

Doyle backed up. He was angry, embarrassed, and impressed. "I have had enough, Dago," he said. "I am happy that you talked me into using the cannon ram." Then he smiled broadly. "I'm pleased to have you on our side. When we can, you can give these Leathernecks some bayonet lessons."

Practically every enlisted Marine in the small unit had, at one time or another, fallen to fisticuffs or brawling with each other. When the fights were over, there were no grudges. Bartolomé thought that this incident might cause friction between him and the Marines. The opposite was true. It made him one of them.

* * *

The next morning, the battery was alerted to British activity about half a mile away. The enemy was attempting to cast up a firing platform for cannon. The river had fallen and the field before the rampart was no longer flooded. On previous occasions, the British had advanced with light field guns and infantry in great columns, and the American cannon fire would drive these formations back. This time, the British were determined to establish a firing platform for larger cannons to batter the American line before advancing with their infantry.

Bartolomé was sent to Battery Number Three to tell that commander on which of the British platforms he was to concentrate his fire. He was told that the battery commander was Captain Dominique. Bartolomé knew the name. Dominique Youx was an associate and, some said, a half-brother of Jean Lafitte. The men of the battery were all men serving the Lafitte brothers. The Lafitte base of operations for New Orleans was Bayou Barataria. Men serving Lafitte made their homes on the bayou and were know throughout the city as *Baratarians*.

When Bartolomé arrived to deliver the message, he approached the captain and announced his purpose. Captain Dominique was standing at the rampart with a glass, examining the British works, with his back to Bartolomé. When he turned around, Bartolomé recognized him as one of the men who had been on the porch with Jean Lafitte. He was even more surprised when Captain Dominique spoke.

"Bartolomé, isn't it?" he said. "Has it become your profession to deliver messages?"

"Sir," Bartolomé replied in the most military manner he could manage. "Lieutenant Thompson's compliments, and he suggests that if you concentrate your fire on the British platform to the left, he will do the same to the one on the right."

"Return to the lieutenant and say that I will do so," Captain Dominique said.

The rest of that day consisted of an artillery duel. Bartolomé had trained on the twelve-pound gun at five of the six positions serving the gun. Each position was named for the act that the position performed. The "worm" was stationed at the front left side of the gun. The "ram" was stationed at the front right of the gun. The "prim" was stationed just left of the touchhole. The "match" was stationed just right of the touchhole. The "powder monkey" was stationed to the rear next to the powder storage box. The "gun captain" was behind the gun and issued all the loading orders and aimed the piece. Bartolomé had never practiced the position of gun captain.

The loading sequence was as complex as the musket drill. It had twelve steps. The last word of the command was emphasized to indicate that the order was to be executed.

The captain would order:

"Advance WORM," and that man would position a wire-tipped staff near the mouth of the cannon.

"Search the PIECE," and the worm would slide the wire end of the staff into the cannon and twist it to catch any bits or pieces of the old canvas cartridge that might have remained from the last firing.

"Advance SPONGE," and the ram would dip the sheepskin tipped end of the staff he carried into a water bucket and place it next to the mouth of the cannon.

"Tend the VENT," and the match would place his thumb over the touchhole so that air would not rush in and out as the barrel was swabbed with the sponge. A smoldering ember might flame up with a rush of air.

"Sponge the PIECE," and the ram would force the wet sheepskin-covered end of his staff down the cannon and give it a twist. This was to extinguish any burning residue that may have remained in the cannon. Once that was done, the ram would withdraw the staff and spin it around to the blunt ram end and give the gun a tap to indicate that he was ready.

"Advance CARTRIDGE," and the powder monkey would remove a canvas-wrapped powder cartridge from a storage box, bring it to the worm, and return to his position.

"Charge CARTRIDGE," and the worm would place the cartridge in the mouth of the cannon.

"Ram down CARTRIDGE," and the ram would force the canvas cartridge to the bottom of the barrel.

"LOAD," and the worm would select a solid ball or shot-filled canister from the pile stored in front of the position. He would place it in the mouth of the cannon and the ram would force the load to the bottom of the barrel. Cannons that were six-pounders or smaller would have the shot stitched into the powder cartridge, making the "load" step unnecessary.

"PRIME," and the prime would push a wire down the vent hole to pierce the canvas cartridge. He would then pour a small quantity of powder down the vent hole until it made a little pile at the top.

"Advance MATCH," and the match, carrying a smoldering wick, would position himself where he could touch the priming charge.

The captain would make such aiming adjustments as he needed and then order "FIRE." The match would touch the smoldering wick to the powder and the gun would discharge. The process was then repeated.

Bartolomé noticed that when the guns were in actual combat, the sequence was not as long or formal. Instead of standing at attention facing the front, the men serving the gun crouched in their positions facing the captain. The noise of the many guns firing drowned out any sound, so the captain simply pointed at the man he wanted to act. The worm and ram could not distinguish the sound of a neighboring gun firing from the one they served, so they rested their hands on the barrel of the gun to feel when it discharged. Every man was careful not to act until directed by the captain.

During a particularly heavy exchange of cannon fire, a British ball flew into Bartolomé's battery and smashed the arm of one of the militia soldiers. Bartolomé and another man began to help the wounded man when Lieutenant Thompson intervened.

"Dago, you stay here. Collins, get another to help bring this man to the surgeon," he said.

After the wounded man was evacuated, Lieutenant Thompson turned to Bartolomé. "Dago, you are too important to be gone from the line. Do not leave this post unless an officer sends you." With that, the lieutenant returned to directing the cannon fire. Bartolomé had not felt that what he did was important. He had not fired a shot. He didn't even have a firearm. All he did was translate and run messages.

By the time it grew dark, the British guns had fallen silent. A cheer was heard along the line as those with glasses reported that the British guns had been dismounted by the American fire. The Americans had won another duel. Bartolomé went to the rear of the battery and sat with one of the Marine privates.

"What is the date of today?" Private McFee asked.

"It is the first day of January," Bartolomé replied, "and of the Year of Our Lord, the one thousand eight hundred and fifteenth."

Bartolomé became lost in thought. It was less than one month ago that he had given Anna the golden bracelet. In his mind, he saw her beautiful face, framed by iron bars. Where was she now? Did they make it to Louisville? It had been just over a week since he bade his mother good-bye on the road by their little farm. How was she faring? Did the English go down to Bencheque?

How could so much have happened in so little time? He had seen men torn to pieces. He had heard steel ball and lead shot whistle by. He had learned to man cannon and watch as the shot he helped send ripped through a line of men, throwing muskets, equipment, and body parts about. He had learned to sleep while rockets flew and cannons thundered. How long would this go on?

"Dago!" It was Lieutenant Thompson. "Go to Battery Three. Captain Dominique wants to see you."

Bartolomé leaped to his feet. It was only two hundred yards to Battery Three, and he ran the distance easily.

Captain Dominique was sitting at a field table. He had a map spread out and he was conversing with several other officers. Bartolomé ran up to the table and came to attention.

Captain Dominique spoke without lifting his head. "Do you have a boat that you can use?" he asked.

"Yes, sir," Bartolomé replied.

"Take this message from General Jackson to Commodore Patterson. You shall find him at the battery on the west bank," he said. "You will be at the commodore's disposal."

Bartolomé took the message and placed it in his haversack and headed for the river. He stopped at the tent he shared with other men and recovered his meager bedroll. He kept the small *pirogue* that he had taken from Bacenaux next to Battery Number One.

As he was pulling it to the river, Sergeant Doyle called out to him. "Where are you bound in such a rush, Dago?" he said.

"Running messages," Bartolomé answered. "I am posted to the west bank for now."

"That is a mighty big river and you have a mighty wee boat," Doyle said. "Keep on top of the thing."

Bartolomé paddled vigorously and took great care to account for the current. It wouldn't do to be swept downstream and into range of British guns. He arrived at the west bank just below the battery that anchored the river end of a crude defensive line. The west bank rampart was not as complete as the Rodriguez line. He noticed that the cannons on the river side battery were situated to fire across the river and onto the British as they advanced against the Rodriguez Canal. If the British attacked the west bank line, the cannon would have to be shifted to defend themselves.

He approached a naval officer. "Commodore Patterson?" he said.

"Yes," was all the commodore said.

"A message for you from General Jackson, sir," Bartolomé said as he handed the paper to the commodore. He then stood at attention as the commodore read.

"This one is for you," Commodore Patterson said as he handed Bartolomé a small folded paper that had been enclosed within the packet.

Bartolomé was mystified. Why would General Jackson have written a message for him? He unfolded the paper. It was in French.

"Shortly, there will be a reconnaissance sent down river. You will accompany it. You will pass the house where you met my brother. Speak with the house girl, Dede. Tell her that you have come for the Star. She will give you a packet. Bring it to me when you are sent back to this side of the river." It was signed "DY."

Dominique Youx, Bartolomé thought. He realized the message was from Captain Dominique. He had added it to the Jackson message. This side trip was not part of the battle plan.

CHAPTER *12*

everal days passed as Bartolomé carried on his mission of translating between the various unit commanders on the west bank. This was a sorry lot compared to the force that defended the Rodriguez Canal. The Louisiana militia was a newly formed unit that could barely march in step. The best firearms they carried were old hunting muskets. The Kentucky militia was even more poorly equipped. More than half of that unit had no firearms at all. Bartolomé was certain that a hundred well-armed regulars could sweep away these eight hundred defenders.

A reconnaissance in force was finally ordered. Three hundred of the best armed men, Kentuckians and Louisianans, were assembled. They set out downriver with Bartolomé along to help the French-speaking Captain Mouton communicate with the English-speaking half of his command. They had traveled about nine miles when they came upon the house that Bartolomé had visited with the message from Mister Too.

The militia leader decided that he would question those found in the house to ascertain if they had seen anything. While this was going on, Bartolomé saw the house girl, Dede. She had just been questioned by Captain Mouton.

"Dede," he said. "Do you remember me?"

Dede nodded.

"I have come for the Star," Bartolomé said.

Dede's eyes widened. She ducked into one of the rooms and returned with a small leather pouch. She cautiously gave the pouch to Bartolomé, making certain that no one saw her do it.

The inquiry over, the reconnaissance continued until the force was at a point on the river just opposite the quarantine station at English Turn. There was no sign of British forces.

On the return trip, Captain Mouton took note of a location along the road that was hemmed in by swamp on one side and river on the other. "This would be a good location to fight a delaying action," he said.

With that, he posted one hundred and fifty men to blockade the road. "If the British come this way, fire a few volleys into their ranks and withdraw to the rampart up river."

The remainder of the force returned to the rampart. Commodore Patterson did not seemed pleased with Captain Mouton's initiative. "If there is no action by this time tomorrow," he said, "I will send for those men to return here."

The next morning was cold and wet. A heavy fog hung in the air. Bartolomé had barely stirred when he was summoned by the commodore.

"Take this message to General Jackson," he said as he handed Bartolomé a folded paper. "You are to remain on the east bank unless ordered back here." Bartolomé noticed that the message had old and smeared writing on the outside of the fold. The commodore had simply written the message on the back of used paper.

Bartolomé collected his meager bedroll once again and launched the *pirogue*. The fog was very thick and he had to estimate his line of travel by the currents alone. The sun had risen, but the fog on the river persisted. He looked for some landmark, as he thought he was approaching the east bank. Finally, he saw the tip of the flag staff that was mounted on Battery Number One. He adjusted his course to land at the foot of the battery.

Just then, there was a great burst of cannon fire. It was quickly repeated along with cannon fire from the British lines. Then there was a tremendous volley of musketry. The British had mounted a major attack that seemed to involve the whole front.

Bartolomé landed his *pirogue* and pulled it a short distance up the bank. He removed the *sunta* from his belt and hung it on his right forearm by its leather loop.

Battery Number One fired the large cannons. Bartolomé knew that it was canister shot by the whistling sound the canister made. Canister rounds were only fired at infantry at close range. The British were assaulting the small redoubt!

* * *

Bartolomé rushed forward with his *magado* at the guard. When he reached the foot of the redoubt that held Battery Number One, he saw a Redcoat trying to scramble up the slope. The Redcoat slipped and, as he did, he turned to see Bartolomé advancing. The ground all about was slick with mud, and both men had trouble with their footing. The Redcoat made a falling lunge with his bayonet. Bartolomé parried it and drove the *magado* into the man's neck. The Redcoat fell silently, with an expression of rage frozen on his face. The noise of the battle around Bartolomé was deafening and continuous. If the Redcoat had made a noise, Bartolomé would not have heard it.

A strange kind of energy filled Bartolomé. It was as if he could see himself standing in the mud at the foot of the redoubt. He moved up the slope of the redoubt to confront several more climbing Redcoats. The nearest one turned and Bartolomé ran him through before the man could bring his bayonet around. Bartolomé caught a movement out of the corner of his eye. He moved to the side just as a bayonet stabbed toward his face. Something struck him on his cheekbone. He grabbed the musket with his left hand and both Bartolomé and his attacker tumbled down the slope.

Bartolomé lost the *magado*, but he held firm to the musket with his left hand as they stopped at the bottom of the redoubt. The Redcoat was attempting to pull the musket free to make another thrust at Bartolomé. The *sunta* slapped against the palm of Bartolomé's right hand. In a second, he had it in his grip and he struck the assailant on the top of the head with the stone-tipped *sunta*. The Redcoat's eyes rolled back into his head and Bartolomé struck him several more times. The musket would not fall from his face, so Bartolomé gave it a twist and it suddenly fell free. He could not see out of his left eye and it felt if some giant was squeezing his face. Bartolomé began to go back up the slope when he saw two Redcoats aim their muskets straight at him.

There was a blast of orange flame from his left and the Redcoats disappeared in a red mist. Bartolomé recovered his *magado* and, instead of climbing the redoubt, he surged toward the ditch where the Redcoats were attempting to cross. The two Redcoats nearest him were climbing up out of the ditch. Bartolomé made a lunge at one of the soldiers that sent the steel blade of the *magado* deep into the man's chest. The other he pummeled repeatedly with the *sunta* until the man was still.

He felt something beside him and turned to see Sergeant Doyle and several American regular soldiers. They formed an impromptu skirmish line and confronted the enemy. A British officer lunged ahead, calling out to his troops to advance. He began to slash at Sergeant Doyle with a saber. Doyle had all he could do just fending off the blows. Bartolomé lanced the officer in the side and, when the wounded man turned to attack Bartolomé, Doyle smashed his skull with the butt of his musket.

As they were about to be overwhelmed by the advancing British, the battery behind them came back in action. A blast of canister fire over the heads of the skirmish line destroyed the British coming up to support those engaged in hand-to-hand fighting with the Americans.

The fog over the river had lifted enough so that the west bank batteries could fire on the British coming up the riverbank as well. Bartolomé was unaware of anything but battling the man in front of him or on either side. Eventually, the British soldiers who had reached the redoubt were forced to surrender or were killed. Bartolomé began to think that he might live.

An American lieutenant from the Seventh Infantry was in command of the platoon of regulars that was sent to clear Battery Number One. The battery had been overrun by the British and he assumed command of the motley group that retook the position. He now commanded the little skirmish line. The Americans advanced a short distance to capture a small cluster of Redcoats trapped in a gap in the fields of fire. If they advanced, they would have to battle the skirmish line. If they retreated, they would have to expose themselves to cannon fire from Battery Number One and the west bank. Totally cowed and with no officers left alive, they surrendered.

Bartolomé pointed his *magado* at one of the Redcoat privates. "Drop your musket and cartridge box," he ordered. The look of fear on the private's face was pathetic. Bartolomé wondered how he could evoke such a response from anyone. They returned to the redoubt with their prisoners. Bartolomé ordered one of the prisoners to help a wounded Redcoat up the slope to the top of the redoubt. The American regulars then marched the prisoners, wounded and able alike, to the rear.

"Look, Dago," Sergeant Doyle said as he gestured toward the battlefield. Until now, Bartolomé had only been able to see the narrow area between the levee and the river. The great, muddy field that lay before the Rodriguez Canal was littered with red, motionless lumps. The firing had stopped. Slowly, some of the lumps stirred. Here and there, a Redcoat would rise and begin to stumble toward the British lines.

"We better tend to that," Sergeant Doyle said, nodding at Bartolomé.

Bartolomé didn't know what he was referring to.

"Tend to what?" Bartolomé said.

"Sit down, lad," Sergeant Doyle said as he gestured for Bartolomé to take a seat on the rampart. "I need to get it out while your blood is still up. If I don't do it now, the surgeon will. It will hurt more then."

"What will hurt?" Bartolomé said. He then realized that he could not see out of his left eye. The left side of his face felt numb and taut.

Sergeant Doyle had two of the militiamen hold Bartolomé's head still. Bartolomé heard a knife being drawn from a scabbard. He felt a streak of coldness cross his left cheek. Suddenly, whatever it was that blocked his left eye was gone.

"Here you go, lad," Sergeant Doyle said. He placed a bayonet in Bartolomé's hand. "You've got a trophy candlestick," he said. The bayonet had been lodged in Bartolomé's cheek just under the skin. The mounting ring of the bayonet had blocked his vision. Sergeant Doyle placed an almost clean cloth to Bartolomé's wound, which was bleeding profusely. Bartolomé held it to his face with his left hand.

Sergeant William Stout came up to the small group that had gathered around Bartolomé. "Let me see your shoes," Stout said.

Bartolomé lifted a foot with quizzical look on his face. Stout had a pair of fine boots in his hands. He placed the sole of one of the boots against the sole of Bartolomé muddy, worn, and ragged shoes.

"A perfect match," Stout said. "They were too big for me. I got them from that British officer Doyle killed."

Stout pulled off Bartolomé's shoes and slipped the boots onto the bare feet. The fit was very good. Bartolomé could feel that the boots were still warm, and the realization of what that meant sickened him. Then shakes began to wrack Bartolomé's body. He was ashamed to have his comrades see him and he tried to steady himself.

"There's nothing to be ashamed of, lad," Sergeant Doyle said. "Your blood's been up for some time. Now that it is all over, the shakes are just the blood calming down. It used to happen to me all the time."

General Jackson came up to the small group. They all stood to attention as the general surveyed the chaos of bodies at the bottom of the rampart.

"Good work, gentlemen," Jackson said. "We feared that the redoubt would fall. Had you not held here, the whole line may have fallen."

Bartolomé remembered the message. "Sir, a message from Commodore Patterson," he said as he handed the folded paper to the general.

"Thank you, Dago," he said.

"Begging your pardon, general," Sergeant Doyle said, "but I think you do the lad an injustice by naming him Dago."

Every man stiffened. A lowly sergeant was addressing a general and in a manner of a rebuke.

Jackson smiled. He had seen the fierce fight at the redoubt. Any brave man there could have his say. "And why do you say that, sergeant?" the general asked.

"Begging your pardon, sir," Doyle said. He stood as ramrod straight as he could. "If the general had seen this man in action, sir, the general would be amazed. Why, sir, he was killing Limeys left and right. Like a fishmonger swatting flies, sir."

Jackson laughed outright. Few things pleased him like a warrior in action. "Right you are, sergeant," General Jackson said. His voice was loud and meant for all to hear. "From this day forward," he said as he faced Bartolomé, "I shall address you as *El Tigre*." He placed his hand on

Bartolomé's shoulder as if he were knighting him. *"El Tigre*, the Tiger of New Orleans."

Bartolomé didn't know what to say. "Yes, sir," was all he could manage.

The general then read the message that Bartolomé had delivered. He spoke to the cluster of officers around him. "Patterson believes that a determined effort will overrun his position. The matter is moot now, gentlemen. The enemy can do nothing but parley a truce to collect their dead and wounded. If they take the west bank, those troops will be in danger of being cut off from the rest of their army."

Just then, the sound of musket fire was heard from the west bank. There was one more volley and then nothing. Presently, activity could be seen on the west bank battery and then a cluster of men rushed down to boats in the river. Redcoats appeared on the west ramparts. Jackson had the battery turn its guns on the west bank and fire on the ramparts. There was no return fire. Soon the boats that fled the west bank came ashore. Commodore Patterson was among them. They and Jackson's entourage retired to the command tent.

* * *

Battery Number One became an attraction as word of the desperate fight there trickled down the line. Nearly every man at one time or another visited the battery, and all were amazed that so few had held the flank against so many. There were more than four hundred dead and severely wounded enemy at the base of the rampart. Sergeant Doyle repeated the exploits of "the Tiger of New Orleans" many times. With each telling, the feats increased.

Bartolomé had to tell his tale many times, as well. However, he didn't think to embellish his version. Most of what he had seen was in his immediate vicinity and he had no knowledge of what had happened on the top of the redoubt. He overheard one Army officer comment that it all must be true for no one had ever heard a Marine brag about anyone other than himself or another Marine.

Bartolomé was finally convinced to visit the field surgeon to have a look at Sergeant Doyle's handiwork. He was able to stop by the command tent for the batteries that Captain Dominique controlled. When he was allowed to enter the tall, walled tent, Captain Dominique told the others gathered there to step outside.

"How are your wounds, *El Tigre*," the captain asked once they had the tent to themselves.

"My wounds are slight," Bartolomé said. In truth, his face throbbed constantly.

"Did you have the opportunity to visit the girl, Dede?" Captain Dominique asked.

Bartolomé removed the leather pouch from his haversack and placed it in Captain Dominique's hand without a word.

Captain Dominique felt the shape within the pouch. "You have done well, Bartolomé deMelilla," he said. "I will not forget your loyalty. What shall I give you as a reward?"

Bartolomé thought for a moment. "There is no need for a reward, sir," he said finally. He could not think of anything else to say.

Captain Dominique waited a moment. "Very well, *El Tigre*," he said. Then he summoned one of his Baratarians. "Go with *El Tigre* to the surgeon," he said. "Then return to me and report on the surgeon's opinion."

Bartolomé strode along, using the blood-stained *magado* as a walking staff. The Baratarian walked to his left and slightly to the rear. It was a sign of respect on the part of the Baratarian. Among warriors, the front right position was reserved for rank and persons deserving respect.

The surgeon was busy tending to the British wounded. The American wounded had been so few that he had finished with them hours ago. He stopped what he was doing and examined Bartolomé's face. Bartolomé had to explain how he had received the wound and about Sergeant Doyle's operation.

"The cut that removed the bayonet was clean," he said. "The wound does need a good washing to remove any bits of fabric or mud. The danger is that the wound may fester. Only time will tell."

Bartolomé returned to Battery Number One and retrieved his bedroll from the *pirogue*. He rolled a blanket out next to one of the cooking fires and went to sleep.

"How can he sleep so soon after all he has been through?" Private McFee asked as he looked down on the slumbering Bartolomé.

"There's your true warrior, McFee," Sergeant Doyle said. "If an enemy gun were to discharge nearby or the camp grow active with alarm, he would be up and at'm like the tiger the general named him."

* * *

Bartolomé slept until the next day. The general had left explicit orders that *El Tigre* was not to be disturbed unless the general himself ordered it, but he was up and about at sunrise. He felt rested, but the wound on his face throbbed awfully. After two days, the throbbing grew worse and Bartolomé felt sick and feverish.

"The wound is beginning to fester," the surgeon announced. He had no advice to offer except rest. When the surgeon was alone with General Jackson, he delivered his prognosis. "If the wound continues to fester, the young man will die. It is out of my hands. He must heal on his own."

Bartolomé only grew worse. He was wracked with fever when Captain Dominique came to see him.

"Captain," Bartolomé said weakly, "if you could, sir, could you have someone bring me to Madam Barbeaux? She is a friend who may be able to help."

In an instant, a wagon and team of horses was summoned and an unconscious Bartolomé was loaded aboard. Captain Dominique personally accompanied the wagon to Madam Barbeaux's door.

"Please, bring him in," Madam Barbeaux said as soon as she saw that it was Bartolomé in the wagon. She led the Baratarians carrying Bartolomé to a back room and had them place him on a bed.

"Madam," Captain Dominique said, "I would consider it a personal favor if you would tend to this man."

"This man is a friend of mine," she answered. "I will draw upon all my powers to save him."

Captain Dominique was surprised. *A personal friend of Madam Barbeaux! The Tiger of New Orleans had powerful friends.*

Captain Dominique left Madam Barbeaux's house and parted company with the rest of the Baratarians, telling them to return to the Rodriguez Canal where he would join them later that night. Dominique walked a short distance to a small blacksmith's shop. He went in through the smith's work area to a room in the back. There he met two men who were waiting for him. One was Jean Lafitte and the other was Pierre Lafitte.

"Dominique, the Delgado house has been ransacked by the British," Pierre said. "Dede and the other servants have been taken away and the house burned."

"Brothers," Dominique said with a smile "look at what I have." He opened the leather pouch that Bartolomé had given him. In it was a woman's necklace. He spread it out on the table.

"Our grandmother's pendant!" Jean said.

The three men gathered around the table to examine the necklace. It was a simple gold chain with a single, small, gold star, a Star of David.

"How did you manage to save it?" Pierre asked.

"We have Mister Too's young messenger, Bartolomé deMelilla, to thank," Dominique answered. "He is the one they now call the Tiger of New Orleans."

"Mister Too said he was a warrior when he vouched for him." Jean said.

"I will send word to Mister Too that *El Tigre* is at Madam Barbeaux's house being treated for his wounds." Dominique said. "Now, I will return to General Jackson's headquarters. He is convinced that the British have not given up on New Orleans."

"All indications are that the British are withdrawing down Bayou Terre Aux Boeufs and then La Loutre to be closer to deep waters, and their fleet, when they evacuate." Jean said. "No doubt they will try another approach very soon."

CHAPTER *13*

adam Barbeaux examined Bartolomé's wound. It was festering badly. She went to her wide rack of powders and lotions and took down a jar that had a cloth covering the opening. She removed the cloth and, using chop sticks, took out several maggots, one at a time. These she placed in the wounds at the most infected locations.

"Pepe," she said to the young black man standing at the foot of the bed. "Come here and watch the maggots. Keep them working in the wound and don't let them close to his eye." Pepe did as he was instructed.

Madam Barbeaux went to the room with the little altar. She placed a cup of rum between the candles and began to call upon Loa Legba to ask permission to enter the spirit world. She closed her eyes and was immobile. After a while, she began moving her lips as if she were speaking. Then she was still once more. The request had been granted and Ogoun was coming. She then fell to her knees as Ogoun spoke to her.

Pepe was still performing the task of herding the maggots when Madam Barbeaux returned to the room. He had been at it for hours and was tiring.

"Go, Pepe," she said. Pepe quickly retreated from the room, fearing madam would devise another arduous chore before he could escape. Madam Barbeaux removed the maggots from Bartolomé's face in the same manner she had placed them there. She covered the jar and returned it to the shelf. She placed a bowl on a stand next to the bed and filled it with rum. She then soaked a linen cloth in the rum and began to clean the wound with it. Bartolomé didn't move or make a sound.

The maggots had done a good job. Ogoun had told Madam Barbeaux that evil spirits were in the wound and that rum would drive them out. She was to clean the wound with rum three times a day for three days. Each time, she was to use a new cloth and fresh rum. After that, Bartolomé would awake in one week or die.

* * *

Bartolomé sat on a bench in the hiring hall. He was naked and the hall was dark on the end where he sat. He looked around, confused and dazed. How had he come to be in the hall? Why was he naked? Where was everyone? He stood on shaky legs and walked toward the lighted end of the hall. Suddenly, a large black figure blocked his path.

"*No hoy* (Not today)," the figure said. He was an African with a large cowhide shield and a long spear. He stood so that Bartolomé could not pass.

Then there was a voice calling him. "Bartolomé, *dónde está* (where are you)?" It was Anna's voice!

Bartolomé looked around. No one else was in the hall except the giant African and himself.

Anna called again.

"*Estoy aquí* (I am here)," Bartolomé called out, but his voice was just a whisper. He realized that Anna was calling him from outside the hall. He could hear her just on the other side of the door that led to the street.

"*Estoy aquí*, Anna! *Estoy aquí! Estoy aquí!*" he kept trying to yell as he pulled at the door latch. At last, it opened.

* * *

Bartolomé awoke looking into the face of Madam Barbeaux.

"Anna is not here, young sir," Madam Barbeaux said.

Bartolomé lay back on the pillow. There were tears in his eyes.

"I thought I heard Anna," he said. His voice was shaking.

"You did hear her," Madam Barbeaux said. "You were in the spirit world. Tell me what else you remember."

"I was in a dark hall, Mister Too's hiring hall. I tried to walk down the hall, but a giant African warrior would not let me pass. Then I heard Anna calling me from outside the hall. I went out to her but I awoke here," he said. "Where am I?"

"You are at my house. The Baratarians brought you to me to treat your wounds. It was Anna who called you back from the dead," Madam Barbeaux said.

It was then that Bartolomé realized that he was, in fact, naked beneath the simple sheet that covered him. He could see his clothes folded neatly next to the bed. His haversack, *magado, sunta,* and knife were in a corner. Everything had been well cleaned, including himself.

"I will bring you some food and water," Madam Barbeaux said. "You have been asleep for a week."

A week! Bartolomé thought. *How can that be?* He dressed while Madam Barbeaux was gone and he was sitting on the edge of the bed when she returned.

"You cannot leave until you have your strength back," she said. "Mister Too has been to see you and he told me that he has sent word to your family that you are recuperating from your wounds. Your family cannot come to see you yet, for the British have not fully evacuated."

He started to rise, but quickly sat back down. "I think you are right, madam," he said. Then he drank the water mixed with wine that Madam

Barbeaux brought and ate the soup as well. He lay back down and was asleep instantly.

* * *

Anna stood on the street in the late evening twilight. The street was unfamiliar and she didn't know where she was. There was a long building in front of her that had no windows. Only a single door opened onto the street. She looked about. No one was on the street.

Faintly she could hear someone calling her. "Anna, Anna," the voice said, "*Vendré para* (I will come for you)." It was Bartolomé's voice. He was far away.

"Bartolomé, *dónde está* (where are you)?" Anna called out. She could hear someone pulling on the door latch.

It is Bartolomé, she thought. *He is coming to me.* Finally, the door opened. An African warrior stood in the opening, blocking any vision of the interior.

"He will come for you," the African said. His English was perfect and it had the accent of a native of Baltimore. "You must be patient. See, you have called him back." The African stepped aside and Anna could see Bartolomé. His face was covered in blood and he looked into her eyes and said, "*Estoy aquí*, Anna."

* * *

When Anna awoke, she was sitting upright in her bed. The sun had risen far enough to cast shadows in the trees outside of her bedroom window. She had been startled by this same dream for three nights running.

There was no nanny to awake her. Miss Wren had been discharged for reasons of economy. Bernard Steward had divested himself of all his property in New Orleans and invested heavily in a millwork shop where they now lived. Anna now helped her mother with the household chores and caring for James.

She helped her mother prepare a breakfast for the family. When Bernard came in, he had a newspaper from the night before. The whole town had been in a state of celebration for some weeks. General Jackson's defeat of the invading British was still the center of discussion. Today, February fifteen, 1815, they learned that the war was over. The United States and Great

Britain had signed a peace treaty. France was at peace. Spain was at peace. All of Europe was at peace. It was if a great weight had been lifted from every shoulder.

"Father, when may we return to New Orleans?" Anna asked.

"I am afraid that we never shall," he answered. "We must make our home here now."

Anna was visibly upset by this bit of news. She had been pining away ever since they left New Orleans. Even the excitement of riding the steamship up to Natchez had failed to lift her spirits. Then there was the long trek to Louisville and then on to the city where they settled.

Bernard gave his wife a telling glance. They had discussed what to do to shake their daughter of her infatuation with the farmer boy, and had reached a decision.

"Anna," Bernard said, "I've received some bad news from Mister Getty in New Orleans."

Anna looked up at her father and waited.

"That young man who would translate for Miss Wren in the market was killed in the Battle for New Orleans," he said.

Anna turned pale and sat down. It looked for a moment that she might faint. "That cannot be true. There has been a mistake," she said. She ran to her room and wept the entire morning.

For weeks afterward, she was inconsolable. Even after she returned to her normal activities, a cloud hung over her. She developed a serious and somber ambiance that remained just below the surface.

"She will grow out of this melancholy, Grace," Bernard told his wife.

"We must hope we did the right thing," Grace said.

In an attempt to change his daughter's mood, Bernard enrolled Anna in a finishing school. There she gained a reputation for being a beauty who was cold and aloof.

The school arranged formal dances so young girls could meet young men of the right sort and in controlled conditions. The miniature balls were, for Anna, joyless affairs. She danced with the young men who asked, and they all wanted to dance with Anna. But she considered them to be mere children.

CHAPTER 14

When Bartolomé, the Tiger of New Orleans, was well enough to leave Madam Barbeaux's house, he visited the general's headquarters in the Cabildo. General Jackson had been slow to release the army that had been gathered under his command. The word of the Treaty of Ghent reached New Orleans in February, but even now, well into April, militia units were being held in service at the many outposts, redoubts, and forts across the Louisiana bayous. Jackson, ever distrustful of the British, would not fully release his forces until both nations had ratified the treaty.

This caused more than a little difficulty for the citizens of New Orleans and the surrounding area. Crops were not planted, fields not tilled, and work was halted as men idled away their time on alert for an attack that never came. Wives and children did what they could, but the chores of surviving as a family required everyone to work.

"*El Tigre!*" Jackson exclaimed as soon as Bartolomé walked into the room where the general and others had gathered for a conference. "Gentlemen, this lad here is none other than the Tiger of New Orleans," he said. He introduced Bartolomé to those present, some of whom Bartolomé remembered from the Rodriguez ramparts.

"Major Latour is composing a magnificent book to preserve our great feat for history," Jackson said.

Bartolomé recognized the major. He was Jackson's chief engineer and practically second-in-command.

"I am taking orders for the book now," Latour said. "Beale here has ordered a hundred copies."

Bartolomé knew Captain Beale as well. He was the commanding officer of the private militia that William Stout served in. Technically, Captain Beale had been Bartolomé's commanding officer when he was stationed at the redoubt that held Battery Number One. This fact was something that Captain Beale emphasized during every recount of the climatic battle of the Eighth of January.

"I had to buy that many," Captain Beale retorted. "For how much is said in this book of a man's actions in the defense of New Orleans will depend of the number of copies he orders today."

"Sir, you wrong me," Major Latour replied. Both men were laughing, but there was a grain of truth in the accusation.

"*El Tigre,* here," Beale continued, "was the man who broke the British assault on Battery Number One. The battle was Thermopylae anew. *El Tigre* waded into the Persians, stabbing and crushing skulls, all the while ignoring the bayonet lodged in his face. The British were filled with fear by the ferocity of our Tiger. Had he not attacked as he did, armed with nothing but a lance and a club, the right flank of the whole army may have been turned. Instead of celebrating a great victory, we all would have been killed or taken prisoner."

"I did nothing but defend myself," Bartolomé said. "The victory was attained by our superior artillery."

"See, gentlemen," Jackson said. "This lad is more aware of modern military tactics than all of Washington's commentators combined."

"Sir, the purpose of my request to speak with you is to beg leave to return to my family," Bartolomé said when the opportunity arose.

"I have no hold on you, *El Tigre*," Jackson said. "Beale here may claim you as one of his corps, but in truth, you are an underage volunteer. Beale tells me that you are fifteen years of age. None of us can claim you against your will. Return to your family, son, with our eternal gratitude."

As Bartolomé walked along the street toward Mister Too's business, he was aware that citizens were often pointing him out to each other.

One young boy called out to his playmate, "It's him! It's *El Tigre.*"

"*Mais jamais,*" said the playmate. "He's not tall enough."

Bartolomé was nearly six feet tall. Few men he knew were taller. How tall was he supposed to be?

"Fool," said the boy. "Look at his face."

It was the bayonet wound on his face that provided proof of Bartolomé's identity to every stranger familiar with the story of the Tiger of New Orleans. The scar that remained was fresh and bright. The color would fade in time, but the wide wound healed in a way that pulled the left corner of his mouth up into a perpetual sneer. Every citizen, even those he had never met, could describe the Tiger of New Orleans in detail.

Mister Too was in the small office just off the hiring hall. Shipping was slowly being restored, but with so many still on military duty, business was slow.

"I thank you for keeping packet safe," Mister Too said. Mister Too had visited Bartolomé several times during the convalescence at Madam Barbeaux's and had retrieved the papers he had entrusted to Bartolomé. He confided to Bartolomé that the packet contained, among other things, Too's last will and testament. What the documents might have said remained a mystery. Mister Too had no family that Bartolomé knew of.

"You go. Care for mother, sisters," Mister Too said. "When militia released, come see me. Please. Most important."

Bartolomé began the long walk back to Bayou Terre Aux Boeufs. He made a stop by Bayou Pecheur and the Steward house. He had learned that Steward had sold the business to Mister Getty and others at a panic price, and moved his family to Louisville, maybe. No one was certain where the family had settled.

He went to the iron-barred window that Anna had named the Weeping Iron. There was no note in the frame. His heart sank. It was going to take a lot of time and effort to find Anna. But he was going to find her. He continued toward home, not knowing what he would find. If Jacques and Maurice were alive, they were most certainly still with the militia. Communication with the small redoubt at Bencheque had not been restored. The handful of men serving there had been forced to retreat in the face of overwhelming odds.

Aimée and the rest were God knows where. They had evacuated to Bencheque, but the British had twice occupied Bencheque for a short time, first as they moved additional supplies to the battle ground and then as they withdrew their forces. Aimée was terrified of the British. She could not speak Spanish, which was the language of Bencheque, nor could any of her children. Bartolomé was certain that his Aunt Marie and other deMelilla relatives would have taken the family in, but what had transpired in the meantime, he did not know.

* * *

Oceane was the first to see Bartolomé coming up the narrow trail along the bayou. *"C'est frère Bartolomé!"* she exclaimed. She dropped the hoe she had been working with and ran through the gate. Leaping into Bartolomé's arms, she held him tightly as he walked up to the porch. She continued to whisper in his ear. *"Mon frère,"* she said, over and over. Aimée came to the front porch when she heard Oceane call out. She had little Inez by the hand. A look of relief swept over her as she realized that her son had finally come home.

"Jules and Gabriel are in the back," she said. It was an effort to keep back the tears. "They are rebuilding the smokehouse. They will be happy to see you,"

They walked through the house to the back door. Aimée led Inez by the hand. Bartolomé carried Oceane. She refused to let go of Bartolomé's neck. He could feel her tears dripping on his neck.

"Jules and Gabriel," Aimée called to them. "Your brother is home."

The two dropped what they were doing and rushed to the house. Bartolomé sat at the little table on the porch with Oceane on his lap. Little Inez clapped her hands and laughed as the family gathered around. They had heard, as had the entire village, of Bartolomé's exploits during the battle.

"Tell us about it all," Gabriel begged.

"I will sometime," Bartolomé said. "Not now, maybe later." He glanced toward his mother and sisters.

Jules prodded Gabriel. "Not now," Jules said as he tilted his head toward Oceane.

"Were you afraid, brother Bartolomé?" Oceane asked without lifting her head from her embrace.

"Yes," Bartolomé said.

"Why did you not run away?" she sniffled.

"I did not think of it," he answered.

"We ran away," Oceane said, lifting her head at last to look into Bartolomé's eyes. "We stayed with your uncle Jose far down the bayou."

"Did you have a nice visit?" Bartolomé said as he attempted to lighten Oceane's mood.

"Your uncle is nice, but he can't speak French," she said.

"Did you learn any Spanish?" he asked.

"*Calma* (Quiet)," she said as she placed a finger over her lips.

"The people in Bencheque hid us from the British. We had to tell the girls not to speak and to pretend to be Spanish," Aimée explained.

The British were allied with Spain in Europe and their officers had thought they might obtain help from the Spanish villages, so they did not harass anyone in Bencheque. Jacques and Maurice had been captured along with the other half dozen militia defenders at the little redoubt. The prisoners were put to work hauling supplies for the British. The last anyone had seen of them, they were carrying British wounded down Bayou La Loutre to be evacuated by boat. They hadn't come back.

"Now that there has been a peace treaty," Bartolomé said, "they will be released." Everyone hoped that would be the case, but no one really believed it.

"We are together now," Aimée said. "Tomorrow we will begin anew."

There was a lot of work to do. The British had stolen everything of value. All the hams and smoked meats that had not been carried to Bencheque were gone. The sow had been confiscated by the retreating British as they passed through Bencheque. The smokehouse had been destroyed. The firewood was gone, and most of the farm tools were gone. The house itself had only minor damage, but all that was saved of the furniture was a table and two chairs. The family had been sleeping on the floor. Jules had hidden the *bateau* in the swamp before they had evacuated, so that was saved as well.

"Tomorrow," Bartolomé announced, "we shall all go into the city to buy supplies."

"We all?" Oceane asked, wide eyed. "Even me?"

"Yes, all of us must go," he said. "We need to get many things and I cannot carry it all by myself."

"The horse was taken, and the wagon, too," Oceane said. She and Inez had never been to New Orleans.

"We are going in the *bateau*," Bartolomé said. "Mama hid our money from the British and it is enough to get a good saw, axes, shovels, and a new sow. A horse and wagon will have to wait. Then we can make some new beds and a smokehouse."

That night, Aimée and Bartolomé went over the list of items they would need to get. The two gold pieces and a few dollars would have to be enough.

* * *

Word of Bartolomé's return had spread throughout the village. The next morning, neighbors came to visit the Tiger of New Orleans and when they learned that he had planned a trip to New Orleans to obtain supplies, several volunteered to accompany him with their boats. The village had been robbed of food, tools, and animals by the retreating British. The great plantations above and below the village fared much worse, having more to lose.

It was decided that those with boats would go with Bartolomé. Those who stayed behind sent lists of their needs and what little money they had. Bartolomé found himself to be the leader of a flotilla of small boats heading upstream to the docks at New Orleans.

The flotilla passed Poche's Ferry, or at least where the ferry had been, for the British had burned it to the waterline. Bacenaux was there, sitting on the steps to his little shack.

"Sir," Bartolomé said as they halted at the landing for a little rest, "I had to take your *pirogue* to escape the British. I shall return it today, or replace it."

Bacenaux shrugged his shoulders. "Consider it my gift to you, *El Tigre*," he said. "I shall not need it. Today, I will start to rebuild my ferry."

The ferry was an important part of the communication line that small farmers and trappers depended upon. The large plantations had their own resources and means of travel. Bacenaux would not be receiving any help from the plantations. The little flotilla pressed on into the river and turned upstream. Bartolomé looked back. He could see Bacenaux still sitting on his steps with his head in his hands.

"He should start if he is to make a new ferry," Oceane observed.

"Starting is the hardest part, *T'Yeux Noir*," Bartolomé said.

In less than an hour, the flotilla had reached the Villere Canal. The British had extended the canal through the levee and banks of the Mississippi River so they could send barges full of troops to the west bank. That mission failed and the British had abandoned half a dozen barges on the riverbank when they retreated. The vessels were more like wide, flat longboats. Each, except one, was about eight feet wide and sixteen feet long. The one exception was about twice the size of the others. All were very flat and slapped together by the British pioneers for the mission of bringing troops across the river.

Several men were standing about the barges. They signaled Bartolomé to land near them.

"*El Tigre*, allow me to introduce myself," one of the men said. "I am Colonel Villere. Please, join us for a while."

Colonel Villere was the commander of the militia regiment that was tasked with closing the canals and guarding the waterways the British had used to invade. The dismal failure to accomplish this mission would haunt Villere for the rest of his life. He could even be tried for dereliction of duty. The happy fact that a great victory was achieved might allow the matter to be overlooked.

"Sir," Bartolomé said, "we are on our way to the city to replenish our supplies and obtain material to rebuild. We cannot tarry, but thank you."

"Materials?" Villere said. "Take these accursed barges. They block my efforts and I know that the timber could be of use."

Timber from river barges had long been a source of building supplies in this part of Louisiana. River men would freight goods downriver with the current, then sell their goods and the riverboat. The trip upriver was too difficult in the wide flatboats. The boats were most often disassembled so the wood and the nails could be used to build houses. These barges would be well received.

Bartolomé consulted with some of the villagers. It was decided that six of the men would tie the barges together and bring them back to the village.

"Give the largest one to Bacenaux," Bartolomé suggested, "so that the people downriver will be able to come to the city by land."

The rest of the boats were to be brought to the church for disassembly and distribution of the lumber and nails. The nails alone were a great find. They had just begun their trip and they had already acquired enough material to meet their needs. Some homes needed repair, furniture needed to be replaced, and a smokehouse rebuilt.

The rest of the expedition continued up the river. They passed the Rodriguez Canal. Bartolomé was relieved to find Bacenaux's *pirogue* where he had left it. He paused only enough to recover the *pirogue*. Sightseers were still about, here and there, in small groups. The redoubt that supported Battery Number One looked very different now. It appeared to be small and unimposing. The slopes on which so many men battled for their lives were beginning to grow a covering of grass. How could anyone perceive the desperation of the fight on slick, muddy slopes and in a blood-filled ditch? Bartolomé had to look away. The angry, stunned face of the British Redcoat he had stabbed through the throat filled his mind.

"Is that little hill where you were, brother Bartolomé?" Oceane asked.

"Yes." Bartolomé replied.

Oceane wondered how such a little mound of mud could have been so important. The full scope of the battle area could not be seen by the little flotilla on the river. To them, it appeared that Battery Number One was all that had stood between New Orleans and the invaders. In a way, it was.

They passed the landing at Bayou Pecheur. The party paused there to talk to those near the landing. Villagers had the habit of sharing news and other information with everyone they encountered. It was how people kept informed. Moine was there, as were several others.

"Good day, Moine," Bartolomé said.

"*El Tigre!*" Moine exclaimed. He didn't know that the famed Tiger of New Orleans was the same young man who had traded in moss. "How have you faired?"

"I am well, thank you," Bartolomé replied. "Tell me, have the Stewards returned?"

"No, sir," Moine replied. "Mister Steward has sold his interest in the business to Mister Getty and he has gone."

"Where did they go?" Bartolomé was developing a sick feeling in the pit of his stomach.

"They were bound for Louisville on the steamboat. The boat only goes as far as Natchez, so I cannot say where they are now," Moine said. He suspected, as did many of the workers and servants for the Steward household, that Bartolomé and the beautiful Anna were more than mere acquaintances. The look on *El Tigre's* face confirmed that suspicion. "If I should hear anything, I shall send word to you," Moine said.

"I would be grateful if you would," Bartolomé said sadly.

"*Allons, frère Bartolomé,*" Oceane called out. The flotilla was underway again.

The landing at New Orleans was bustling. Riverboats were arriving from upriver and goods were being loaded, unloaded, and carried about by sweating men, black and white. A small guard was left at the landing to care for the flotilla as the rest scattered about to find the goods needed to replenish the village. Bartolomé and his family went to the market. They found William Stout at his usual stall. He saw the family coming and rushed over to greet them.

"*El Tigre,*" Stout called out in a loud voice. Many in the market had already recognized Bartolomé. The feats of battle attributed to him had grown with every telling. He found it embarrassing to be lauded when all he was doing was trying to survive.

"I am glad to see you well," Stout continued. He was no longer Sergeant Stout of Beale's Rifles. He had returned to being Mister William Stout, produce merchant.

Bartolomé introduced his family. Mister Stout had never met the little girls or Aimée. Jules and Gabriel had been to the market before, though. Mister Stout commented on how much they had grown.

"Are Jacques and Maurice well?" Stout asked. He asked in English, thinking that only Bartolomé would understand. But Aimée knew what was being said because she heard the names of her husband and stepson. She put her hands to her eyes.

"We do not know," Bartolomé said. "The British captured them. The last word we had was that they were being forced to carry British material during their evacuation."

"*Choses amélioreront* (Things will improve)," Mister Stout said, switching to French, at least his version of the language, so that Aimée and the others could understand.

"We are in the need of several supplies," Aimée said. Now that French was being used, she was ready to get to business. It would help her put her fears for Jacques and Maurice to the back of her mind. "Where may we find a good sow?"

Mister Stout directed her to a livery nearby that had several pigs for sale.

The shopping that day was done by the family as a group. For reasons that none could explain, the efficiency of splitting up into smaller groups to collect what was needed was not even discussed. Saw, axes, shovels, hammer, vegetables, dried meats, and, finally, a young sow and hog were acquired. They returned to the boats on the river loaded down with what they had purchased. The two gold coins had gone a long way. Every stall or shop that they visited recognized Bartolomé. Each had a little food or drink to offer, particularly for Oceane and Inez. As soon as all was loaded, they cast off for home. The flotilla had waited on them so long that the villagers were wondering if they should send people to find the family.

The trip back to Bayou Terre Aux Boeufs was festive. Most of the villagers had purchased only a few items or bartered with some of the goods they had brought along. Even so, the boats did ride a little lower on the trip downriver and the spirits of the people were a little higher. When they passed landings or groups along the bank, the waves and greeting were more joyous than before. Hope was returning. Recovery was underway.

When they reached Poche's Ferry, two of the boats had to put people ashore to decrease draft enough to cross a shallow shoal at the entrance to Bayou Terre Aux Boeufs. The river had fallen during the day. Once past the shoal, everyone re-embarked and they continued down the bayou.

Bacenaux was hard at work converting the barge that had been delivered to him into a proper ferry. He was nearly in tears as he hailed the little flotilla to the bank. He thanked each and every villager personally. To each, he vowed free passage on his ferry for the rest of their lives. Bartolomé thought of how important the role of the little ferry was in the lives of the people down river. Communication was the cement that held communities together.

The flotilla began to break up as it passed the homes in the village. When Bartolomé guided the *bateau* to the bank at the farm, it was getting dark. It had been a long day. Oceane and Inez were sound asleep in the bow. Jules and Gabriel carried them up the bank and to the house. Aimée and Bartolomé tended to the livestock first. The rest of the goods could stay in the boat until later.

As soon as had they managed to get the animals up the bank, Jules came rushing out of the house. "They are back! They are back!" he was crying. "Papa and Maurice are back!"

Aimée dropped the tether to the sow and rushed to the house. Bartolomé had to scramble to catch the sow and herd both pigs to the rear and get them in the sty. He could hear the joyous shouts of the family from within the house. He took the time needed to inspect the sty and ensure that the pigs would stay. Then he went into the house.

Jacques and Maurice were sitting on the only two chairs that had survived the marauding British. The men were gaunt and clearly exhausted.

Both men gave Bartolomé a hug when he entered the room. Jacques noticed the ugly scar on Bartolomé's face.

"What happened to you, my son?" Jacques asked.

"There will be time to tell the story, Father," Bartolomé replied. "Now we need to get the few blankets and other goods we purchased into the house. A good night's rest and tomorrow we can build some beds."

"We spoke with the villagers at the church where people have begun to recover lumber and nails from some old barges. They said we could have all we needed," Maurice said.

Maurice looked at Bartolomé closely. "They said that you had been in the thick of it," he said. "When Papa and I were carrying a wounded Redcoat, he talked all the time to a comrade who walked along with us. One of the militiamen, Etienne Solis, who was captured with us, could speak English, but the Redcoats didn't know it. Etienne said that the Redcoats told of a wild man who attacked them with a spear and a club. Even though the man had a bayonet lodged through his head, he stabbed and clubbed them into retreat."

"There was much smoke and confusion," Bartolomé said. "Things sometimes appeared different than they really were."

That night, the family slept on the floor in one room. The next day, each was assigned a chore and everyone went to work. Even little Inez helped her father build the beds. She would catch the ends of the rope he laced through the side frames and send it back though the next hole. Together they made the heavy rope netting that supported the moss-stuffed mattresses.

After a week of work, the farm had nearly returned to normal. One or two crops would generate enough money to buy the remaining replacement tools the farm lacked. The smokehouse was finished, but there would be no hams to cure this year. Several neighbors brought some venison to be jerked, so the smell of smoldering oak returned.

It was almost fall before life had returned to a normal routine. Then, one morning, a man came to the house. He had a letter for Bartolomé, only he said it was for "the Tiger of New Orleans."

Bartolomé eagerly open the letter. He prayed it was from Anna or it was about where she had gone.

The letter was from Mister Too. "Please, if you can, come see me. I have business," was what the letter said.

Bartolomé was somewhat saddened that it was not about Anna. But still, business meant money and this family could use some money.

"I shall go to New Orleans tomorrow," Bartolomé announced. "Mister Too has some business for me."

CHAPTER 15

Jean and Pierre Lafitte sat at the small table in the back of the blacksmith's shop. They were joined by their half-brother, Dominique Youx, who entered from a side door. The activity of the busy street could be heard beyond the walls. Life in New Orleans was beginning to resume. General Jackson was gone, martial law had been lifted, and the city was beginning to enter into the summer doldrums of 1815. Now that Europe was at peace, the men had a business problem. No war meant that there would be no letters of marque to thinly disguise the true nature of their business, which was piracy and smuggling.

"We will have to invest what we have left in some legal enterprise in which we have some level of experience," Jean said. "Shipping is what we know, but our competitors may harbor some resentment. This will make an entry into the legitimate shipping trade difficult."

The brothers had lost a considerable portion of their wealth in the war. What wasn't destroyed in the raid conducted by Governor Claiborne was consumed by the battle. Fully half the cannon shot and powder expended on the line at New Orleans had been the private property of the Lafitte brothers.

"I have been talking to Mister Too," Dominique said. "He has been doing quite well in the short haul business. He is convinced that river traffic will become very profitable if we can acquire steamboats. The courts have annulled the contract that Fulton had with Louisiana that granted him exclusive rights to use steamboats on the Mississippi. Captain Shreve has already introduced a boat into service."

"Let us see if we can form a company with Mister Too," Pierre said. "Our part must be unknown. Offer Mister Too this: We will finance two steamboats to start. Mister Too will establish the network of merchants we need. We will ship cotton from the plantations, hard goods from New Orleans, grains from the Missouri valley. We will make money going upriver and down."

That afternoon, Dominique's small town buggy stopped in front of Too's hiring hall. The men gathered in front of the hall abandoned the steps and cleared the doorway. Many removed their hats, and one man assisted the driver by holding the horse's bridle as Dominique stepped down from the buggy. There was a murmur from inside the hall as word of the distinguished visitor filtered through the building. When Dominique entered the hall, Mister Too was waiting at the door to the inner office to usher him in.

Dominique sat across the small desk from Mister Too. He had explained the offer of financial backing of a pair of steamboats in partnership with Mister Too. Too would provide the river and barge shipping connections. The Lafittes would provide the cash.

"I do it," Mister Too said. "But we need better man. I no talk to rich planters, cotton traders. We need man all respect. I know who."

Dominique was not surprised when Mister Too suggested that Bartolomé deMelilla, the Tiger of New Orleans, should be the man to head the operation. "He is young, but he has the mark of a leader," Dominique said. "They tell me that he led an expedition of people from his village to collect supplies to rebuild. Young as he is, the people accepted his leadership. He is courageous, yet thoughtful. In battle, he is as fierce as Louis Chighizola, but he can control himself. He is well spoken and willing to work. But, will he do it?"

"I send for yesterday. He come here soon," Mister Too said. "I ask. Then we know."

* * *

Bartolomé stopped for a moment near the alley that led to the rear of the Steward house, or what was formerly the Steward house. He could not find anyone who knew where the Steward family had resettled. Bartolomé had not been able to track their movements beyond boarding the *New Orleans* bound for Natchez. If he were to find Anna, he would have to go to Natchez and perhaps beyond.

He no longer carried his weapons, the *magado* and *sunta*, for the war was over. Deserters from the British force, and there were many, were no threat. These men only wanted to settle peacefully, and were considered good employees by those that took a chance with them. Not that he was unarmed. He still carried the great knife that he had acquired in the fall of 1814. That was almost a year ago, but it seemed to have been a lifetime. The walking staff he used to aid his travels, in his hands, was as lethal as any sword. He did not carry his traditional weapons of war, but he was far from unarmed.

He found Mister Too sitting in the office in the hiring hall. Summer was a time of reduced activity and the hiring hall was empty. The sugar plantations were short-handed, so many of the bargemen were hiring out as day laborers. The plantations downriver from the Rodriguez Canal were trying to rebuild. Most lacked slaves to do the work of recovering from battle damage. The British had not only destroyed some buildings, taken furniture (which fueled their camp fires), silverware, tools, and slaughtered animals of all kinds, they had carried away all the slaves that would go with them, which was most.

"Bartolomé, welcome back to my humble place of business," Mister Too said. His broad smile was genuine and Bartolomé knew it. "I have job, you take?"

"That would depend upon the job," Bartolomé said. In truth, the difficulties that the farm suffered as a result of the invasion were serious. In order to help his family, Bartolomé was going to accept any reasonable employment. He was not ready for what was to follow.

"I start Cathay Steamboats. I build steamboats for river. I have investors. We have money. We need face," Mister Too began. "You talk good. You smart. You be our face. You arrange shipments, schedule stops, talk businessmen."

"I do not think businessmen along the river will put much stock in a young boy scheduling shipments," Bartolomé said.

"You Tiger of New Orleans. All men respect you, fear you," Mister Too said confidently. "My investors want you."

"Who are your investors?" Bartolomé asked. He had decided that, if Mister Too couldn't trust him with that information, he would decline.

"Must be secret. I tell you, you no tell anyone," Mister Too replied. Bartolomé nodded his head. "Investors Jean and Pierre Lafitte and Dominique Youx," Too said in a hushed voice. "They all know you. All want *El Tigre* be face of Cathay Steamboats."

"I do not know the first thing about shipping or cotton markets or gentlemanly behavior," Bartolomé protested.

"Not worry," Mister Too said. "We have hired lawyer Edward Livingston to teach you. Get you started. We pay you one hundred twenty dollars a month and expenses."

One hundred and twenty a month was as much as a good doctor or lawyer would make. He could send half to the farm every month and they would be well on the way to recovery.

"I will take the assignment," Bartolomé said.

"Good," Mister Too replied. "Here is address for Mister Livingston. He know you come this week. He explain better." Mister Too handed Bartolomé a slip of paper with an address on Levee Street. It was in an area that specialized in sailors, ships, and riverboats.

"I will meet him today," Bartolomé said.

Mister Too nodded until Bartolomé thought his head would come off. "We do good. We make business, *El Tigre,*" Mister Too said as he guided Bartolomé out the door.

Bartolomé strode along toward the river until he arrived at Levee Street. He then turned upriver, looking for the address that Mister Too had given him. Most of the buildings were without addresses of any kind. Some bore the sign of the business housed there. Every now and then, a sign would be displayed on a pole over the door and perpendicular to the street. It seemed that every fifth establishment was an ale house.

Finally, he arrived at a building with a newly painted sign and an address that matched the note in his hands. The sign had the words "Cathay Steamboats" over a picture of a smoke-belching side-wheeler. The picture matched Jacques' description of the machine he'd seen that day in the market. Bartolomé had never even seen a steamboat. Fulton's steamboat, *New Orleans*, had only begun regular service to New Orleans in 1812. Bartolomé and the steamboat were never in the city at the same time. Through some sort of monopoly or patent, only Fulton could have steamboats in operation in Louisiana until the courts tossed out the restriction this year. Now the race was on to get into the business.

A bell over the door jingled as Bartolomé entered. The receiving room had a small railing that isolated a sitting area from a receptionist's desk. A door to an interior office lay on the other side of the receptionist's desk. There was no one at the desk. To the right of the office door, there was a stairway that led up to a closed door. The door to the office opened, and a slender, hawk-nosed man entered the room. His face was ruddy and his forehead protruded beneath a receding hairline.

"*El Tigre*, no doubt," the man said. "Allow me to introduce myself. I am Edward Livingston, attorney for Cathay Steamboats, at your service." Livingston extended his hand as he spoke. They shook hands across the railing. Bartolomé was not quite comfortable with the fact that he was known everywhere he went.

"Pardon me for my poor manners," Livingston said. "Please come into my office." He opened the gate in the railing and ushered Bartolomé through to the office. Livingston invited Bartolomé to take a seat in a padded chair near a wide desk. Livingston sat in the high-backed chair behind the desk.

"I assume, because you are here, that you have accepted the position that Mister Too had offered," Livingston said.

Bartolomé replied that he had.

"Then we have a lot of work before us," Livingston continued. "If it meets with your approval, we have reserved a few rooms upstairs for your quarters. You will have to go out to eat, for there is no kitchen attached to this property."

"I am interested to learn of my duties," Bartolomé said.

"In time," Livingston replied. "You will be provided an expense account at Armond's tailor shop, where I have directed that you be provided with sufficient clothes in keeping with a business man. If the clothing he has provided is not satisfactory, just visit his shop for a fitting." Livingston made a show of noticing that Bartolomé was barefoot. "A cobbler has also been hired to provide you with shoes."

"I have a fine pair of English leather boots at home," Bartolomé said. He was a little offended by Livingston's distain for his apparel.

"Is that so?" Livingston said as if such a thing was unimaginable. "I've often wanted a pair. They are expensive."

"This pair cost me nothing," Bartolomé said.

"Wonderful," Livingston replied. He wondered if Cathay Steamboats had hired someone with a checkered past. Then he remembered who the investors were.

"Next, you have fencing lessons three days a week under the guidance of Bernard deMarigny. He will also introduce you around society as the opportunity may arise. The office in which we now sit will become yours as soon as we have determined that you have been polished enough. I have arranged with a court to have you declared an adult under the law when we need to do so. You will then be able to enter into contracts and act as an officer of the company," Livingston concluded.

* * *

Bartolomé returned to the farm that evening to retrieve his few personal items from the cramped quarters he shared with his stepbrothers. He planned to spend the night and return to the city in the morning. The family gathered around him eager to learn of his new position.

"The salary is excellent," Bartolomé said. He was speaking to Jacques, but the family could hear every word. "Mister Livingston has given me this letter of introduction for you." He handed a folded paper to Jacques. "The next time you are in the city, go to the Hall Bank and present this letter to the clerk. He will open an account in your name. I will deposit sixty dollars a month in this account for the family."

Jacques and Aimée hugged each other. This royal income would insure that the family would never want.

"If you wish to contact me, send a letter or message to the Cathay Steamboats office in New Orleans. It will get to me." Bartolomé looked at each the family members. "I shall be off before dawn tomorrow," he said.

Oceane began to cry a little, but she contained herself. "Will you ever see us again?" she sniffed.

"Yes," he said. "I promise."

"More than once?" she asked.

"Many times," he gave her an assuring hug. "I will be away quite often, but I will visit when I can. There will come the time when I will not need to travel anymore."

"You will become one of those gentlemen dandies and forget all about Terre Aux Boeufs," Maurice said. He was surprisingly moved by the circumstances.

"I may become a gentleman, but I shall never be a dandy," Bartolomé said with a laugh. "I have been instructed that I am expected to bathe at least once a week."

"A dandy, to be sure," Jules said.

The sun was just beginning to break the horizon when Bartolomé passed Bayou Pecheur. In an hour or so, he would be settling down at Cathay Steamboats. For the first time in his life, he was to have a room to himself, an entire room to sleep in and another to work in. He carried the fine boots over his shoulders as he plodded along. His haversack bulged with every item he could call his own.

When he arrived at the office, he found a clerk seated at the desk in the reception area.

"*El Tigre*," the man exclaimed as he jumped to his feet. "I was told to expect you today. My name is Jon Loitan. I am the head clerk for Cathay Steamboats."

"Call me Bartolomé, sir. How many clerks do we have?" Bartolomé asked.

"I am all there is, for now. I am confident that we shall grow," Loitan answered.

Bartolomé went up the stairs to his quarters. There were several sets of clothes hanging in a wardrobe. He managed to satisfactorily dress himself. He slipped on the boots and looked in the mirror that was attached to the back of the door on the wardrobe. A rugged, scar-faced, and well dressed young man stared back. When he returned to the reception area, he found Loitan talking to a well-dressed gentleman.

"*El Tigre*," Loitan said, "may I introduce you to Don Bernard deMarigny."

Bartolomé gave a little bow, "Bartolomé deMelilla, at your service, sir," he said.

"Bartolomé, they tell me you are an *Isleño*," deMarigny said as he extended his hand.

"My father was born in Aguimes, Grand Canaria. I am a native of Bayou Terre Aux Boeufs," Bartolomé replied.

"That was my meaning," deMarigny continued. "My wife's family is from the Canarian archipelago as well. She is of the Morales family."

DeMarigny walked around Bartolomé, inspecting him. "You are not so much the *coonée* as I had been led to believe," he said finally. Bartolomé flushed at the left handed complement. "I think you shall pass for a gentleman quite well. Today we will visit a few coffee shops and I will introduce you to the right people," deMarigny said. "These will be the cotton traders, sugar barons, and shipping masters that you will need to know to arrange the shipments on the river. They tell me the boats will be ready to sail by January, so there is no time to waste."

* * *

There did not seem to be a gentleman in New Orleans that deMarigny did not know. It was more than a little disconcerting that every man that deMarigny introduced knew Bartolomé already and addressed him as *El Tigre*. Bartolomé noticed that a special deference was given to deMarigny by all they met.

During a conversation at one of the coffee house visits, Don deMarigny had excused himself for a moment when the subject of fencing came up, and Bartolomé learned that deMarigny was one of the finest duelists in the city.

"One time, he was escorting the beautiful Lady Anna Morales, now his wife, to a ball," one gentleman confided. "He would not permit any other man to dance with the lady. As she was not even his fiancée at the time, the act was considered impertinent. Six men challenged Don deMarigny to duels. The next day, he met them all, and dispatched them all, one at a time."

At the mention of the name "Anna," Bartolomé instantly thought of his own Anna. She was far away and only God knew where. He vowed that at every port he visited during the development of Cathay Steamboats he would search for Anna. He was determined to find her one day, and God had given him the means to do so.

The months that followed were hectic with learning. Fencing, etiquette, business management, and steamboat construction were just a few of the things Bartolomé had to master. Each time, he was tutored by an expert in the field. He visited the cotton exchange and the sugar exchange, where a year's supply of the commodities were bought and sold, sometimes before the products came to the port. The man who could ship these and other commodities quickly up and down the river would make a fortune. Cathay Steamboats was going to do just that.

The tradition of fall and winter formal dances in New Orleans was one business opportunity that could not be ignored. These balls were where young men met eligible ladies, and family elders arranged both marriages and business mergers. It was during one of the etiquette and formal dance lessons that Bartolomé had the opportunity to meet the wife of Don deMarigny.

Edward deMarigny strode into the small studio where Bartolomé was practicing the waltz to the rhythm of the dance master's clapping hands. He was escorting a lady who appeared to be about twenty years Bartolomé's senior. To say she was beautiful would be an understatement. Bartolomé could see how a man would challenge six rivals for this lady.

"*El Tigre*," deMarigny said. "I must interrupt your work for only a moment."

Bartolomé approached the couple and gave a small bow to the lady.

"My dear," deMarigny continued, "may I present to you Bartolomé deMelilla y Bourg, the Tiger of New Orleans. Sir, my wife, *Señora* Anna Morales y Mathilda deMarigny."

"I am your servant, *Señora*," Bartolomé said with a deep bow. She offered her gloved hand, palm down, and he kissed the white cotton covering her knuckles.

"*He aprendido de usted* (I have learned of you)," the *señora* replied.

Bartolomé responded in Spanish, "Stories often grow as weeds and hide the truth."

"In your case, I think not," *Señora* deMarigny continued in Spanish. "My husband speaks perfect Spanish, but the dance master and his assistant do not. I say this so you may speak freely. I have been told that you are the grandson of Don Diego deMelilla of the Spanish Louisiana Regiment."

"That is so, *señora*," Bartolomé said. He was curious about just how much was known of him.

"Don Diego saved my father's life at the battle of Pensacola," she said. A tear formed in the corner of her eye. "It was a debt that he was never able to repay. I was saddened to hear of Don Diego's death last year. My own father had died only a year before that sad news reached me."

Bartolomé was astonished. Bartolomé remembered his grandfather's story of the siege of Pensacola very well. Don Diego had rushed into the open to pull a wounded *soldado* into the safety of a siege trench. Although Diego had insisted there was really no danger, for the British were reloading their cannon, Morales insisted upon telling everyone that Diego had saved his life. *Señora* deMarigny was the daughter of that *soldado*, Morales.

"My grandfather spoke of your father often. He told me that the favor had been returned many times," Bartolomé said. In actuality, his grandfather had mentioned Morales only that one time. He had described the *soldado* as very young and severely wounded.

"You are kind to say so," she replied.

"We must now depart, dear," deMarigny interrupted.

"Yes, my husband," the lady said obediently. "Good-bye, *Senor* deMelilla."

"I have been honored to meet you, *Señora* Anna Morales y Mathilda deMarigny," Bartolomé said with a deep bow. He watched the couple depart. How could deMarigny, married to this beautiful lady, own several mistresses?

* * *

Bartolomé had learned many things about the Creole gentry from deMarigny. He had decided to only adopt those practices necessary to gain access to the business of shipping. He vowed to shun those vices that plagued the idle rich. The practice of owning people was repugnant. Forcing a slave to become a mistress was worse.

The rural farmers, Spanish and Acadian alike, were working families. Husband and wife labored together to raise crops and children. The shared hardships of a working farm bonded man and wife in a comradeship that surpassed simple love. Besides, no one had any time for dalliances. Infidelities did occur, but they were uncommon and hidden. The Creole elite openly kept mistresses. Their wives were expected to ignore the young girls their husbands boarded in city apartments.

Gambling was another vice that Bartolomé could not understand. The Creoles would gamble at every conceivable opportunity. Cards, dice, horse racing, duels, and any other occasion having a questionable conclusion were wagered upon. The sums hazarded were staggering. The plantations that supplied the wealth had been established generations ago. Bartolomé learned that those who inherited wealth were often ignorant of the value of money and hard work.

Dueling was expected. The Creoles concept of honor was, to Bartolomé's thinking, warped. It seemed that if a slight of honor did not occur within a certain term, then one had to be created. Duels were formal affairs, like a dance. The offended party, no matter how trivial the offense, would challenge the offender. It was presumed that the parties involved would be too incensed to converse, so seconds would be chosen to arrange the terms of the duel. The party challenged had the choice of weapons, but rapiers were the favorite of most. The duel would end when blood was drawn, so most encounters were not fatal. Bartolomé determined that he would never challenge anyone to a duel. He had more important things to do than indulge in petty squabbles.

The Creoles considered reading an activity reserved for priests. The crowded coffee shops and shipping exchanges were never witness to discussions of any works of literature. Books, philosophy, and science were of no use to the Creole. Trading commodities, gambling, breeding horses, dogs, and octoroon mistresses were paramount. Bartolomé wondered if some of the wealthy plantation owners he met could even read.

The Creoles were rich. Many of the men Bartolomé met had more wealth than any prince of Europe or Asian potentate. Perhaps it was the wealth and idleness that festered into the vices that plagued the New Orleans aristocrats. They would conduct business with Bartolomé because he was a known associate of Jean Lafitte and because of his fame as the Tiger of New Orleans. Bartolomé would be allowed to do business with these people, but he would never be one of them.

Non-Creoles were considered foreigners to be tolerated if money could be made. Americans, the Spanish Canary Islanders, and even the French-speaking Acadians were held in contempt by the haughty Creoles. Bartolomé's accented French branded him as an Acadian. He would not attempt to change his accent. He refused to wear a top hat. The Creole considered the ridiculously tall head cover to be high fashion. Bartolomé would don a farmer's straw hat when visiting the docks or a boatyard. His evening dress cover was a woolen garrison cap. He was determined to make it clear that he was not a Creole *gentilhomme*.

It was the fashion statement of a garrison cap that seemed to irritate some he met the most. DeMarigny had introduced Bartolomé to a group of sugar speculators when one of the *gentilhomme* by the name of Francois Dargaray commented that the cap Bartolomé wore was nothing more than a sack.

"In many ways, you are correct, sir," Bartolomé replied with a smile. "Indeed, I must turn up the sides to see."

"My only use for a sack is to carry horse shit," Dargaray said.

"You must do so out of necessity," Bartolomé said, "there being no room in that fine top hat for any more." The ambiance shifted from frivolity to menacing.

"How dare you, *coonée*," Dargaray sputtered. "You are a bumbling fool."

"I thank you for the complement, sir," Bartolomé replied.

"You fool, I insult you and you thank me?"

"It is my opinion, sir, that insults from a scoundrel can bestow on a man more honor than praise from a dozen honest men."

Dargaray stood. His chair fell to the floor and the room became silent. He was a heavily built man, muscular, dark, and only slightly shorter than Bartolomé.

"You insult me, sir. I demand satisfaction," he said with a sneer. "Name your second."

"My second is *Monsieur* deMarigny," Bartolomé said. He stared straight at the fuming Creole. "My choice of weapons is hammers, in the street, and now."

DeMarigny laughed and announced, "Hammers, in the street and now."

* * *

Bartolomé marched out of the coffee house. He had noticed when he and deMarigny entered the crowded little coffee house that some carpenters were repairing the siding on the adjacent building. He took two hammers from the startled men and went to the center of the street. He gave the hammers to deMarigny when he and the others arrived in the street.

The eldest of the gentlemen in the street was chosen as the moderator or judge. It was the moderator's assignment to see that the duel was conducted according to custom. The duel could be avoided if the conditions of honor were met. The offending party could apologize or the offended party could withdraw the challenge.

Bartolomé would not extend an apology and Dargaray would not withdraw his challenge. DeMarigny presented the hammers to the moderator. Dargaray's second was offered first choice. The man knew nothing about choosing hammers for combat. He shrugged, selected one, and brought it to Dargaray. DeMarigny gave the other hammer to Bartolomé. The moderator directed the combatants to positions in the middle of the street and about ten feet apart.

"*En garde*," the moderator commanded.

Dargaray crouched, with his hands held wide. In his right, he held the hammer ready to strike down. His empty left hand was open and ready to deflect any blows.

Bartolomé crouched, as well. He kept both hands close to his chest. His right held the hammer. His left was clenched into a fist.

The moderator took a deep breath and then commanded, "*Engager!*"

Bartolomé rushed forward, hard and low. Dargaray attempted to strike at Bartolomé's head, but his blow was easily blocked as Bartolomé's left arm shot up into Dargaray's forearm.

Bartolomé didn't swing at Dargaray's head, as was expected. Instead, he thrust the hammer that he held close to his chest straight up into Dargaray's chin. The power of the blow smashed the man's chin and collapsed his lower jaw into the roof of his mouth. Blood and teeth sprayed out in all directions. Dargaray fell without a sound. He lay motionless in the mud and filth of the street. It had happened so fast that some of the crowd had not even finished their wagers.

Bartolomé returned to the coffee house. He tossed his hammer to a stunned carpenter, walked through the doors, and sat at a table. He drank from a cup and then braced himself for the shakes that were sure to come. When they did come, he struggled to remain still.

DeMarigny came in and sat across from Bartolomé. If he noticed that Bartolomé was shaking, he didn't mention it.

"Dargaray is dead," deMarigny said.

CHAPTER 16

On January fifteen, 1816, Cathay Steamboats received the first of two boats that had been ordered. She was christened the *August Moon* at the landing across the road from the Cathay Steamboats' office. She was a wide, long, and shallow-draft side-wheeler. Livingston and Too were there to sign the papers and officially receive the boat. They gave Bartolomé a nod and set off for the office. Bartolomé stepped aboard. He met the captain, Albert Christen, and the first mate.

"Gentlemen," he said, "please make for Natchez." Bartolomé had been assigned the task of making the maiden voyage up to Natchez. He was to stop at various plantations and ports along the way to arrange for shipments of all sorts. He also would pass the word that anyone wishing to make a dollar or two would need only to stack firewood at a landing, and the *August Moon* would pay handsomely for the fuel. They reached Natchez in only four days. Bartolomé felt as if he were flying.

He had scheduled shipments of cotton and other staples to New Orleans and taken orders for sugar and hard goods for the return trip upriver. The *August Moon* would not move a mile, up or down the river, unless she was loaded with goods. There were passenger berths, as well. A dozen staterooms and a cramped dining area occupied the second tier over the open cargo decks. Bartolomé had a cabin reserved for him just aft of the captain's berth. The captain's berth was directly beneath the wheelhouse and was connected to it by the means of a hatch and ladder. The wheelhouse had exit doors on both sides where others could enter from the roof of the second deck. Stairways on the left and right led from the second deck to the roof near the wheelhouse.

The crew used nautical terms such as "hatch" instead of "door," even though the hatches to the wheelhouse appeared no different than a door one might find in a small Rampart Street cottage. Everything on the boat was "port" or "starboard," "aft" or "forward," "stem" or "stern." "Deck" meant "floor," "overhead" meant "ceiling," and so on. Bartolomé absorbed this language quickly. Before the *August Moon* anchored for the first night, as the captain did not yet trust traveling the river at night, he was conversing with the hands as if he had spent his life aboard a ship.

Natchez was a small town clinging to the bluffs overlooking the Mississippi River. Bartolomé finished his business with several plantation owners and was free to stroll about the town. He was committed to dine with a select group of businessmen later that night, but for now, he was free. He went straight to the largest bank in town. He asked to speak with the bank manager. Even here, he needn't introduce himself. The manager recognized him as *El Tigre* of Cathay Steamboats.

"Tell me, sir," Bartolomé began, "have you a depositor by the name of Bernard Steward?" He asked the same question at every opportunity.

"No, sir." It was the same reply every time: "I have never heard of the name." Natchez proved to be no different. Bartolomé resolved that the trip would continue to Louisville. When the *Evening Star* came into service, Bartolomé was determined that it would travel the route between New Orleans and St. Louis. He was personally going to scour the Mississippi, Ohio, and Missouri valleys. One day, somewhere, someone would recognize the name Bernard Steward.

* * *

Louisville proved to be more of a town than most that the *August Moon* had visited along the Mississippi and Ohio River valleys. The Ohio River was not passable to sizable boat traffic at Louisville because of a series of rapids. A portage was required, and the town of Louisville grew up at the site. Riverboat traffic down from Pittsburgh was interrupted at Louisville. There, the goods being shipped would be unloaded and carried by hand or cart or sled to a dock below the falls. Then the riverboats, now floating high, would be gently guided down the rapids and reloaded below the falls.

River traffic was almost exclusively downstream until Fulton's invention made travel against the current practical. Now, a steamboat service was being developed between Louisville and Pittsburgh above the falls, and between Louisville and New Orleans below the falls. Bartolomé had finally reached Louisville to carve out a share of that shipping for Cathay Steamboats.

It was the summer of 1817 when the *August Moon* moored at Louisville. Cathay Steamboats' reputation had preceded Bartolomé's visit. The *August Moon* and the *Evening Star* were already shipping goods down from the Midwest and up from New Orleans. Manufactured goods, such as shovels, plows, nails, and other necessities were being distributed across the Mississippi and Missouri valleys. Raw products such as cotton, sugar, and timber were going upriver in great quantities for the first time in history. Cathay Steamboats was in the forefront of this exploding trade.

Something new was happening at Louisville. There was talk of constructing a canal and lock system that would bypass the falls. Once this was done, river traffic would be uninterrupted between Pittsburgh, New Orleans, St. Louis, and beyond. In all those places, new settlers would need hard goods and an outlet for their products. Cathay Steamboats was going to move as much of it as possible.

Bartolomé walked into the office of John Bucklin. Bucklin was a banker and businessman of great influence in Louisville.

Bartolomé was expected. *"El Tigre,"* Bucklin said as he extended his hand. "I am John Bucklin. It is a great pleasure to meet you."

"And I, you," Bartolomé replied. "I understand that our correspondence has reached you. I would like your honest opinion of our offer." Both men took chairs across from one another at a wide, oak table.

"We have studied the offer. Your shipping fees and the host of customers you provide are most persuasive," Bucklin replied. Offering to ship goods was one thing, but Cathay Steamboats had also provided a long list of purchase orders for the goods to be shipped. John Bucklin was eager to sign a contract with the young representative of Cathay Steamboats. Bucklin studied the young Louisianan. He noted the man's rugged and heavy frame, his light colored hair and eyes, and, of course, the prominent scar that went from near the left corner of the man's mouth almost to the ear. It gave *El Tigre* a permanent sneer. Bucklin assessed the man's age to be twenty-three years or so.

"It is our intent to provide two more vessels to our line below Louisville and two above. All four vessels will be sternwheelers. It is our experience that sternwheelers can be loaded and offloaded faster than side-wheelers. Also, sternwheelers can more easily accomplish shore landing where no dock exists," Bartolomé explained. Steamboats would often make unscheduled stops to pick up fuel or passengers. Nosing a sternwheeler into the shore kept the paddle wheels further from the shallows and reduced the exposure to damage that the same maneuver presented to a side-wheeler.

Papers were signed and a parade of clerks moved about as the shipping contracts were completed. Bucklin noticed with interest the name printed on the documents identifying the man he knew only as *El Tigre*. "Bartolomé deMelilla" had a distinctly Mediterranean ring to it. The young man before him was tall and powerfully built, with features that suggested a Scotch-Irish lineage. Bucklin was one of only a handful of men who had cause to see Bartolomé's full name. To everyone doing business with Cathay Steamboats, Bartolomé was known as *El Tigre*.

When the paperwork was done, over three hundred thousand dollars of business had been contracted. That was more money than was on deposit at the Bank of Louisville. Bartolomé had concluded eight similar contracts between New Orleans and Louisville in the short time Cathay Steamboats had been in existence. Some were for more, a lot more. He had been so successful that he had been made a full partner and acting director by Mister

Too and the Baratarians. None of the men doing business with Cathay Steamboats would have guessed that the young *El Tigre* would reach only his eighteenth birthday this summer of 1817.

"Now that we are concluded, sir," Bartolomé said, "I would like to ask a question of personal interest to me."

"Certainly," Bucklin replied. "I welcome the chance to be of assistance."

"Tell me, sir," Bartolomé began his standard question, asked at every new port. "Do you know of, or have you heard of, a man by the name of Bernard Steward. He would have arrived here from New Orleans in the early spring of 1815."

"I regret to say that I have not. Many from New Orleans passed through Louisville during that time to escape the British invasion of New Orleans, which you, sir, crushed," Bucklin said as if *El Tigre* had stood alone against the British.

"And where, sir," Bartolomé inquired, "would you suppose such travelers would be bound?"

"I believe that most continued up the Wilderness Road through the Cumberland Gap and on to the east coast," Bucklin speculated. Few continued up the Ohio because of the hardships of upriver travel at the time. Steamboats will change that."

The east coast! Bartolomé had hoped that the Stewards had settled here. The east coast was vast and heavily populated. The Appalachian Mountains created a barrier between the east coast and the great river valleys more formidable than a wide sea.

"I will continue up the Ohio, sir," Bartolomé said. "Should correspondence for me reach you, please forward it on to Pittsburgh. I am to contract the construction of our upper Ohio boats in Pittsburgh."

"We intend that your boats be afforded passage around the rapids in a few years, sir," Bucklin boasted. "It will be to our mutual benefit when the Cathay line is free to ply the rivers from Pittsburgh to New Orleans unfettered."

"That is our anticipation as well, sir," Bartolomé said as he rose to leave.

"If you are to be here in Louisville until the morrow, perhaps you would like to join me and my family at a small dance we are having tonight. Nothing as grand as the balls in New Orleans, but it will be a festive affair, I assure you," Bucklin said.

* * *

At almost every town Bartolomé visited he was offered, and expected to accept, invitations to the local dances. He accepted Bucklin's offer without hesitation. He would attend. Perhaps he would dance with one or two of the ladies and talk business with the elders. Most of the dances were imitations of the formal balls for which New Orleans aristocrats were famous. The young ladies would gather on one side of the dance floor and the young men on the other. The elders would occupy the area nearest the entrance, and farthest from the band. A young man would send a servant to this lady or that with an invitation to dance. If the lady accepted, she would write the gentleman's name in a little card that hung from her wrist. The returning servant would then inform the gentleman that he had been reserved a dance for the third or fourth waltz, as the case might be.

Bartolomé made it a point to request dances from ladies who did not seem to have many reservations on their cards. He did this so that he would not interfere with any budding romances. It would be very bad for business to have to duel someone's son who might have felt compelled to compete for a lady's attention. He happily discovered that these wall flowers were often excellent dancers and conversationalists.

The Louisville ball was as expected. Word had been passed that the famous Tiger of New Orleans would be at the dance. The ladies were giddy with anticipation and the young men apprehensive. Bartolomé danced with a few nervous ladies, but never more than once with anyone. The ladies were disappointed and the young men relieved.

As soon as it was proper, he retired to the elders' section of the ballroom and met more of the leading businessmen of Louisville. One of the men he was introduced to was Andrew Guthrie. A man of about thirty, he was the son of a shipping magnate out of Baltimore. He had come downriver from Pittsburgh to explore the possibility of expanding into river shipping as well. Eventually, Bartolomé decided that he would join Guthrie on the return trip through Pittsburgh and evaluate the possible ties that might be made to the east coast. If nothing else, Cathay Steamboats would have east coast connections.

Andrew proved to be a pleasant traveling companion, although the choice of horseback as the means of travel to Pittsburgh was the least favorite means of travel for Bartolomé. Unlike the landed gentry who provided most of the business leaders, Bartolomé grew up afoot. He had never been on a horse until deMarigny's effort to mold a gentleman out of a farm boy. As far as Bartolomé was concerned, horses were for pulling wagons and plows.

Both men were aware of the dangers associated with travel in the wildernesses between settled areas. The trail up to Pittsburgh was crude by any measure. Protection from highwaymen or other two-legged dangers was best provided by numbers, so they traveled in a small caravan of returning boatmen. Soon Cathay Steamboats would become the most convenient, safe, and secure means of travel up or down river between islands of civilization. Until then, the small but well armed caravan would have to do.

Every night, Bartolomé and Andrew discussed the prospects of shipping from the east coast to the Gulf of Mexico. The consensus developed that goods from Europe could land at New Orleans and be shipped inland as far west as the confluence of the Kansas and Missouri Rivers, where a strong settlement was developing. Goods produced west of the Appalachians or in the Great Lakes region could easily be distributed throughout the Louisiana Territories by steamboats. East coast manufactured goods were better distributed down the Ohio than shipped by sea around to New Orleans. Pittsburgh would be an ideal location for the production of durable goods and development of overland ties to Philadelphia. The Pennsylvania Road that connected Philadelphia and Pittsburgh was nearing completion. Once that was done, the east coast would have a connection to the rest of America that could not be blockaded.

Bartolomé decided that he would continue traveling with Andrew through Pittsburgh, Philadelphia, and on to Baltimore, to explore the possibility of coordinating European shipping and the exploding American river collection and distribution network. The steamboat had converted the one-way, downriver commerce of raw goods to a two-way exchange of goods. America was going to become rich and Cathay Steamboats was going to lead the way.

* * *

Pittsburgh was a small town with much promise. There were several successful businesses operating in or near the town, producing such things as steel wire, shovels, plows, and all types of iron goods. It was situated at the confluence of two small rivers that joined to form the Ohio. Overland travel came to Pittsburgh from Philadelphia on the east coast, and down from the Great Lakes before continuing down the Ohio. That traffic would soon be two-way.

Much to Bartolomé's relief, the trip from Pittsburgh to Philadelphia was by coach. The Pennsylvania Road was essentially completed and well traveled. Inns and towns were frequent and travelers sped along at the rate of twenty miles a day or more.

"I had received a curious report," Andrew began as they bounced along in the coach. "The Europeans have devised a means of using steam power to move coaches."

Bartolomé was instantly intrigued. The greatest burden to communication in the vast continent of America was cumbersome land travel.

"It seems," Andrew continued, "that a steam engine has been developed that turns the wheel of a coach much the same way as a paddle wheel."

"That is not particularly new," Bartolomé answered. "Such models have been around for some time. The difficulty lies in controlling the direction of the contraption."

"That is what has been solved," Andrew replied. "The contraption, as you say, operates on a road made of parallel rails, like a mine car. This type of road is less expensive to build than a canal and simpler to maintain. I have heard that the rails could be made of iron instead of wood."

"It will be some time before we will see such a thing," Bartolomé said. It was an intriguing thought. Travel could be straight between cities and not subjected to the meanderings of rivers or the expensive effort required in building canals and locks. Something like that could travel over twenty miles in one hour. He reserved the thought for further consideration.

Philadelphia was a city that surpassed New Orleans in size. Until now, all the towns that Bartolomé had visited were compact frontier settlements. Philadelphia was a city. Andrew was well known in the business centers of the city. Quarters were arranged at the house of Thomas McKean, a business associate of the Guthrie family. The McKean family was prominent and politically active in Philadelphia, so it was not surprising that, the following night, a Friday, a ball had been planned to honor a visiting gentleman.

"I think you may know the guest of honor, *El Tigre*," Thomas said. The Americans seemed to insist on using the phrase *El Tigre* as if it were one word. "It is General Andrew Jackson. He has just returned from Florida, where runaways and renegades are a threat to decent people. He is campaigning to garner political support for an expedition against the Seminole and resurgent Red Sticks, as these renegades have come to be called."

The true Red Sticks were a cult of the Creek nation that had rebelled against the rest of the tribe and white settlements. A short civil war of sorts had ensued, during which many settlers were killed, along with a great many Creeks. Jackson destroyed the cult in 1814, just months before defending New Orleans

"I doubt that the general should remember me," Bartolomé said. "There were thousands of soldiers in New Orleans and I was just a messenger."

"You need not be humble, *El Tigre*," Thomas said with a smile. "Even here, we have heard of the Tiger of New Orleans. Please, do come as my guest. Andrew and I will be seeking to dance with every lady we can. Having the Tiger of New Orleans in our company will ensure our popularity."

"I have already spread the word, my friend," Andrew added. "If you deny our request, we will be shamed as braggarts."

It was late November, and Bartolomé felt as if he had been traveling all of his life. He was tired and would have preferred to rest. Even so, he could not refuse. "I will attend, gentlemen," Bartolomé replied, "but do not be surprised if the general does not recognize me."

* * *

The next day was spent at several coffee houses and pubs, as Andrew and Thomas introduced Bartolomé to the influential men of Philadelphia. By the time evening arrived, Bartolomé had made several promising contacts for east coast overland shipments to Pittsburgh and Cathay Steamboats. The east coast ports were eager to increase trade with the exploding American interior. The question was how. Canals were under construction that could bring the New York coast trade to the Great Lakes. However, there was little hope for a canal network through the Appalachians. New Orleans was drawing the bulk of the interior trade away from the east coast. Philadelphia, Boston, and Baltimore wanted in on that trade. Bartolomé was going to position Cathay Steamboats so they could provide transport both ways, from the Gulf of Mexico to the Atlantic coast, right through the heart of America.

The ball was a crowded affair. The general and his wife had formed a reception line at the entrance to the ballroom, and the line had extended well into the lobby. Bartolomé, flanked by the grinning Andrew and Thomas, took his place in line. As they approached the general, each gentleman gave a card bearing his name and the name of his lady to a servant. The servant, in turn, would whisper the names of the guests to the general just before they shook hands.

"You need to write your name on this card," Thomas said to Bartolomé. Andrew, who was escorting a lady, was in the process of presenting his card to the servant.

"I fear I haven't the time," Bartolomé said. He was certain that the name Bartolomé deMelilla would not be recognized. He turned around from his conversation with Thomas just as the general finished greeting Andrew's lady.

"*El Tigre!*" the general fairly shouted, "My friend!" He stepped forward and took Bartolomé's hand as if he were greeting his brother. The general turned to his wife. "My dear, this young man is none other than the Tiger of New Orleans. The slayer of the invaders! The Leonidas of Battery Number One!"

Rachel Jackson gave a respectful curtsy and then offered her hand. "My husband has told me of your exploits many times," she said with a genuine smile.

"Madam," Bartolomé said as he kissed her hand, "the general is generous with his praise. Your husband is the one who stood against the British successfully, which was more than Leonidas did against the Persians."

"El Tigre," the general said, "Please, could you and your friends join us at our table tonight. I have heard that you have successes of your own in the operation of steam-powered shipping. I find the subject very interesting. We must talk about the rivers of Florida."

"Of course, general," Bartolomé said. The general's table was in a prominent location. Thomas, Andrew, and his lady beamed with pride as they gathered around the guest of honor's table.

"I shall not be denied a place on dear Becky's card tonight," Thomas whispered to Bartolomé. Becky was a lady Thomas had been pursuing. She was coy and lovely. Thomas was smitten and showed it.

"She will dance with no other, I am certain," Andrew said. "Invite me to the wedding. I will come all the way from Baltimore to see it."

"See it?" Thomas replied, "I shall condemn you to be my best man."

The night was pleasant enough. Bartolomé danced with several wall-flowers. Thomas did indeed monopolize the lovely Becky.

As the night ended, the general turned to Bartolomé. "What are your plans, sir," he asked, "if I may be so bold as to inquire?"

"I had intended to travel to Baltimore in search of trade opportunities, sir," Bartolomé replied. "Andrew Guthrie has offered accommodations at his home for a fortnight. After that, I'm bound for the National Road through the Cumberland Gap and to the Ohio River. The steamboat *August Moon* will provide my passage back home."

"A lady awaits your return?" Rachel asked with a smile.

A sad shadow passed over Bartolomé's face, which he quickly replaced with a smile. Rachel perceptively regretted the question.

"In fact, there is," Bartolomé said. "Two very young ladies, Oceane and Inez. My sisters are promised presents upon my return."

"It falls right!" the general exclaimed. "We are bound for Baltimore on Monday, another political visit in the midst of Whig territory. Please join us. There is to be another blasted ball."

"I must accept the offer, sir," Bartolomé replied. "Baltimore it shall be."

"Perhaps the general will accept my invitation to sail with us," Andrew said. "We have a vacant stateroom on our schooner."

"I accept your kind offer," Jackson replied.

CHAPTER 17

The trip from Philadelphia to Baltimore was quite pleasant. They traveled on a topsail schooner, one of Andrew's coastal traders. The accommodations were comfortable and the weather cooperated, even though it was the last week of November.

The general was constantly on deck, observing the operation of the vessel with some admiration. Andrew took a turn at the helm, as did Bartolomé. This was Bartolomé's first time in the open sea, though they were never more than a mile or so from land at any time. The unconfined waters allowed full use of the wind, quite different from the narrow, confined waterways of inland navigation.

Baltimore was a city as modern and advanced as any in America. The port was full of shipping, and commerce was conducted at every turn. Andrew delighted in escorting Bartolomé to the coffee shops and ale houses. The general had arranged for quarters at the finest hotel in the city. General Jackson and Rachel visited the many shops. After a day or two, political meetings began to absorb the general's time, so Bartolomé and Andrew began to see less of General Jackson or Rachel.

The ball scheduled for that evening was the talk of the town. Baltimore had performed very well in defense against a British invasion. The prospect of hosting the commanding general of the great victory at New Orleans was an opportunity few would miss.

The newspaper had the event as the headline. The ball was to be Wednesday night, December third, 1817. Along with the particulars of the event was a small listing of those to be in attendance. There were several paragraphs extolling Jackson's exploits in New Orleans and, most recently, in Florida. Several prominent civic and business leaders were also featured. There was even a report that the "Tiger of New Orleans, the Franco Patriot, will be a special guest of the General. Young ladies wishing to practice their French will have the opportunity this night."

Andrew pointed out the report to Bartolomé. "You must not reveal that your English is better than most of the citizens of Baltimore. It will be amusing to hear the candid discussions of the ladies," he said.

"I think not," Bartolomé said. "It will be enough to hear Yankee French attempted."

Andrew laughed, "You will find the French spoken in Baltimore is not very different than your home. Many Acadians have settled here as well."

The sun had barely set when Bartolomé and Andrew made their way to the opera house. Andrew was escorting a lady, Miss Belle, this night, as well. He had bragged to Bartolomé that he had a lady friend in every port on the east coast. Thus far, his boast has been proven true. It was going to be a cold night and everyone hurried to get into the foyer and out of the cold wind.

"El Tigre! Come join us!" It was General Jackson. He was waving Bartolomé to the reception line that was in process in the foyer. Andrew and Miss Belle greeted General Jackson and Rachel, then continued into the ballroom. General Jackson placed Bartolomé next to him so that the servant passing the introductions spoke into Bartolomé's ear.

"*El Tigre*, here is Mister George Craft, his wife Lily Craft, and their daughter, Prudence," the servant read from the card he had been handed. Bartolomé shook the gentleman's hand, and kissed the hands of the ladies while expressing what a pleasure it was to meet them.

Bartolomé then turned to General Jackson and recited; "General Jackson may I introduce Mister George Craft, his wife Lily, and their daughter, Prudence."

The general smiled broadly and said, "Welcome, thank you for coming tonight. Please meet my wife, Rachel." This act was repeated for every person wishing to meet General Jackson.

Between greetings, the general could say only a few words to Rachel or Bartolomé before the next guests were introduced. "You have missed a full half of the guests who are already in the ballroom," Jackson whispered.

"I do apologize, sir," Bartolomé replied. "I misjudged the shipping time between the Guthrie Estate and the Opera House."

The general smiled and retorted, after greeting another august pair, "You will now have to make amends by remaining until the bitter end."

"I am your servant, sir," Bartolomé said with a deep bow.

The last of the guests were welcomed, and the general took Rachel's arm and motioned for Bartolomé and Andrew to follow them into the ballroom. The room had already divided into sides. Young men were to the right, the elders near the doorway, the musicians on the far side of the dance floor, and the ladies were to the left.

Bartolomé approached Andrew, who was in an animated conversation with a group of young men that had gathered around him, when he felt a strange sensation. He turned to look across the dance floor. Servants were busy bringing dance requests to the covey of young ladies, when he saw a red-haired beauty holding her gloved hands to her face. Her green eyes were wide and she appeared to have seen a ghost. There stood Anna Steward!

* * *

Bartolomé strode directly across the floor. *"El Tigre,* where are you going?" He did not heed Andrew's call. Servants scattered to clear his path, and the covey of ladies divided before him, their fans covering their shocked faces. This was a serious breach of protocol. Anna did not move. Bartolomé walked up to her until they were nearly touching.

Anna looked up at him. A tear trickled down her face. "Bartolomé," she said quietly, *"Mi amor. Mi corazon y alma* (My love. My heart and soul). They told me you were killed." She removed the glove from her right hand and gently caressed his scarred face.

"I have come for you, Anna," he said as he pulled her closer to him. She fit into his embrace as if she were sculpted for him alone.

The shocked guests could not believe their eyes. The cold and aloof beauty, Anna Steward, was having a conversation in Spanish with the Tiger of New Orleans. They did not understand a word, but it was obvious that the conversation was intimate. What happened next drew a gasp from the crowd, and a laugh from General Jackson.

Bartolomé kissed Anna full on the mouth. The kiss was earnestly returned. The stuffy protocol of the ball was not just broken; it was smashed.

Bartolomé took Anna's arm into the crook of his elbow and led her across the dance floor through the stunned ball room to General Jackson and Rachel.

"General Jackson," Bartolomé said formally, "Madam Jackson, it is my pleasure to introduce you to my lady, Anna Steward."

"I assume that you are old friends," the general said. His eyes danced with delight. *Oh, to be young,* he thought. "Dear lady," he said, "you have captured the Tiger."

Rachel moved closer to the general as she spoke to Anna. "I am familiar with your plight, dear child," she said.

"Please excuse us, sir," Bartolomé said. "Anna and I would like to retreat into the foyer for a moment."

"We understand, sir," Jackson said. "Please do, by all means."

Bartolomé and Anna walked through the doorway, arm in arm. When they entered the foyer, they resumed their conversation, in Spanish. The doors were not quite closed and many strained to hear what was said.

A desperate search was made for someone who could translate what was being overheard. A servant was found who could. When the orchestra began to play, they were quickly silenced.

"*Anna, he buscado por mucho tiempo,*" Bartolomé whispered as he held Anna close.

"He said that he has searched for her for a long time," the servant said to the crowd.

"*Bartolomé, mis sueños son verdaderos,*" Anna replied. She stroked his face.

"She said that her dreams are made true," the servant translated.

"Now that I have found you, I will not let you go," Bartolomé said.

"You could not drive me away, my love," Anna said. "I still wear the chain that you gave me three years ago this very day. It has bound me to you."

"Will you marry me? Now, tonight?" Bartolomé said. "Will you come with me?"

"I will go with you, even if you do not marry me," Anna said, and she kissed him again.

They returned to the dance hall just as the last translation circled the room. Andrew stepped forward. "It so happens, my friends, that a church is but across the street and a priest is in the rectory."

"Please send for him," Bartolomé said as he looked into Anna's eyes. She gave her consent with a tearful smile.

"Tell him he is to save a man's soul this very night," Bartolomé added.

The priest arrived confused and flustered. When the situation was explained, he began to waiver. "Is this lady of age?" he said.

"Today is the eighteenth anniversary of her birth, sir," Bartolomé said.

"Who gives this lady to this man?" the priest said.

"I give myself," Anna replied. "Conduct the ceremony or I shall leave with him and marry at another time."

"Come with me to the church," the priest said. "There are papers to be written."

Nearly all of the guests trudged across the street to the church. After the somewhat shortened ceremony, the couple completed the paperwork. Andrew Guthrie and General Andrew Jackson signed as witnesses. The entourage returned to the Opera House and the ball resumed as a wedding feast.

The evening was nearly over when Anna's parents arrived. The matron who served as Anna's chaperone had sent for them. They were shocked and hurt by the news that their daughter had married a stranger without so much as a word to them.

Bernard rushed in to discover that it was not a stranger at all who had married his daughter. It was the farm boy from the bayou. He then knew that his lie to Anna had been discovered.

"How could you?" Grace asked. "Without a word to your father and me."

"Mother, I was devastated by your deceit," Anna said. "You both saw how I suffered and yet you continued the lie. Be content that I will forgive you, in time."

"Madam," Bartolomé said, "we are to depart for New Orleans in a week. Until that time, we will visit with you both and young James so that we may part without bitterness. Anna is my wife now, and that will not change as long as I live. I pray you, do be content."

* * *

Bartolomé and Anna stayed in Baltimore for a full two weeks. The fact that Bartolomé was rich, famous, and had powerful friends did much to mollify Anna's parents. Her public elopement was the talk of the town and a source of pride for the local gentry. After all, the ladies of Baltimore were so alluring that even the Tiger of New Orleans was instantly captivated.

None of the chatter mattered to Bartolomé or Anna. They visited the Steward house several times and began to make their good-byes. Bartolomé had business to attend to on the Mississippi River. They began to prepare for the long haul on the National Road through the Cumberland Gap and on to Louisville. It was late December and many of the would-be pilgrims had decided to spend the winter in Baltimore and set out in March.

For several days, Bartolomé and Anna visited the local stores and trail-fitters. Bartolomé had most of the rugged equipment needed for a winter trip, so the activity involved getting cold-weather gear for Anna. In addition to a heavy cloak, Bartolomé insisted that she have a pair of men's boots, long underwear, and men's trousers. He also bought her socks to wear instead of the thin stockings she was accustomed to. He did not admit that he had only just begun to wear socks himself.

"I cannot go about in men's trousers, *novio*," Anna said with a smile.

"I intend for you to wear a dress and cloak over everything, *novia*," he replied. "You will look like a walking *wigwam*, a warm and comfortable *wigwam*."

"And now, a special gift for you," Bartolomé said. He handed Anna something wrapped in a fine leather belt.

She unrolled it. "A knife?" she said in surprise.

"It is a lady's bodkin, *novia*," he corrected. The small stiletto was beautiful. The scabbard and belt were meant for a lady's waist. She drew the blade. It was about nine inches long, six inches of which were fine Spanish steel, razor sharp and double edged. It was no wider than an inch at the hilt. The grip was tightly wrapped in black leather from the diamond butt to the quillion.

"I don't know how to use a knife," she said with a puzzled look.

"That we will correct before we depart, *novia*," Bartolomé said. He considered the use of weapons vital to anyone's basic education. He was not about to allow his wife to go about unarmed and unprepared.

Later that night, lessons in the proper use of the knife in defense began. "Wear the sheath on your left side so that when you draw the blade with your right hand, it is ready to use," Bartolomé said as he guided Anna's hand. He had her grip the handle so that the quillion rested across the base of her thumb and the second knuckle of the forefinger. Held like this, Anna could point with the blade much like a conductor scolding with a wand.

"Never hold the blade forward or away from your body," he demonstrated. "You may put your left hand forward to fend the enemy away or grab him. Keep the knife close to your side until you stab straight ahead. No slashing, just a forward punch. If your attacker should grab your left or rush at you, pull him toward you and punch with the knife."

"Pull him to me?" Anna asked. "Why do that? Is it not better to run away?"

"He would expect that and he would eventually catch you," Bartolomé explained. "To pull an attacker to you would be unexpected. It will be a surprise. An attacker is likely to be larger than you, with a greater reach. If you pull him close, that advantage is gone. The distance you must stab will be shortened and that will reduce his opportunity to block the thrust."

Anna could see that a knife used in this way would be very hard to fend off. After she was comfortable pulling the blade and assuming the guard position, Bartolomé replaced the knife with a small, tightly rolled towel. He then had her practice stabbing and defending until she could deftly drive the rolled towel into his ribs. The lesson deteriorated into a wrestling match, laughing, and finally, lovemaking.

* * *

Anna became accustomed to wearing the delicate stiletto under her cape. She never went out without it. Bartolomé also carried a dagger, the cane sword, and, sometimes, a small pistol. He had one with the new cap lock that did not need a pan primed with dry powder to discharge. Every gentleman in Baltimore went about armed, as did most of the ladies. Bartolomé often commented that he felt more armed with his walking staff than anything else. Anna did not tell him that she had witnessed his fight in the alley. She knew how dangerous he was with a simple walking staff.

The overland route through the Cumberland Gap to Louisville required detailed planning. Unlike river or sea travel, baggage had to be kept at an absolute minimum. The choice of weapons was limited to those essential for the passage through the gap. Bartolomé decided to carry the pistol, a knife, and a hatchet. Anna armed herself with the stiletto. They conferred for hours on the choice of what else to bring. They were to be on horseback, but would have a wagon available. What did not fit in one small trunk would be slung behind the saddle or worn.

The supply wagon carried all the provisions of their fellow travelers. A troop of federal Dragoons had been dispatched to Louisville to join the garrison at a fort there. It was a small force of two dozen men, commanded by a new lieutenant. Dragoons were a rare sight on the National Road, where the mountainous terrain was better suited to infantry than cavalry. Upon General Jackson's recommendation, the lieutenant had invited Bartolomé and Anna to join them for the trip.

Anna and Bartolomé said their good-byes to Anna's family and their host, Andrew Guthrie, at the small way station on the outskirts of Baltimore. The troop had assembled there to prepare for the long trip. It would be six weeks or more before they reached Louisville and the Ohio River, about the end of February.

Anna was an accomplished rider, and she rode in formation next to Bartolomé, who occupied the center of the road just in front of the wagon team. Troopers were stationed before and on both sides of their civilian guests. The National Road was well traveled and it was punctuated with many way stations, and even an inn every now and then.

The first leg of the trip went well. Even though it was winter, the small force occasionally met other travelers along the road. Those bound for Baltimore gave reports of the road conditions ahead. Most of the winter travelers to Louisville were much slower than the fast-moving troop of

Dragoons. These would pull to one side of the narrow road, when conditions permitted, to allow the troop to pass.

The people they met were concerned about the news of the Seminole War. The Seminole in Florida reminded people of the Creek Nation's Red Stick rebellion a few years before. It had raised fears among travelers even this far north. Runaway slaves, renegades, and some Cherokee and other southeastern tribes had formed their own loose alliance in Spanish Florida. Napoleon had left Spain destitute, and it had no resources to properly garrison Florida. The land had become a lawless region. The British operated there freely, providing guns and sowing discontent among the renegades. Raids into Georgia, and even Tennessee, had become too common. General Jackson had sworn to end the raids, and the resulting Seminole War was now in full bloom. All the travelers were happy to see an army troop, and the little band was often greeted with huzzahs.

Most nights were spent in trail camps. The troop was well provisioned, and accomplished at camp living. Bartolomé had provided a personal donation to help fund the force, as money from the federal government was notoriously slow to arrive. The cold nights were no match for the heavy blankets and tightly closing tents the wagon carried. Way stations, when they were found, provided wooden walls, dirt floors, and a dry place to spread a blanket before a hearth.

They had begun the downward leg of the trip when a young man rode up to the troop. "Sir, sir, you must help," he pleaded to Lieutenant Adams. "There's some kind of a fight going on ahead of us. We have heard several gunshots."

"Ahead of who? How many gunshots?" the lieutenant asked. The boy was part of a small caravan that was about two miles ahead. The shots and yells came from around a bend in the road. The boy didn't know much except that they were afraid.

"Sergeant Cahill, you and Fisher stay with the wagon and our guests," the lieutenant ordered. "Continue as best you can. I'll take the rest of the troop up ahead to see what we are up against." He then ordered the troop ahead at a gallop.

Bartolomé didn't like splitting up the troop, but the wagon was too slow and he understood the lieutenant's reasoning. Anna's horse had been acting lame and she had taken a seat on the wagon next to the driver, Trooper Billy Whittington. Her horse was tethered, and trailed behind the covered wagon. Bartolomé assumed a position on the left front. Sergeant Cahill took the center and Trooper Fisher took the right. They continued at a reasonable pace down the steep grade of the road. The road was very narrow and winding at this point. They listened as the rest of the troop disappeared ahead.

CHAPTER 18

Tall Wolf watched as the band of mounted men rode by. He knew where they were headed. He and four others had broken away from a group of renegades that had just attacked a caravan. The defenders were able to arrange a strong position on the far side of the road, and he had told the others that it would be a waste of time to try and attack, but they rejected his advice. Now more were rushing to help the defenders.

"See, the others will now have to flee for their lives," he said to the four who stayed with him. "You must have a plan before you attack."

They rested for a while. They were in a desperate way. Game was scarce along the road, for every traveler foraged for fresh meat. There had been little to eat for days. They had been traveling south for a month, to join the Red Stick remnants. Now they were hungry, cold, and tired. Then Tall Wolf saw the wagon and a small vanguard.

"Now we will eat," he said. "It is five against four. If we take the wagon, the other three must come at us. I will send an arrow into the driver. Padum, you must rush the driver if he is not killed. Bricks, you will go around the wagon, pull the woman off, and attack the driver from the other side."

Tall Wolf did not yet completely trust Bricks. He had joined the band of renegades only a week ago. Bricks had been traveling north when he came into Tall Wolf's camp. He told Tall Wolf that a woman came to him in a dream and said that Tall Wolf would lead him to a great reward. Because of a dream, this runaway was going to turn around and trudge back south from where he came. He claimed that a spirit called Kalfu was his protector.

"Kalfu told me in a dream that no man could stab Bricks, no man could put an arrow or bullet into Bricks, no man could harm Bricks in any way," the runaway bragged to the camp. Tall Wolf was suspicious of dreamers, so he gave Bricks a part that was not critical to the plan.

"Ming," Tall Wolf continued, "you will run to the rear of the wagon and climb on. Make certain no one is in the bed. Cheche, you will come with me to the rear of the wagon. Ming will join us if there are no men in the rear of the wagon. When the driver is dead, it will be five against three and we will have the wagon to hide behind. They will not know how many we are. The narrow road will hinder the horses. The three will have to come at us in the open or run away. If they come at us, we will shoot them down before they can get close to us. Then we will eat and maybe sell the woman, later."

It was a good plan. Mounted men on the steep, narrow road were at a disadvantage to men in cover and armed with bows.

When they had moved into position, Tall Wolf let fly an arrow at Billy Whittington and they all rushed forward with a whoop.

* * *

Madam Barbeaux had gathered a few of her most trusted followers in the small altar room at the front of her house. Standing near the altar was the slave, John, the carpenter of the Poche plantation. He was big, wide, and strong. He had come straight from Africa as a small boy. Now he was a skilled carpenter. His owner had turned down a five thousand dollar offer for him. On the other side of the altar was Elisa Ferrier. Elisa was a free man of color and owned his own blacksmith's shop near the lower end of Rampart Street. Elisa was powerfully built, with broad shoulders and massive forearms.

Two women slaves occupied the first chairs. Della and Rosa were trusted house slaves, the property of two different families in New Orleans. They were also apprentices of Madam Barbeaux. Seated in the chairs behind Della and Rosa were two white aristocrat ladies of the city. One was a young, dark-haired Creole who nervously fanned her face. The other was an elderly lady dressed in mourning black and fully veiled. The ladies were to be witnesses to the ceremony. The men were "champions." Their job was to protect those in attendance from Madam Barbeaux.

Today, Madam Barbeaux was going to perform the ritual of *monter* with a loa. She had performed *monter* many times. Today was different in one way only. She was going to invite evil Loa Kalfu to occupy her body.

In a *monter*, the mambo invites possession by a selected loa. The normal ceremony would require contact with Legba, the gatekeeper, to receive permission to invite the loa chosen for the *monter*. But Kalfu was a gatekeeper, as well. He controlled access to those desiring less than honorable favors from the spirit world.

The loa would accept the invitation if the mambo had a special experience to share. When in possession of a mambo, a loa could taste, feel, and experience physical pleasures through the host's senses. A possessed mambo could perform many strange contortions and consume vast quantities of food and drink with out feeling anything. The loa felt it all.

Madam Barbeaux was going to offer Kalfu rum and the *Tchmench*-aged ham. She lit the candles, sipped some rum, and began the incantation.

"Kalfu, evil one," she prayed. "I have rum for you and blood-red ham filled with vapors from the *Tchmench* tree."

The "champions" bracketed Barbeaux, ready to restrain her if she should break for the women. Elisa held a bucket of water. He could break the possession by pouring the water in Barbeaux's face.

The mambo's eyes fluttered, and her arms and legs began to twist as if someone was attempting to dislocate every limb. Her joints seemed to dislocate and her body twisted until her arms and legs formed impossible angles. Even in this contorted condition, she began to eat the red, aged meat. Every bite elicited a moan of pleasure. She drank rum from a bucket until more than a gallon had been consumed.

This went on for a full hour, until all of the ham had been eaten. There must have been fifteen pounds of meat. Then Kalfu left. Madam Barbeaux fell to the floor, moaning as her limbs slowly returned to normal.

Elisa and John helped her to her feet. She was drenched in sweat, breathing heavily. Though tired, she showed no signs of the vast quantities of rum and meat she had just consumed.

"Kalfu has gone," she said. Those in attendance began to talk all at once. The veiled lady did not say a word. She sat unmoving in her chair. Barbeaux showed no sign of ill effects from the great quantity of food and potent drink, or the impossible contortions. Her followers gathered around her, embracing, kissing, reassuring.

"I have done what must be done," Madam Barbeaux said.

* * *

The arrow caught Billy Whittington in the left bicep. He had been in the act of slapping the reigns and his arm covered his chest. The arrow passed through his arm and grazed his chest.

"Look out, Miss Anna," Billy yelled and he gave her a push away from him. Anna jumped down and ran toward the rear of the wagon only to meet the runaway, Bricks, as he rushed toward the front. He raised his club to strike the woman. He expected her to turn and run. He planned to kill the driver and then collect the woman later. To his surprise, she didn't turn away from him and run; she rushed straight at him. She grabbed a fold in his cloak with her left hand and began to punch him in the chest with her right. They both fell to the ground and rolled until they were under the wagon, with Bricks on top.

Why is she punching me? Bricks thought. Her blows were light. Bricks laughed until he realized that she wasn't punching him. She was stabbing him! He tried to raise up to hit her with his club, but his head struck the bottom of the wagon. Anna took advantage of the opening and stabbed up into the runaway's throat. The narrow blade drove into the man's brain and he fell dead on top of Anna.

Ming ran to the rear of the wagon. He could see Padum struggling with the white man. He had to hurry. The wagon was still rolling, and he attempted to climb on the rear gate. He stepped on something and felt a slap on his leg. He looked down at Bricks on the ground.

What is he doing on the ground? Ming thought as he tried to get up on the wagon. He slipped on something and tried to climb on again. Again, he slipped down. The rear of the wagon was awash with blood. Then he felt something warm flowing down his leg. He looked to see a river of blood gushing from his leg. He grabbed the wound and looked at Bricks. Then he saw the woman under Bricks. She had a knife.

The wench stabbed me, Ming thought. He pulled his own knife and rushed toward Anna, only to fall inches from her. He mumbled something and was silent.

Things had not gone as Tall Wolf had planned. He and Cheche gathered behind the wagon ready to ambush the riders. He expected the other renegades to join them, but there were no others. He knew that it was two against three now. They still had the advantage. The two renegades prepared to send a volley of arrows at the mounted men, who were now only yards away.

Tall Wolf hid against the rear of the wagon. He had an arrow nocked and was ready to fell the rider he heard approaching. As soon as the horse began to pass the wagon, Tall Wolf let fly. The arrow passed over an empty saddle. Then he saw a white man with a scarred face. He saw no more.

Bartolomé had leapt from the horse as he came abreast of the wagon, for he did not trust his riding skills in any kind of a fight. He saw an Indian fire an arrow over the saddle. The Indian looked astonished when Bartolomé struck him full on the face with a hatchet. The hatchet lodged in the man's head, so Bartolomé threw the body into the other renegade who was preparing to fire an arrow at one of the troopers.

The renegade turned to see what had fallen into him. Bartolomé drew a pistol from his belt and fired into the man's face just as Trooper Fisher slashed the man across the neck. The shot was at such close range that the man's headscarf caught fire and smoldered. Sergeant Cahill emerged from the rear of the wagon and tossed a body to the ground. He had dispatched the renegade who was struggling with the wounded Whittington.

Bartolomé was terrified for the first time in his life. "Anna," he cried out. "Anna, where are you?"

"*Estoy aquí*," a voice called back. She sounded far away.

"I see her," Trooper Fisher yelled. He was the only one still mounted, and he rode up to what looked like a pile of clothes in the middle of the road. Fisher dismounted, and rolled over the body of an Indian. The body was ashen and the man had died gripping his groin. He could see Anna's red hair. He rolled over the other body, a black man with a gaping gash in his throat.

Anna stood up just as Bartolomé reached them. "Thank you, Trooper Fisher," she said as she straightened her blood-soaked dress. Her hair, face, and shoulders were covered in blood that steamed in the cold air.

"Anna, are you hurt?" Bartolomé said as he quickly hugged her. He and Fisher began to search her for wounds. They both knew that the wounded often feel nothing at first.

"I am not hurt, husband," she said. She calmly reached down and cleaned her stiletto with the edge of one of the dead men's coat. She sheathed the blade and looked into Bartolomé's eyes. Then she began to shake violently. Bartolomé held her tightly until the shaking passed.

"Your blood is still up," he said. "Many experience such a thing after a fight." Bartolomé attempted to wipe the blood from Anna with a bandana. When he had cleaned her as much as he could, he tossed it onto the road.

* * *

Whittington was badly hurt. The feathered end of the arrow was exposed on the outside of the man's arm. The shaft had passed through the man's arm into his side and skipped along the ribs. The arrow head protruded from his chest. His arm was pinned to his side. The thick clothes had helped. Anna hurriedly climbed onto the wagon to tend to Whittington. He had fallen back in the bed of the wagon. It was hard to find room for him to lie because of all the gear. She attempted to stop the bleeding, and Bartolomé joined her.

"We need to draw the arrow out," he said. He took out his knife and broke the arrowhead off where it protruded from the wound. Bartolomé carefully shaved the splintered end until it was smooth. He then managed to find a bottle of whiskey in the stack of stores.

"Take a pull on this," he said to Whittington. Whittington took a big gulp. Bartolomé then poured some of the whiskey on the shaft of the arrow and the wounds it had made. Anna held the trooper's head as Bartolomé pulled the shaft out of the man's chest and arm.

"The whiskey will chase away the evil spirits," Bartolomé said. "A doctor told me that once and it worked for me." He poured some more whiskey on the wounds in Whittington's arm and chest. Then he gave the rest of the bottle to Whittington.

"I'll stay with him a while," Anna said. "I can comfort his head as we travel."

Bartolomé nodded in assent and joined the others who were collecting the horses and debris from the fight.

It had begun to snow. "Let us move the bodies off the road before they are covered," Sergeant Cahill said. The men pulled the bodies, one at a time, until all five lined the edge of the roadway.

Lieutenant Adams rode up with the troop. They had easily overpowered the renegades and rescued the cornered travelers. The renegades who were not killed had been captured, trussed up, and left in the care of a small militia party that had come up from a nearby hamlet to joint the fight.

"Sergeant Cahill, what has happened here?" Adams asked when he halted by the wagon. The sergeant made a full report of the fight to the lieutenant, while Trooper Fisher filled in the enlisted men. The sergeant's report was short and factual. Trooper Fisher's story was much more graphic. He explained how Anna had killed two of the renegades with the little knife she carried, and *El Tigre* had slain another two while the fifth was dispatched by Whittington and Cahill. His description, which drew a nervous laugh from the huddled troop, emphasized the condition of the second man Anna had killed.

The lieutenant had the men tie ropes to the feet of the bodies, and hung them from the trees along the road. He said it was to keep the animals from eating the bodies until the local militia could bury them. As this was taking place, the group of travelers the troop had passed some hours ago came upon the sight.

They spoke in hushed German as the men, women, and children studied the bodies that hung by the feet from the roadside trees. It was decided that they would stay with the troop.

Other travelers joined the caravan as they continued on to Louisville, and the troopers slowed their pace so everyone could keep up. Word had spread of the fight at the Gap, and fear was mounting that there were other renegades about.

Anna turned to Bartolomé as she held tight to his arm. "I am ashamed of myself," she said.

"There is nothing to ashamed of, *novia*," Bartolomé said as he kissed her temple. "You had to kill them to save yourself."

"I am not ashamed for having killed them, *novio*," she said as she stared at the hanging corpses. "I am ashamed of how much I hate them, even now, for forcing me to do this terrible thing."

"It is not wise to hate an enemy, *novia*," Bartolomé said. "Hate clouds the mind. It may make you vulnerable. If you must kill, do so quickly and as violently as you can. As for these men, they are beyond hate."

Anna noticed that the men were much more respectful of her, not that they had ever been rude. It was just that they seemed reverent and very formal when they spoke with her now. Bartolomé had grown accustomed to this sort of deference, but it was new to Anna.

Some of the women in the ever-growing caravan offered to tend to Whittington so that Anna could ride a horse. Another trooper had been assigned to drive the wagon, so there was a good mount to spare. Bartolomé rode next to Anna, but they spoke very little.

Bartolomé was proud of Anna. He was relieved that she had reacted as he had taught. Her experience with weapons was limited. It bothered him that Anna had depended so much on the little training that he had been able to provide. What if it had been the wrong thing to do?

His instinct guided them to the center of the road where they would be furthest from ambush. He would have to teach her a little every day, as his grandfather had taught him.

They made it to a small town before nightfall. The streets were crowded with travelers, and the camping lots at each end of town were filled with tents and wagons. The troop moved to the western end of town and began to pitch camp. As they were doing so, a group of townsfolk introduced themselves to Lieutenant Adams.

After a short conversation, Adams turned to Bartolomé. "*El Tigre*," he said, "these folks have offered you and your lady a room in their inn. Mister

Goodly here owns it. It is well built and even has a wooden floor. If you refuse, I think he may be offended."

Bartolomé looked at Anna. She was disheveled and covered with dried blood. And she was beautiful.

"Sir," he said, "I should like that very much, but I do not want to put anyone out. I will pay the normal fee."

"Sir," Mister Goodly replied. "A room was reserved for you and your wife the moment the news of the fight at the Gap reached our ears. It is our gift to you. I pray, do accept. Those renegades have been of great mischief lately. We are grateful to be shed of them."

"Go, sir," Adams said. "The troop will wait for you in the morning."

The inn was Spartan compared to the hotels in Baltimore, but quite lavish by frontier standards. Anna and Mrs. Goodly excused themselves and disappeared into a back room. Bartolomé and several townsfolk visited in the big room which served as a tavern. The story of the fight had to be repeated many times. Another tale was to be memorized and repeated as if it were an epic poem. Bartolomé thought of his grandfather's many tales. He wondered how many he would collect. No more, he hoped.

Anna and Mrs. Goodly reappeared. Anna had washed her hair and cleaned up as much as she could. Her cloak and outer garments were being washed. Tonight, she would sleep in a warm bed with her husband. A wave of relaxation swept over her. Now it was Anna's turn to tell the tale to a rapt audience. Bartolomé listened intently as Anna painted the picture of her desperate fight, a fight that had taken place out of his view.

Finally, with reluctance, Bartolomé and Anna retreated from the big room to the sleeping quarters in the rear of the combination inn and ale-house. They slept well for a while, but Anna awoke twice with a start. Bartolomé comforted her each time with assurances that the nightmares would end. He hoped that would be the case. He still occasionally dreamed of the look of rage on the British soldier's face as he drove the *magado* into his neck. He never told Anna this.

CHAPTER *19*

The next day, all were up with the sun. Bartolomé and Anna felt rested and eager to continue to Louisville. They rejoined the troop of Dragoons and the growing caravan. The day was clear and cold. Everyone bustled about. There was a week's worth of travel left to reach Louisville. Most in the caravan were destined for points much further west. Bartolomé looked forward to the comforts of travel on a Cathay Steamboat.

"Good morning," Lieutenant Adams greeted the deMelillas as they came into the camp. "Mister Goodly tells me that the local store has sold all of the daggers and knives they had in stock. It seems that the ladies of the caravan have decided that a blade is in fashion for the National Road."

"It is wise to be prepared," Bartolomé said. "It is not enough to arm. The ladies need to know how to use their decorations."

They were happy to see that Trooper Whittington was able to continue the trip. They had worried that he might have to convalesce for some time. That was not the case, for Whittington was slumped on top of the baggage in a crudely formed perch while Trooper Snyder drove. A young German girl from the caravan that joined them just after the fight was sitting next to Whittington to tend him on the road. The man reveled in the attention.

"This trip will not be long enough to please young Billy," Bartolomé whispered to Anna. They both smiled at the beaming trooper. The horrors of the fight at the Gap had begun to fade away.

Louisville was as busy as Bartolomé remembered it. After all, it was only last summer when he had left it for Pittsburgh. John Bucklin met the caravan at the town's edge. The fight at the Gap was the talk of Louisville. A somewhat romanticized version of the incident had even been published in the Louisville Gazette.

"My dear," Bartolomé said, "I would like you to meet John Bucklin, a business associate of Cathay Steamboats here in Louisville."

John kissed the back of Anna's hand. "It is a pleasure to meet you, madam," he said. "Louisville is open to you. I have a buggy here for your use and I have reserved a room for you both at Hotel Ohio, the very best in town."

"When is the *August Moon* scheduled to dock?" Bartolomé asked.

"In three days," Bucklin said. "You will be able to see her dock from the balcony of your hotel room. The office that you requested has been furnished and a clerk, sent up from New Orleans by Mister Livingston, has been busy arranging schedules."

"You will have to introduce me to the clerk, as I do not know the gentleman Mister Livingston has hired for the position," Bartolomé said. He had been moving so fast that he had only been able to send letters to New Orleans from the many towns that he visited. Correspondence to him simply could not catch up. He felt a little out of touch.

"The man's name is Pierre Barbe. His English is very good; better than mine," Bucklin replied. "We can go by the office now, if you would like."

Barbe! Bartolomé thought. *Could it be?* Barbe was an alias often used by Dominique Youx. It was not possible that Dominique Youx could pose as a clerk. He was well known and weathered. Bartolomé dismissed it as a coincidence.

"I think we will settle in at the hotel this afternoon and we can visit Mister Barbe tomorrow," Bartolomé said. He could see that Anna was exhausted and could use a little rest.

The troopers located Anna's small trunk and the rest of Bartolomé's gear in the pile of goods in the wagon, and transferred it to the back of the buggy Mister Bucklin had provided. It was a two-bench buggy, so there was ample room for everything. Anna's horse was recovering, but not yet ready to ride. It, along with Bartolomé's mount, was tethered to the back of the buggy. The hotel had a livery stable that would care for the animals. They would sell both of the horses to the stable owner, at a buyer's price, before boarding the *August Moon*.

Parting with the troop and the impromptu caravan was a boisterous affair. Mister Bucklin handled the reins as they rode along the column of the caravan. Bartolomé and Anna sat on the second bench seat. As they passed this group or that, a great huzzah would be called. Lieutenant Adams saluted with his saber and every trooper waved his hat, including Whittington, who had recovered enough to ride on the wagon's bench.

The room at the Hotel Ohio had a large bed, an armoire, a small writing desk, and chamber pots in night stands on both sides of the bed. Anna removed her riding cloak and boots, and flopped down on the top of the bed covers. Bartolomé busied himself with hanging clothes from the trunk so they might air out a little. When he turned to talk to Anna, he saw that she was sound asleep. He pushed her over to make room for himself and quickly joined her in sleep. They did not awake until sunrise the next morning, Wednesday.

* * *

The hotel had a small dining area where a breakfast of ham and greens was available. After eating, Bartolomé and Anna crossed the street to the Louisville office of Cathay Steamboats. Pierre Barbe was there. He was a young and bright man, in his twenties or so.

"*Monsieur et Madame deMelilla!*" Barbe called out as soon as the couple had entered the office. Mister Bucklin had advised Barbe that Bartolomé was traveling with his wife. He continued in French, "I am Pierre Barbe, the Louisville shipping director for Cathay Steamboats. The adjoining office is yours, *Monsieur deMelilla*, whenever you are in Louisville. I have been holding some correspondence for you. You will find it on the desk."

Finally, somebody had addressed him by his name. "Thank you, Pierre," Bartolomé said. "If you can, sir, please use English. We will be shipping for Americans in America. You will need to be fluent in the language of America." He examined the man closely. "Now tell me if your father's name is Dominique." The resemblance was very strong.

Pierre cast a glance at Anna.

"My wife knows all there is to know about me. I have no secrets from her," Bartolomé said.

"I am Pierre Youx, as you have guessed," he admitted. His English was good enough. "My father and uncles have decided that I am better suited for this business than any other."

"This business will suit you well, if you work at it," Bartolomé said. "Now tell me about the shipping schedule you have arranged."

The three gathered around a table where Pierre spread out the schedule he had devised. Anna was interested in Cathay Steamboats and Bartolomé's role in that business. She was insightful and a quick study, so Bartolomé included her in his work as much as possible.

"You are well suited for this business, Pierre," Bartolomé said when the review of the schedule had been completed. "Anna, please hand me the Baltimore papers."

Anna handed a packet of papers they had carried in the trunk from Baltimore. It contained shipping contracts for a conglomerate of overland freight haulers that were originally destined for St. Louis. Cathay Steamboats would load the freight in Louisville and steam down the Ohio, then offload it to wait for the *Evening Star*. She would load the cargo and bring it up the Mississippi to St. Louis while the *August Moon* continued on to New Orleans. The shipment would be in St. Louis in about a third of the time it would have taken to make the trip overland.

"Here are some more orders that need to be accommodated," Bartolomé said as he handed the packet to Pierre.

"I am glad that we have added another boat to the Ohio Valley," Pierre said. "It is the *South Wind*. She is a sternwheeler and can carry twice the freight of the *August Moon*. I will see to these orders immediately."

"Anna and I will go over the correspondence that has collected," Bartolomé said as he rose to go into the adjoining office. "After that, I shall ask that you book us on the *August Moon* for her return trip to New Orleans."

Pierre rose, "Sir, it has already been done. I received word of your pending arrival some days ago." Pierre paused. He added, "Sir, my father has spoken often of your courage at the rampart. I do not intend to flatter, but the reports of the fight at the Gap have indicated to me that you have married well."

Anna blushed at the compliment. "Sir," she said, "I assure you, I am no heroine. I was just trying to stay alive."

Bartolomé gave Anna a knowing look, and a smile. He took her hand and led her into the adjoining office, closing the door behind them. Once the door was closed, he kissed her deeply.

"Lets get to work," he said.

The correspondence was piled high. Anna opened the curtains to let more light in and then they sorted through the papers to separate personal letters from Cathay Steamboats' business.

As Bartolomé read one of the letters, his face became ashen.

"What is it, *novio?*" Anna asked.

"This letter is from the priest at Terre Aux Boeufs," Bartolomé said sadly. "He says that my mother has died."

Anna leaned over and held Bartolomé. She could not think of anything to say.

"We shall be off for New Orleans on the *August Moon* by this time tomorrow," Bartolomé said.

CHAPTER 20

Thursday, February nineteen, 1818, broke bright and clear. Bartolomé and Anna were on the balcony to their room when the sun rose over the Ohio River. They paused to enjoy the scene. It was comforting to know that the long, overland trip from Baltimore to Louisville was finished. It had been harrowing and laborious.

"We can load our goods after breakfast, *novia*," Bartolomé said. He held Anna close to him as they enjoyed the view in the morning breeze. It was cold, and Bartolomé had wrapped a blanket around them both. Anna's red hair wafted across his face. He drank in her scent, reluctant to end the moment.

"The *August Moon* is scheduled to arrive sometime today," he continued. "It will take hours to offload goods and people. Then she will take on provisions and fuel. Then all the goods bound for downriver will be loaded. That leaves us the morning to take in the sights."

"This sight is enough for me, *novio*," Anna said dreamily. "Perhaps, we might go by the post and take our leave of the Dragoons that escorted us here?"

Bartolomé smiled. The proposal was proper and thoughtful. "It is right that we do so," he said. "We shared a desperate battle. That will bind us as comrades forever."

Just as they were preparing to go in, Bartolomé noticed a thin trail of smoke to the southwest. He looked closer and he could see a dark, square shape on the river.

"Here she comes now, *novia*," he said as he pointed out the distant shape. "I will wager that the distant object we see is the *August Moon*."

"If it is, she must have run at night," Anna said. She remembered hearing Bartolomé say that steamboats often tied up to the bank at nightfall rather than run in the dark.

"The moon was nearly full last night," Bartolomé replied. "It was clear enough to run all night."

They left the balcony and finished dressing. In a few moments, they had loaded the single trunk and were prepared to depart. They went down into the lobby.

"Please see to it that our trunk is delivered to the *August Moon*," Bartolomé told the clerk. Then he and Anna departed for the stables. The stable hand took only a few minutes to hitch a horse to the buggy that John Bucklin had loaned them. The trip to the small redoubt that was locally called a "fort" was over in twenty minutes. The troop of Dragoons had formed up for morning muster just as Bartolomé and Anna came through the open gate.

"Troop," Lieutenant Adams barked. "Atten–TION. Sergeant Cahill, POST!"

Sergeant Cahill spurred his mount to the front-center of the line of troopers and halted with a salute.

Adams returned the salute and then rode over to the buggy. "Come to say good-bye, *El Tigre?*" Adams said with a sad smile.

"We have, lieutenant," Bartolomé said. "We are bound for New Orleans on the *August Moon*. We depart before one in the afternoon."

"Well then, climb down and we will say farewell," Adams said. Then, out of the corner of his mouth he ordered, "Sergeant Cahill, have the troop dismount."

Cahill drew a breath and then ordered, "Troop, Dis–MOUNT."

The troopers dismounted and stationed themselves each at the head of his mount. Bartolomé and Anna walked over to Sergeant Cahill and then to each trooper in turn. Bartolomé shook each hand and Anna curtsied.

To each, Bartolomé said, "Sir, I was honored to ride with you." Anna said, "We shall miss your company."

Trooper Billy Whittington, who was wounded at the Gap, was the last to say good-bye. "Take care, ma'am," was about all he could muster up.

Bartolomé and Anna returned to the buggy. Lieutenant Adams ordered the troop to mount and Bartolomé drove the buggy before the formed Dragoons as if performing a military inspection. The troop gave three huzzahs as the buggy passed the formation and out of the fort.

Bartolomé looked at Anna. Her eyes were damp. "You shall never form friendships as deep and as quickly as amongst comrades in arms," he said.

"As are we, *novio*," Anna said.

Anna took his arm and put her head on his shoulder as they returned to the Louisville dock and the *August Moon*.

The bustle about the dock was hectic. Being a side-wheeler, the *August Moon* had moored by the bow. The shallow water next to the pier would have damaged the side-wheel paddles had she docked by the beam. Dock workers were hustling cargo off along two gangplanks that connected the dock to the boat's deck.

Bartolomé and Anna had gone by Mister Bucklin's office to say farewell. Mister Bucklin sent a stable hand to accompany them to the dock, help with transferring their things to the boat, and return the buggy. When Bartolomé and Anna approached the boat, the dock workers ceased their activity and stood aside so the couple could board without having to push their way through. Every man removed his hat as Anna passed by. They had all heard the report of the fight at the Gap.

Bartolomé lead Anna up a stairway to the passenger deck, and then forward and up to the pilothouse.

"*El Tigre*," said a jovial bearded man. "I am Captain Donaldson, David Donaldson, at your service."

"A pleasure to meet you, sir," Bartolomé replied. "May I introduce my wife, Anna deMelilla."

Anna offered her hand, palm down, which the surprised boat captain kissed.

"Pardon me, madam," Donaldson said. "I was not aware that *El Tigre* was married."

"The captain of this boat was Mister Albert Christen when I left her last fall," Bartolomé said. "I hope that he is well."

"He is well, indeed, sir," Donaldson replied. "He is now the master of the *South Wind*. We will pass her at some time on our way downriver. You will see what a fine boat she is."

"I assume that the berth just aft of yours is available," Bartolomé said. He liked the cabin and it had enough room for two.

"It is, sir." Donaldson said. "I have orders that it is to be reserved for you or other officers of Cathay Steamboats at all times. Let me show you some of the additions that have been made since your last accommodation."

A high rail now circled the roof of the passenger berths so that people could take in the sights along the river. One need only climb one the stairways to the pilothouse doors and then, instead of turning in, continue aft to access this new observation area. The passenger deck had been expanded aft so that the dining lounge was lengthened. The meals that were served were mostly stews, hardtack, and smoked meats. Passengers would easily obtain food along the way. The boat would land daily, sometimes several times a day, to take on fuel or cargo. These impromptu ports often had a farmer or his wife selling vegetables and prepared foods.

* * *

Travel on the *August Moon* was not luxurious or as roomy as an ocean-going ship, but it was infinitely more comfortable than trudging along a mud and plank road. Passengers could not go below to the main deck, as it was crammed with cargo of all sorts. A spiral staircase led from the rear of the new dining area to the "conveniences." The stairway ended in a narrow alley of cargo on one side and a wall of four doors on the other. Each door opened to a small cubical with a wooden seat. The river water could be seen through the hole in the seat.

At one in the afternoon, the *August Moon* slipped her moorings and began down the Ohio River. Bartolomé and Anna had joined the captain in the pilothouse. The man at the helm was an apprentice named Joshua.

"I feel as if I'm flying," Anna said as the wind rushed through the open pilothouse window and blew her hair in a long, red stream.

"I'd estimate we are doing ten knots. Add to that a river current of three knots and you can understand why the shore seems to run by. If all goes right, we will make New Orleans in eight days. Less, if the nights are clear, for the moon will be full tomorrow night and we can run all night," Donaldson said.

There were a few stops on the Ohio River. At every one, something was unloaded and something else added to the freight. Each stop had a gaggle of folks selling foodstuffs or arranging shipments. Sometimes, a passenger would depart or another come aboard. A tally clerk busily logged all on and off, both passengers and cargo. He was writing on a large slate in chalk.

"Why, sir, do you not enter the tally into a book using ink and quill?" she inquired. Anna had leafed through some of the large tally books at the Louisville office. She wondered how the clerks were able to enter all of the information in the books so neatly.

"Madam," he replied, flattered that the lady was interested in his work, "these notes are temporary. Once we are underway, I will retire to my cabin. At my desk and out of the weather and river spray, I will transcribe what is noted in chalk into the bound tally book."

He then made a series of coded marks by an item to indicate that it had been offloaded in good condition and that the recipient or a stockman ashore had accepted it. Rural landings handled the cargo from many farms, stores, or people living in the vicinity. Not everyone could be present to receive their shipment. A stockman, often a nearby resident, would be entrusted with receiving the shipment and paying the bill.

They reached the Mississippi in only two days. The landing at the confluence of the two great rivers was no more than a cluster of tents. Cargo from Louisville and destined for St. Louis was being stored there until the *Evening Star*, bound for St. Louis, could take it on. Other cargo destined for Louisville awaited similar transport. In a few short years, upstream shipping had been completely captured by the steamboats. Downriver barges, though reduced in number, continued to travel, one way, on the rivers.

In less than an hour, all shore business was concluded and the *August Moon* continued down the Mississippi River. Bartolomé and Anna had settled in the dining area to visit with some new passengers who had come aboard at the "canvas" landing. Paul Shaw, a merchant, his wife, Prudence, and their daughter, Elizabeth, who was about ten or so, had boarded, bound for Vicksburg. Anna enjoyed the company of Prudence and Elizabeth. Until they boarded, Anna had been the only woman aboard.

A deckhand came in and announced, "*El Tigre*, the captain presents his compliments and asks if you and the lady could come up to the helm. He says that the *South Wind* is on the horizon."

"Tell him that we are coming. See if there is room for a few others, as well," Bartolomé answered. He took Anna's hand and placed it in the crook of his elbow and turned to the Shaws, saying, "Please join us if you would like to see the *South Wind.*"

"How can you see a south wind?" Elizabeth asked. Her eyes were wide with wonder.

"She is a steamboat, my dear," Anna replied. "I am told she is twice the size of the *August Moon.*"

Paul and Prudence declined, satisfied to watch the passing through the window. They permitted young Elizabeth to go to the pilothouse in Anna's care.

Bartolomé hoisted Elizabeth up onto a cabinet top so she could see well ahead down the wide Mississippi River. In the distance, they could see what appeared to be a square house, streaming smoke. It quickly grew until the shape of a wide and tall steamboat filled their view.

"Say hello, Joshua" Captain Donaldson said.

Joshua pulled a rope that was hanging near his left. A loud whistle sounded and Elizabeth covered her ears. One long pull, a pause, and then another. They could see a spout of steam issue from the top of the *South Wind* as she answered with the same signal. It took only a few seconds for the sound to reach them.

"We shall pass her holding to our starboard. She shall do the same," Donaldson explained. "It has become a habit on the river that all traffic will bear to the starboard."

The *South Wind* fairly flew by, no more than two hundred feet away.

"I'll wager she is doing ten knots against the current," the captain said.

The boat was driven by a single great paddlewheel in the stern. She was the first sternwheeler Bartolomé had seen underway. A large swell of foaming water came off the paddles and the rhythmic churn of the drive piston intermingled with the sound of water. Passengers on the top deck, all smiles, waved their hats and handkerchiefs to those on the *August Moon*. In what seemed an instant, she had passed. Joshua turned the helm to the port so that the *August Moon* would take the passing wake head on. A few bumps, and he turned to the starboard again.

"I shall never forget such a grand sight," Elizabeth said.

"Nor I," said Anna. She reflected on her many conversations with Bartolomé about the new age of rapid communications. In as little time as a week, news, goods, and people could be transported from the heart of the continent to the coast. Communication is the foundation on which to build a great country, Bartolomé often said. The Romans did it. Now it was America's turn.

CHAPTER 21

Vicksburg was reached in a few days. There, the Shaws disembarked and the boat began to take on bales of cotton. Even though it was the last week of February and the cotton fields were newly planted, many farmers kept shipments of cotton in reserve to get a better price. The ships in New Orleans bound for France and even England would not have a full cargo this time of the year were it not for such reserved cotton.

Two more days of travel, and the *August Moon* docked at a small landing not far above Baton Rouge.

"Take a walk with me, *novia*," Bartolomé said. "The boat will be here for an hour and there is something I want you to see."

Anna took Bartolomé's hand as he led her down the gangplank and up a steep trail. They stopped at the top where a wooded plateau spread back from the top of the bluff, a hundred feet or more above the river.

"The bayou flowing into the river that we just passed is called Tunica Bayou after the people who lived here before the Chickasaw drove them west. The Tunica are a handsome people and good farmers. There used to be a small Tunica farm here. The remains of a Tunica cabin is there," Bartolomé said, indicating what appeared to be a tangle of vines.

"This is the last place on the Mississippi where the eastern bluffs come right to the river bank," Bartolomé explained. "Down from here, the bluffs pull away from the river and the land is low on both sides. Here, even in summer, the air blows cool from over the river. There is room here for a fine house and a small farm."

"The view is beautiful," Anna said as she gazed down onto the *August Moon*.

"Do you like it?" Bartolomé asked.

"Yes, very much," she answered.

"Good, for it is ours," Bartolomé said. "I purchased the forty acres where we stand on the way up from New Orleans. I shall build our summer home here, if it pleases you."

Anna hugged Bartolomé tightly. "It pleases me, if you are with me," she said.

"When we arrive in New Orleans," Bartolomé continued, "we shall visit my stepfather and my kin in Bencheque straight away. Then we will have to be content to be a little crowded in my apartment at the Cathay Steamboats office until we can find a suitable house. I'm afraid I married without a home to bring you to."

Anna just laughed and held Bartolomé's arm.

He continued, "We will live in New Orleans during the fall, winter, and spring, for that is where I must work. In the summer, we will come up here to escape the heat and pestilence of the city. It is the practice."

"Who will care for the house when we are away for so long?" Anna asked.

"I will hire a couple to tend the house. There are many who would be pleased at such an assignment," he said.

"My father would have bought some house servants, but you plan to hire?" she observed.

"I will not own anyone. It is not the *Isleño* way," Bartolomé said. "God has given each of us free will; who are we to take it from others?"

Anna smiled and held Bartolomé closer. It was a side of him that she loved and treasured. She knew him to be courageous, self-educated, witty, and all things that were admirable. But it was his sense of decency that she admired the most. He was, above all else, straight through and through, a man of honor. That was something that could not be taught. She vowed to prove herself worthy of such a husband.

"That attitude may not sit well with the gentlemen of New Orleans, *novio*," she said.

He looked into her eyes. His face was stern and the perpetual snarl that the scar gave his face hardened. "They shall have to deal with it on my terms," he said.

"I do love you so," was all Anna said.

* * *

It was the first week in March when the *August Moon* moored at New Orleans. The office of Cathay Steamboats was just across the levee road from the landing. Mister Livingston was dockside to welcome the boat and to see if Bartolomé had finally returned. He was happy to see the tall, rugged gentleman that Bartolomé had become descend the landing plank. He was surprised to see him in the company of a beautiful, red haired lady.

"*El Tigre*," Livingston said, extending his hand, "welcome home."

"Thank you, Mister Livingston," he answered. "And may I introduce you to my wife, Anna."

Livingston took Anna's hand and kissed the back of her fingers. "A pleasure and a pleasant surprise, madam," he said. "Your husband has surpassed all our business expectations on this trip, madam. Now those successes pale by comparison. Welcome to New Orleans."

"Thank you, Mister Livingston," Anna replied. "I lived here for a few years before the battle, so I am not a stranger to this city."

"Indeed," Livingston said, "we are richer for your return. Then I shall say, welcome home."

They crossed the road to the office where John Loitan and two assistants were laboring away over shipping documents. They all jumped to attention when Bartolomé came in. The office had all the trappings of a busy and profitable company. After introductions were finished, Livingston called Bartolomé and Anna into the private office.

At first, Livingston was reluctant to discuss business with Anna present. Most of the gentlemen of New Orleans refused to have their spouses exposed to their business activity. Often their slave mistresses knew more about their business affairs than did their wives. During the short time that Bartolomé was being introduced to life in the high business world of New Orleans, he had been frequently offered the purchase, or the rent, of a comely quadroon slave at a good price. He declined. Had he not been the Tiger of New Orleans, his manhood might have been questioned. As it was, no man dared to question his motives.

"I assure you, Mister Livingston," Bartolomé said, "Anna is my closest confidant. I have no secrets from her.'

Mister Livingston shrugged. Bartolomé, he had learned, was nothing if not unorthodox.

"Mister Too has offered to buy out the other investors," Livingston said with a glance at Anna. "The Lafitte brothers have accepted. It seems that new business offers west of the Sabine have their attention. Mister Too would like to offer you a 25 percent ownership. That is fifty shares for one hundred dollars a share."

The offer was a bargain and Bartolomé accepted. He was going to be a wealthy man. John Too had plans to add two more sternwheelers to the Cathay line this year. Every boat in the line moved cargo every time the boilers were lit. Too's barge business between the river and the ships that moored in the coastal bays was the largest such operation in New Orleans. Louisiana had entered into an era of peace and prosperity never seen before.

Lodgings were found in an apartment building facing the *Place D'Armes,* where Bartolomé had witnessed General Jackson's address almost four years ago. The next day, Bartolomé hired a buggy to bring them to the village on Bayou Terra Aux Boeufs. The ride took them past Bayou Pecheur. The house that Anna's family had owned was visible from the road along the river.

"*Puedes recuerda el hierro llorar, novio?*" Anna said as she leaned close to Bartolomé. The conversation had switched to Spanish.

"Yes, I remember the weeping iron, *novia,*" he answered. "Did you think that I could have forgotten?"

"I lived for the little notes that we passed," Anna said. "Perhaps, I shall write such cryptic notes to you again, *novio.*"

* * *

When they arrived at the farmhouse where Bartolomé had grown up, Oceane was on the porch. She leapt up when she saw that it was Bartolomé in the buggy.

"*Mon frère*, Bartolomé," she called out. "Papa, my brother Bartolomé is here!"

Oceane ran to the buggy and jumped up on the step as Bartolomé was attempting to step down. She held him tightly until he had to pick her up and step down holding her on his hip. Bartolomé thought that she must have grown a foot taller in the short time he had been away. He helped Anna down while holding Oceane. By the time they reached the porch, Jacques and Inez were there to greet them. Soon Jules and Gabriel joined them. They had run all the way from the fields when they heard the commotion.

"Who is this lady with you?" Oceane asked when things had settled a little.

"She is my wife, your sister-in-law," Bartolomé replied. "She does not speak French, so I will translate."

Bartolomé introduced Anna around. Jules and Gabriel were taken aback, but Jacques recognized Anna instantly.

"Where is Maurice?" Bartolomé asked.

"He is visiting a friend in Bencheque," Jules said with a smile. "A special lady friend."

"He's going to get married, too," Oceane said. The sisters giggled at the thought.

"And who does he court?," Bartolomé asked.

"Isabel Aguilar," Jacques said.

"I know her," Bartolomé said. "He had better treat her well. She has seven strong brothers."

"She leads him around by the nose," Jacques said.

Bartolomé translated the conversation as best he could for Anna. He felt uncomfortable with her missing so much.

"*Aprendo Español* (I learn Spanish)," Oceane said with a clap of her hands. Maurice would sometimes bring Oceane along when he visited Isabel. The children in Bencheque would play with Oceane and make a game of Spanish lessons.

Anna's face lit up. "*Puedo hablar Español*, Oceane," she said. Oceane's Spanish was rudimentary, but it gave Anna a chance to join the conversation. She, Oceane, and Inez went into the house while Bartolomé and the others stayed on the porch.

"Do you know the cause of my mother's death?" Bartolomé asked.

Jacques shrugged. "One night she grew feverish. She died before dawn. God knows why; I do not. It is hard now. My daughters need a mother, but I think I shall never marry again. I have buried two good wives. I am done."

"Let me take Oceane and Inez into my home. Anna will raise them well, and I can afford to send them to school," Bartolomé said.

"They will learn to read?" Jules said. Such a thought amazed him.

"They will learn to read, Jules," Bartolomé said. "It would not hurt you and Gabriel to learn the art as well."

"*Mais jamais* (But never)," Gabriel exclaimed. "I am a working man."

"You should ask your wife, son," Jacques cautioned, "before you commit to such a thing. If she agrees, I will accept your offer. I cannot raise young girls properly."

When Anna returned to the porch, she accepted the offer readily. Bartolomé spoke to her in English so that she would be free to object.

"To tell you the truth, *novio*," Anna confided, "I was going to make that same offer myself."

The sisters were delighted with the idea as well, provided that they could visit Papa often. It was decided that Bartolomé and Anna would continue on to Bencheque to visit Bartolomé's relatives there. They would pick up the sisters on the return trip.

"It is a good thing that we rented a large apartment," Bartolomé said with a laugh.

"Yes," Anna said. "We shall have to build an even larger house." Anna looked at Bartolomé with a smile, but the nuance in her words escaped him. *He is all man*, she thought.

Bencheque was not prepared for the couple that arrived by buggy over a trail that rarely saw anything better than an ox cart. By the time word spread that Don Diego's grandson, the Tiger of New Orleans, was visiting, the entire community had gathered at Aunt Maria's little house. Everyone had to gather in the yard. Maurice was there with Isabel Aguilar. They looked as if they belonged together.

Anna was introduced around. Everyone was pleased that she spoke Spanish. Thankfully, the news of the fight at the Gap had not reached Bencheque or Terre Aux Boeufs, so Anna did not have to repeat the tale of that harrowing experience.

Even so, it would not be long before that news would arrive. The *August Moon* carried news along with cargo. When she docked, word of the fight at the Gap would flood through the town. It would greet the deMelillas when they returned to the city with the sisters in tow.

CHAPTER 22

A carriage with covered windows drove up to Madam Barbeaux's house. It was drawn by a matched team of black geldings, and driven by a tall, muscular black man dressed in a coachman's uniform. A footman jumped down from his riding step before the carriage came to a full stop. The footman scurried to the carriage door while the stately driver went to the door of Madam Barbeaux's house and spun the bell.

Madam Barbeaux opened her door; only then did the footman open the carriage door. The lady he helped down was dressed in black. Her face was concealed by a dark veil.

"Please, my lady," Madam Barbeaux said as she bowed. "Do come in." She stepped aside to allow the lady, escorted by the black footman, enter.

"Wait at the carriage," the lady said. Soon she was alone in the candlelit chapel room with Madam Barbeaux. The lady lifted her veil. It was obvious that she had been a beauty in her youth. Now, age and an unrelenting sadness filled her face. Her countenance was wracked with sorrow.

"You sent me a message that you have news to tell me," the lady said.

"Yes, my lady," Madam Barbeaux replied. "That which you have contracted me to do has been done." She handed the lady a page of a newspaper: the *Louisville Gazette*. "Does my lady read English?" Madam Barbeaux asked.

"I do," the lady replied as she accepted the paper.

"I am ignorant of the language, my lady," Madam Barbeaux continued, "but I am told that there is a story in this newspaper that is proof of my service."

The lady read the paper. One of the articles was titled "A Desperate Fight." It chronicled an ambush that had taken place on the National Road just west of the Cumberland Gap. Several renegades had attacked a caravan of pilgrims. Fortunately, a troop of Dragoons was nearby and the attack was defeated.

Another small band of brigands had fallen on the troop's baggage wagon. The entire renegade force that attacked the baggage wagon was killed. A few of the renegades involved in the attack on the pilgrims had been captured. The identity of two of the five renegades killed at the wagon had been learned from these prisoners. One of the dead was Tall Wolf, a notorious raider of innocents. The other was the runaway slave known as Bricks.

The lady sat upright, here eyes wide. "Among the dead was a runaway slave known as Bricks," she said aloud. She looked at Madam Barbeaux's quizzical expression. The lady repeated the phrase in French.

"I am told that was the news, my lady," Madam Barbeaux said. "I have made my contract."

"You have, and I shall be faithful to our contract," the lady said. She reached into her handbag and withdrew a bank draft. She gave it to Madam

Barbeaux. "This check is drawn on the Hall Bank for the amount of ten thousand dollars," she said. "I know that your religion dictates that solemn contracts must be paid in gold, so I also give you these seven gold Spanish doubloons as well."

The lady stood. She paused for a moment and lowered her veil. "Thank you, madam," she said. "Please call my footman to the door."

Madam Barbeaux did as she was asked. She stood in the doorway as the lady was escorted to the carriage. The footman and driver did not look at Madam Barbeaux. Then the carriage was gone.

Madam Barbeaux returned to her chapel room. It had been a very profitable assignment. The money from this one client would provide for Madam Barbeaux and her family for the rest of their lives.

It had been difficult. The lady had never told Madam Barbeaux why she sought the life of the man named Bricks. But the spirit Kalfu had, in an unguarded moment, revealed the truth to her. Though Kalfu did not know all there was to know because Ogoun had kept it from him, he laughed as he told of the runaway Bricks and how that wild man had violated and killed a young slave girl who belonged to the rich widow. The lady had borne only one child. Her son had died at the age of seventeen. He had been a wild young man who left nothing behind but a daughter by one of the house girls. The young slave girl who had accompanied the lady everywhere, the innocent child whom Bricks had killed for sport, had been the lady's granddaughter.

Bricks was pure evil and a mindless fool. He believed in the dreams that Barbeaux had invaded, dreams that sent him to Tall Wolf, dreams that put him in the path of *El Tigre*. What Madam Barbeaux had not foreseen was that it would be a woman who sent Bricks into the underworld. It would have been perfect if that woman had been a virgin.

One cannot have everything, she thought to herself. Madam Barbeaux smiled. What was done was enough.

Historical Note

The Canary Islands are a volcanic archipelago located in the Atlantic Ocean less than a hundred miles off the west coast of Africa. Few in the Western world knew of the existence of the islands and their mysterious inhabitants until they were "discovered" by the Romans in the first century. Prior to that time, these islands were only the subject of rumor and speculation. Perhaps they had been visited by the Phoenicians; maybe by others.

The islands had been populated for at least three thousand years. Who these people were and their origin is unknown. There may have been a record of these islands in the great Library of Alexandria, but the library was destroyed. After the fall of Rome, the Western world slipped into the dark ages. The Canary Islands, sometimes called the Fortunate Islands, remained an isolated and rarely visited corner of the world. They were off the beaten path and forgotten.

Europe began to climb out of the abyss. Europeans, eager to explore the western sea and a route to the Orient that avoided the Islamic monopoly on the spice and silk trade, rediscovered the islands in the fourteenth century. The tiny, Mediterranean island kingdom of Majorca even established a settlement on one of the islands in 1312.

The kingdom of Castile wanted the islands as a staging port for westward discovery. That power financed an invasion in 1402. Full conquest of the Canaries required ninety-three years. Castile had united with Aragon to form Spain, and by 1495, the seven populated islands had become colonies of Spain.

The original inhabitants of the Canaries, the *Guanches*, suffered disease, enslavement, and injustice, but they survived. Eventually, they intermarried with the Spanish conquerors. Their ancient languages, customs, and religions faded and almost disappeared.

Nearly three centuries passed, during which the Canary Islands developed into the primary staging port, a gateway for Spain to her rich American colonies. Canary Islanders were compelled by economic circumstances to fill the ranks of Spain's exploring forces as deck hands, soldiers, and settlers. Then the Western European colonies in the New World began to change. Events across the Atlantic would impact the Canary Islanders.

France and Great Britain concluded a war in Canada with a treaty in 1763. Louis XV, King of France, feared he might lose the Louisiana colonies to Britain. Before negotiating the Treaty of Paris, he granted the vast territory to his relative, Charles III, the Bourbon King of Spain. Charles III began to recruit settlers and solders to garrison Louisiana. Included in the new colonists were over two thousand families from the Canary Islands. Forty years later, Louisiana became the property of the United States, and her citizens, Americans. The Canary Islanders who had been recruited to serve the King of Spain would become citizens, and soldiers, of the great experiment in democracy.

The deMelilla Chronicles are the histories of a particular family of *Canarios,* from the time of the Spanish conquest to the westward expansion of America. This was the story of an American, Bartolomé deMelilla, born in Spanish Louisiana.

About the Author

Stephen Estopinal grew up in the swamps and bayous of Saint Bernard and Plaquemines Parishes. He is a graduate of Louisiana State University (class of 1968), a US Army veteran (Combat Engineers 1969-1971) and is a Land Surveyor and Civil Engineer employed by the SJB Group, LLC, in the Baton Rouge area.

Mr. Estopinal was a living history volunteer at the Chalmette Battle Field National Park and a black powder expert. His love of history, particularly the history of colonial Louisiana has prompted him to write a series of novels to bring that history to life. A descendent of Canary Islanders (*Isleños*) transported to Louisiana by the Spanish during the American Revolution, he draws on extensive research as well as family oral history to tell his stories of Colonial Louisiana from a Spanish point of view.

The first of his novels was ***El Tigre de Nueva Orleáns*** published in 2010 and has been approved for sale by the National Park Service at the Chalmette National Park Visitor's Center. It has been followed by a novel every year. ***Incident at Blood River*** was published in 2011, ***Anna*** in 2012 and ***Escape to New Orleans in 2013.*** Collectively, the novels are known as the **deMelilla Chronicles.** The novels are all historical fictions of 18th and 19th Century. They tell the story of the *Isleños* settlers in Louisiana and their struggle for survival. Writing historical fiction has provided Stephen Estopinal with an enjoyable hobby and a means of keeping the diverse history of colonial Louisiana alive. All of Mr. Estopinal's books are available at Amazon.com and BarnesandNoble.com.